The Kidnapping

She had been brought to the hideout in the cave by men with guns. She did not try to resist. She would have been easily overpowered.

Finally she stood face to face with the infamous El Diablo, a man who was known to kill his enemies with a shrug of the shoulder.

"Let's get down to business," Skye said coolly, looking into his fierce eyes. "How much ransom will you demand for me?"

El Diablo gave a little laugh.

"You are unusually straightforward," he said. "And what if I am not interested in money?"

"What else could you want?" she asked impatiently. She did not want to play games with this detestable man.

"You are a beautiful young woman," he answered steadily. "Have you no imagination?"

Also in Pyramid Books

by

BARBARA CARTLAND

THE KISS
OF THE
DEVIL

Barbara Cartland

PYRAMID BOOKS
NEW YORK

THE KISS OF THE DEVIL

A PYRAMID BOOK

Pyramid edition published February, 1972
Sixth printing, February 1975

ISBN 0-515-02635-2

Printed in the United States of America

Pyramid Books are published by Pyramid Communications, Inc.
Its trademarks, consisting of the word "Pyramid" and the portrayal
of a pyramid, are registered in the United States Patent Office.

Pyramid Communications, Inc.,
919 Third Avenue, New York, N.Y. 10022

1

"I hate men!"

"Nonsense!"

"It's true. They're all the same—wanting to get their hands on me or on my money."

Jimmy Donaldson threw back his head and laughed so much that his horse pranced uneasily from side to side, startled by such exuberance.

"A cynic at twenty-one!" he gasped at last.

"If telling the truth and using a little common sense means that I'm a cynic, then I'm content to be one," came the reply, as Skye with a flick of her riding-whip rode on ahead.

Too late Jimmy realized that he had offended his young cousin.

But she was so exquisitely lovely, with her tiny tip-tilted nose in an oval face and fair hair which curled riotously over her small head, that the mere idea of her being created for anything but the delight of mankind seemed ridiculous.

Yet Jimmy knew Skye well enough to be aware that she was not joking when she said she hated his sex; so, curbing his laughter, he rode after her.

He caught her up just as they reached the top of the rising ground, from which they had a magnificent view of one of the great fertile valleys which made Mariposa one of the most beautiful countries Jimmy had ever encountered in his long life as a diplomat.

Rugged rocks rising in the distance to the height of small mountains were rusty red in colour against the vivid blue of the sky, while below lay a lush, semi-tropical vegetation with flowers starring the ground in vivid profusion and butterflies of every shape and colour hovering above them.

It was awe-inspiring in its loveliness, and as he reached Skye's side he heard her draw in a deep breath and her voice was lilting with joy as she said:

"Isn't it wonderful? Just how I knew it would be."

She had evidently forgotten her indignation, and watching her parted lips and shining eyes, Jimmy wondered, as he had wondered so often before, why she always had the facility to surprise him, not once but a dozen times every day they were together.

"It's a magnificent country, isn't it, Jimmy?" she insisted as he said nothing.

"Magnificent," he agreed drily, "but so are its neighbours, Uruguay to our left and South Brazil to our right. And, as I have told you before, they are far more savoury spots than this in which to go sight-seeing."

"You are an old woman! That's what is the matter with you," Skye retorted scornfully.

"Such a remark would undoubtedly incense me to madness if I were twenty-five," Jimmy remarked philosophically; "but at fifty-five I can afford to ignore it. I grant you that Mariposa is very pretty; but having said that, let me ask you once again to come to Chile with me and look at the scenery there."

"Oh, be quiet, Jimmy! You know my answer. You have bored me enough already with your objections to my plans and nothing you can say will make me change my mind. I have been wanting to come to Mariposa for years; and now I am here, not even an army of croaking cousins would stop me exploring the country."

"My dear child, you simply don't know what trouble you may be walking into," Jimmy protested, "besides, there is nothing to see that you have not seen already."

"But I haven't seen anything," Skye cried. "You don't think I am going to be satisfied with just looking at American cars rushing up and down the streets of Jácara, do you?"

"But in Heaven's name, what else is there to see?" Jimmy enquired. Jácara is the only decent town in the country—if you can call it a town—and the rest of Mariposa is very much what you see here—flowers, butterflies and rocks."

"I don't know what Grandmamma would have said to you," Skye smiled. "She used to tell me stories about

Mariposa and they were the most thrilling, exciting tales I have ever heard."

"Things have changed since your grandmother was here," Jimmy answered.

"But for the better," Skye flashed at him. "After all, she and my grandfather were frightened of being killed by Indians. A poisoned arrow in the back was what they expected in those days."

"The result isn't much different from a gun bullet in the front."

"How you do go on! Just because there was a revolution here a year ago."

"There is always a revolution of some sort taking place in Mariposa," Jimmy explained patiently. "That is why the country is so backward and from what I hear its present dictator has a very precarious hold on public opinion."

"So the shooting is due to start at any moment," Skye mocked. "But why shoot me? I'm bringing money into the country—you saw what a reception we had when we brought the yacht into the harbour. Nice, fat American dollars, Jimmy! Nobody's going to be so foolish as to bump off the goose that lays the golden eggs."

"If I could stay here with you, I should feel differently about it," Jimmy said; 'but you know I have to leave for Valparaiso tomorrow."

"I know, and although I shall be sorry to lose you, I am really rather looking forward to seeing the country on my own. Does that sound very selfish and ungrateful?"

Skye looked at him from under long eyelashes to see if he was annoyed, and then she laughed and held out her left hand in its leather riding-glove.

"Dear Jimmy—you have been so kind and so patient; but you know I intend to have my own way in this, so really it is a waste of time arguing with me."

"I am afraid you always get your way in everything," Jimmy complained.

"Not really," Skye replied. "I have had to wait until I was twenty-one, for instance, to come to Mariposa. I suggested coming years ago, but my aunt was simply horrified at the idea. She thinks everyone who lives in South America—or in the North for that matter—is a savage."

"Hilda is a sensible woman," Jimmy said, "I am extremely fond of her."

"So am I," Skye agreed; "but you must admit she has

very little imagination. So different from my American grandmother. You would have loved her!"

"I wonder; I am very English you know, in some ways, one being that I disapprove of young ladies who, with too much money and not enough sense, go careering about the world by themselves."

"There speaks all my English relations, ancestors and for-bears," Skye laughed. "When you talk like that, Jimmy, I find myself being extremely glad that I am half American."

"All the same, you will be sorry one day that you have not listened to me."

It was not surprising that he was worried, he told him-self as he watched her. She was, in her pink, white and gold beauty, enough to turn any man's head and he had seen the bold glances her slim, sweetly curved figure just blossoming into maturity received from the dark-eyed Mariposans with Spanish blood coursing hotly in their veins.

The horses were moving forward down the incline of the hill. As they went, Jimmy looked back and saw over his shoulder that their escorts, two Mariposan boys who had been sent with them as guides, were talking together and pointing to the distance; then, as he turned away, he heard one of them come cantering up behind.

"What is it?" he enquired in Spanish.

"*Excusa,* Señor," the boy said in his soft, deep voice, "but it is best that you and the Señorita should go no further."

"Why?" Jimmy started to ask, only to be interrupted by Skye.

"We are going on," she said in fluent and beautifully enunciated Spanish. "It is still early in the afternoon and the Señor and I wish to see the country."

"But, Señorita . . ." the boy started to say.

"That is what I command," Skye said imperiously and, spurring her horse, she galloped off ahead.

It was a little time before Jimmy could catch her and when he did they cantered for some way over the soft springing turf before their horses settled down to walk more quietly beneath the shade of some trees.

"Why did he want us to turn back?" Jimmy asked when he could get his breath.

Skye shrugged her shoulders.

"Maybe he wants his *siesta,* who knows? Or perhaps he feels we have had our money's worth out of the horses;

but, as I explained when I hired them, I need horses that can carry me all day if need be, and mine is certainly not tired as yet."

She bent forward to pat the glossy neck of the beautiful animal she was riding, and then she looked at her cousin's face and guessed his thoughts before he spoke them aloud.

"You are sensing danger, Jimmy, and you are wondering what arguments you can use to persuade me to turn back. You need not speak the words I see trembling on your lips. I know exactly what you will say and it is quite useless."

"In that case, I suppose we go on."

There was a slight irritation in Jimmy Donaldson's voice. He had been a diplomat all his life, but sometimes he found his young cousin's flouting of the conventions and her utter disregard for danger extremely irritating.

He was very fond of Skye. He had known her since she was born, for her father had been his first cousin and they had more or less been brought up together.

But whereas Arthur Standish had been an easy, good-natured, uncomplicated character, his daughter was very different.

"Yes, it is my American blood," Skye said aloud, again sensing what Jimmy was thinking, and added, "I wish you had known my mother—well, I mean."

"She was a very lovely person to look at."

"She was lovely in herself, too; so gay, so brave and exciting to be with. Oh, Jimmy, if only she had not died when I was too young to appreciate her!"

"It was a tragedy," Jimmy agreed, "and yet the accident might never have happened if she had been a little more careful."

"I could never imagine my mother being particularly careful about anything; but I had so little time with her, especially as I was only allowed to be with her in America for a part of my holidays."

Her eyes darkened for a moment and Jimmy Donaldson thought, as he had thought before, how miserable it could be for the children of divorced parents, with their divided loyalties and their feeling of instability without a proper home and a proper background.

"I suppose in a way everything connected with my mother seems to be brighter, more glorious simply because I saw so little of her," Skye said honestly. "My upbringing in England certainly always seemed very tame compared with the excitements I could find at my grandfather's house in Long Island or on his ranch in California. And you must remember those visits were very rare after my mother died; but now, as I look back at them, they are indivisibly mixed in my mind with my grandmother's stories of Mariposa."

"Did she come out here when she was a girl?" Jimmy asked.

"No, no; when she was first married. My grandfather was a mining engineer and they came out to try to discover gold for some firm in New York. It wasn't very successful, but they had wildly exciting adventures with the Indians on their trek into the interior.

"My grandmother had never left home before she married, and what was more, she had always lived in a town. The butterflies, birds and flowers here made her feel as if she were walking into a fairyland. She used to describe them to me so vividly that now I feel as if I have seen all this before in some previous existence."

"How long were your grandparents here?" Jimmy enquired.

"Only two or three years; then they went back to America and as you know grandfather discovered oil. I can't feel very excited about that part of their lives. Oil is so dirty and ruins the look of the land. But gold is different. There are even diamonds and rubies hidden away in those mountains—that's romantic, if you like."

"There may be unexplored mineral wealth that we still know nothing about in all these South American countries," Jimmy said, "but the Spaniards, when they first came, were full of grandiose dreams of treasure trove, only to be disappointed."

"As you are quite sure I shall be! It's no use, Jimmy. I don't want gold—heaven knows I have got enough of that, but I would like to have adventures like my grandmother had."

"Adventures are usually only fun when one talks about them afterwards," Jimmy said.

"Dear, dear, how prosaic you are!" Skye mocked at him. "Well, I'll have my adventures first and write about them afterwards; and if it's a best-seller, you will be proud to know me."

"I'd much rather you would read about adventures and listen to other people's stories than try to live them yourself," Jimmy said. He looked over his shoulder as he spoke and said, "By the way, what has happened to our guides? They don't seem very pleased about something."

"They're just lazy," Skye said quickly—too quickly—so that Jimmy looked at her speculatively and said:

"You know what is wrong! Now tell me, because otherwise I shall go back and question them."

"No, Jimmy, don't do that," she pleaded. "There is nothing the matter, really, I promise you."

"Tell me," he said, "I insist on knowing."

"All right, then," she capitulated; "the man from whom we hired the horses did murmur something about not going too far into the interior. He said there were bandits or . . . I don't quite know what he did say. I didn't catch the words properly. Anyway, he inferred that it was wiser to stay near Jācara."

"Exactly what I said to you," Jimmy said; "and now we will go back."

"You can go back. I'm not stopping you; but I have no intention of doing anything of the sort. Who wants to sit in Jācara when there is all Mariposa to explore?"

"I told you, there is always trouble of some sort going on in this country and you don't want to be mixed up in it."

"How do you know I don't? I like the Mariposans, what I have seen of them; and if I get the chance, I shall give them some good advice and that is to get rid of their present dictator."

"General Alejo? He won't last long—they never do! But I don't expect he is any worse or any better than those who have held the position before him."

"What they want in this country," Skye said seriously, "is someone with initiative and courage, someone who will do something for all those poor people we saw hanging round the harbour."

"What are you asking for—a government of the people by the people for the people?" Jimmy teased.

Skye shook her head.

"No, I don't believe, from what I have seen of them, that they are capable of governing themselves yet; but I don't think that Alejo is of the slightest use to them. I saw him drive along the harbour road in his car yesterday. I am sure it was because he was curious about the yacht; but he looked arrogant, fat and oily, and I saw a lot of those beggars spit after he had gone by. They obviously have no love for him."

"Dictators don't expect to be loved, my dear, they only wish to be obeyed."

"Well, I hope there are quite a lot of people who are prepared to disobey him. Look! What a perfect place to ride."

She urged her horse forward as she spoke and Jimmy followed her.

The trees were left behind and now they had come into the open country. There was thick grass, a small winding river and the golden sunshine flooding everything with a hazy beauty.

It was good cattle country, Jimmy thought, and wondered why the Mariposans did not make better use of their land. Skye was leading the way in a wild gallop. On they went, the sweet fragrance of the grass seeming at times almost overpowering as they moved through it.

Then, ahead, Jimmy saw Skye rein in her horse. She was looking at something, and as he came up to her he saw that she had stopped beside a dead tree.

It must have been struck by lightning for the shattered trunk was scarred and burnt; but it stood there, a bitter contrast to the lush, live loveliness of everything else around it.

As he drew nearer, Jimmy saw there was something else to look at besides the tree. He had a quick impression of horror in Skye's wide eyes before he heard her voice, quick and urgent, ask:

"Jimmy, is he dead?"

He saw then that hanging from a bough of the tree was a dead man. He was swinging a few feet above the ground, a rope round his neck, his face distorted by the agony in which he had died.

There was no need for Jimmy to touch the cold hands, tied together behind his back, or to feel the stillness of his heart to know the man was dead. He had been hanged, perhaps two or three hours earlier and extremely effectively without there being the slightest chance of his being able to escape strangulation.

"Yes, he's dead, Skye; and now come away."

"But . . . but oughtn't we to do something?"

Skye turned to her cousin in a perplexity which made him realize that she was in many ways very young and very inexperienced.

"There's nothing we can do," he replied.

"But surely we should report his death . . . to someone?" she asked. "Who can have dared to do such a thing?"

The colour was coming back into her cheeks and once again there was a ring in her voice.

"It is nothing to do with us," Jimmy said quietly; "we are strangers—visitors—to this country. It is always best to remember that our ideas of justice may not be other people's."

"Justice!" Skye cried. "Do you imagine they gave him a trial of any sort? And now he will hang here until . . ."

She glanced up at the sky. Jimmy followed her gaze. As he expected, there were two vultures hovering above them, waiting until they should move away.

"It's horrible! It's bestial!" Skye exclaimed.

She wheeled her horse round slowly. With an obvious reluctance the guides were following them. Skye rode a few paces towards them.

"Who has done this?" she asked as soon as she was within earshot. "Who is responsible for such an outrage?"

She pointed to the corpse as she spoke. The two boys looked for a moment, then glanced at each other. One crossed himself surreptitiously, but the other looked round quickly, as if in search of an enemy.

"Who could have done such a thing?" Skye repeated.

The boys looked at each other again and hardly above a whisper, one said, almost as if he spoke to himself:

"El beso del diablo!"

"The kiss of the devil?" Skye translated. "What does that mean?"

"I shouldn't ask too many questions," Jimmy said warningly in a low voice.

"But I want to know," Skye retorted. "Surely things like this can't happen, even in Mariposa, without some explanation?"

"We know nothing, Señorita," the older boy said with an air of defiance. "We should go back. It is not permitted to go any further."

"Not permitted by whom?" Skye asked.

"I don't know—but it is not permitted."

His face had assumed the obstinate look which Jimmy recognized as being an almost universal mask when natives of any country wished to avoid giving explanations.

He knew only too well the toneless voice, the furtive

movements of the eyes and the air of stupidity not to realize that further questioning would get them no further.

"El beso del diablo!" the younger boy whispered again, only to be shouted into silence by his companion.

For a moment it looked as if a quarrel would flare up between them—the younger answered the older and in a moment they were shouting and snarling at each other like two angry puppies; and then, as quickly as the storm blew up, it vanished again.

One moment the air was noisy and resonant with their raised voices and the next minute they were suddenly silent, their eyes staring ahead; and then they had turned their horses and were galloping away as hard as they could go back the way they had come.

For a moment both Skye and Jimmy were too astonished to say or do anything and then, simultaneously, they turned their heads to see what caused the flight of their guides. Coming towards them through the flowered grass were several men on horseback.

"Who are they?" Skye asked.

"I have no idea," Jimmy replied quietly, "but I think it best not to retreat. Let us ride towards them, smile and appear friendly. On no account ask them any questions."

He moved his horse forward as he spoke and Skye, drawing a little nearer to his side, went with him.

There was nothing, at first glance, to warrant the terror which the approaching group had inspired in their guides.

Riding spirited horses, the men appeared to be ordinary *gauchos* or cowboys of the South Americas. Their clothes were the usual hotch-potch of ancient and modern—wide sombreros, the loose trousers called *bombachas* tucked into boots of horsehide, and factory-made tweed jackets.

Only at festival time does the *gaucho* nowadays appear romantic.

Then, as the party came closer, both Skye and Jimmy saw that one man was different from the rest. He was riding in the centre of the group, and it was obvious without words or actions that he was the leader.

One glance at his handsome, hawk-like features and broad shoulders was enough to confirm that they were in the presence of some striking personality.

He had a red scarf wound negligently round his neck, well-cut European tweeds and the light polished boots of a man whose life is spent in the saddle.

In his hand he carried a *rebenque*—the inevitable riding-whip glistening with silver ornamentation, and his saddle and stirrups were also encrusted with silver. Whoever these men might be, here was their leader.

When the newcomers were directly in front of them, Jimmy and Skye reined in their horses. Jimmy raised his hat.

"Buenos dias, Señor."

For a moment there was no answer, then the leader of the *gauchos* spoke.

"You are not permitted on this land. You will return immediately to Jácara."

His voice was deep, vibrant and imperious.

"We are strangers here," Jimmy said quietly, "so we must crave your indulgence, if we unwittingly are trespassing. We apologize, Señor, and will return to Jácara as you suggest."

He turned his horse as he spoke, but Skye remained where she was.

"Does this land belong to you?" she asked.

The leader of the men glanced at her as if for the first time. His eyes, deep-set and dark in the shadow of his wide-brimmed hat, seemed to take in every detail of her appearance.

"It belongs to the people of Mariposa," he replied.

The words were simple enough, but somehow they were a challenge. Their eyes met and for the first time in her life Skye was conscious that a man was looking at her, not in admiration but with what seemed to her to be dislike.

There was something else, too, in his expression, something to which she could not put a name and yet instinctively she defied it.

She threw back her head, forgetting caution, forgetting that a moment before she, too, had been a little frightened when their guides had run away.

She stretched out her hand and pointed towards the dead man dangling from the tree.

"And does that, too, belong to the people of Mariposa?" she asked.

The expression on the face of the man to whom she spoke did not alter, but she fancied that for a moment his eyes narrowed. Then, as she waited, wondering what answer he would give, his voice came quietly from between his lips.

"That is the way, Señorita, that the people of Mariposa treat traitors."

Skye had not thought it possible that so much could be conveyed by so few words—cruelty, disdain, tyranny! She could sense his pride and she hated the insolent arrogance of his manner, knowing in that moment full well who was responsible for the man's death.

She wanted to say more, she wanted to defy him, to challenge his right to such an action, to tell him what she thought of such a crime; but before she could speak, Jimmy's voice came clearly to her.

"Come at once, Skye—at once!"

He spoke in English and though the men might not understand, there was no mistaking both the command and entreaty in his tone. For the first time since they had met, the *gauchos* and their leader seemed to relax their tension.

It even seemed to Skye that a faint smile flickered over the hawk-like face before his hard lips parted and he said:

"That's right; run along like a good little girl and don't interfere with things which do not concern you."

A sharp movement from Skye made her horse rear up in astonishment, but not before the men watching her had seen the colour flame up in her cheeks.

As she turned and rode away, following Jimmy, she could hear their laughter and felt her own anger, wild and fiery, bring the words spluttering to her lips.

"How dare that man behave in such a way! It was he who had that wretch hanged from the tree—do you realize that? And then to turn us back with such insolence! He has no right, I am sure of that. I have a good mind to go at once to General Alejo and tell him what I think of such behaviour."

She went on talking for several minutes before she looked at Jimmy and realized that he was very pale and that beads of sweat were standing out on his forehead. She suddenly became silent and her anger died away from her. Jimmy would not be so afraid without good reason for it.

They reached the shelter of the trees before she looked back, only a quick glance. The men were still there and couldn't have moved since they left. The sunshine was very golden, the grass was very green and the butterflies glinting in the sunshine were lovelier than ever, and yet there was something menacing over the land which had seemed so peaceful and beautiful but a few minutes before.

Skye felt herself shiver as if from cold; and then, as Jimmy wiped his forehead, she asked:

"Who is he?"

"How should I know?"

Jimmy's tone was irritable and so she was silent until, passing through the wood, they came upon their guides waiting for them. Shamefaced and yet hiding their shame behind volubility, they hurried forward.

"It is time for the Señorita to return. It is a long way home and sometimes the evenings grow cool—it would be best to make a good speed."

They spurred their horses as they spoke, but Skye interrupted them.

"Who was that man?"

They did not pretend not to understand her. They glanced at each other and the elder of the boys shrugged his shoulders.

"We do not know, Señorita."

"Very well, if you do not wish to tell me," she said sharply, "you can keep the name to yourself. It is a pity you are not more obliging, for we have enjoyed the ride and would have rewarded you well for looking after us."

The boys looked at each other, obviously disconcerted by such a direct attack.

"Won't you tell me his name?" Skye asked more quietly of the younger guide, "and tell me the truth, for I don't want to hear a lot of lies."

She had seen him cross himself at the side of the dead man and guessed that he was a Catholic and for that reason, if for no other, he might be less experienced at lying than his tougher friend.

For a moment he hesitated and then, glancing over his shoulder as if afraid they might be overheard, he whispered two words, *"El diablo!"*

"The devil!" Skye ejaculated. "That is ridiculous, as you well know. How can an ordinary human being be the Devil?"

"That is what he is called, Señorita, and that is all I know."

There was a simplicity about the way he spoke which told Skye that this was the truth. When they were out of the wood, she rode ahead with Jimmy and told him what the boy had said.

"We will make enquiries," he said. "I imagine the man is some local bandit. He may be a landowner or a farmer in a big way, but somehow I doubt it. If he was, these town boys would not be so frightened of him. I wish to goodness I had asked the Embassy for a confidential report on Mariposa before we left New York. But if you remember, you told me only that you were going to cruise through the Caribbean."

"Which we did," Skye interposed.

"But you didn't add, until you got me well away to sea, that you intended to stay in Mariposa. Now perhaps you will change your mind, so one good thing has been gained by this ride."

"Change my mind?" Skye ejaculated. "If anything this has cemented my desire to see more and yet more of the country. If you think the first twopenny-ha'penny bandit I meet is going to frighten me out of Mariposa, you are much mistaken."

"Well, I suppose there are other directions in which you can ride," Jimmy sighed.

"When I think of that man," Skye said, "it makes me so angry that I can understand anyone shooting a brute like that. If I had a revolver on me, I think I should have put a bullet into him."

"I shouldn't try tricks of that sort," Jimmy said drily. "All the same, when you go riding in future, it might be a good idea to take a revolver with you! For goodness' sake, though, don't shoot anybody; but at the same time, a shot fired into the air will often scare a hostile crowd."

"I don't believe an atom bomb would scare that lot," Skye replied, "but I'll take your advice."

"I don't know what to do about you, I don't really," Jimmy said with a groan. "You would think that this incident would show you that Mariposa is not entirely a land of milk and honey. Please come to Chile with me, Skye; and later, if I get some leave, I will bring you back here again."

"Dear Jimmy, I should hate to interfere with your diplomatic career."

"Bother my diplomatic career," Jimmy said; "you are more worry than all the Diplomatic Service put together. What you want is a husband, and the sooner you get one the better."

Skye laughed.

"So you think that only a husband could protect me from the band of robbers. Don't worry, Jimmy, I can look after myself. I am not afraid of any man—not even El Diablo himself!"

2

"I'm alone!"

Skye said the words aloud as she awoke to the sound of the waves lapping against the sides of the yacht. Then she sprang out of bed and ran to the open porthole to feel the breeze from the sea fanning her face.

"I'm happy—so, so happy!" she cried to the sea.

It had been almost breathlessly hot the night before; but now, although the sun was blazing, the air was cool, and Skye stretched her white arms high above her head. It was the ecstatic action of someone tinglingly alive with the joy of living, reaching out towards the unknown.

"Alone! Alone!"

She turned from the porthole and had a sudden glimpse of herself reflected in the long mirrors over the dressing-table.

Her chiffon nightgown, blown by the wind, clung to her figure and the sunlight shining through the sheer transparency of it revealed the beauty of her body—the small, firm, tip-tilted breasts, the tiny waist, the exquisite curves of her hips. She was as beautiful at that moment as a Greek goddess; but Skye's thoughts were very far from appreciation of her own beauty.

She was alone at last! She was alone to do as she liked, her own mistress, her own keeper.

For years she had chafed against the careful chaperoning of her guardians. When her father was killed at Dunkirk, she had been left in the care of her aunt.

Skye had loved her father's only sister, and yet at the same time she had felt stifled by the soft gentleness which dominated her existence and the conventions which Aunt Hilda would not set aside however much she protested against them.

"I don't think we will do that, dear!" she would say quietly but with an inflexible determination behind the sweetness of her smile.

When Skye's American grandfather died and she became heir to his great fortune, she found things no easier for her in America. There were always relations, lawyers, bankers and financial advisers of all descriptions directing her life, telling her what she should do, forbidding her the very things she wanted most—solitude and the chance to see the world.

"No! No! No!"—how Skye hated the word!

But now at last she was her own mistress, alone on her own yacht, thousands of miles away from England and New York. Even Jimmy had gone, poor old worried Jimmy, who had argued with her up to the very moment of his departure the night before in an aeroplane which had been sent up for him from Valparaiso.

"Please take care of yourself," he begged when all his pleadings that she should go with him had failed.

"I'll do that. Don't worry," Skye answered.

It had been easier to say than for him to believe. Skye knew that from the frown between his eyes. Impulsively she pressed her cheek against his.

"Dear Jimmy! You've been so kind to me," she cried. "I won't forget. I will try to keep out of mischief."

"Pray Heaven you do," he said. "But if you are in any trouble, you know where to get hold of me. If I leave the Embassy even for a night or two, I will let you know by telegram exactly where I can be found."

She waved until the aeroplane was out of sight and then went back to the yacht, guiltily conscious of her relief and with a sense of rising excitement.

Now she could begin to do what she wanted. How tired she was of hearing the eternal croakings of her relations, however well-intentioned they might be!

She had dinner alone and then sat on deck, looking out over the sea gleaming silver beneath the light of the stars; but as she sat there, she saw against the beauty of the night a man hanging by his neck from a dead tree, his mouth open in agony, his eyes protruding from their sockets.

"The kiss of the Devil!" What bitter irony there was in those words.

Over and over in her mind she reiterated what had been said by the man with the hawk-like features, the man who, the frightened boy had told her, was called "El Diablo".

Who was he? Where did he live? What was his power? She saw again the cruel line of his lips, the steel of his eyes, the arrogant assurance of his manner. He had seemed so at ease, so utterly sure of himself, while Jimmy had been humiliatingly humble before him.

"El Diablo!"—a fitting name for a murderer; and she knew too, that she would never forgive the manner in which he had insulted her. "Run along like a good little girl!"

Her cheeks flamed in the darkness and she felt the hot anger rise in her throat. If only she could punish him for that!

Then she had an idea. She would expose this man! She would find out all about him, discover what hold he had upon the people, by what assumption of authority he might hang a citizen of Mariposa from a tree, and why nothing was done to stop him.

The government should be forced to act. Alejo should be shamed into protecting the liberty of the individual. Not unless he were forced would there be much hope of help from Mariposa's dictator.

Standing high above the town and harbour, the great Palace, which had originally been built by the Spaniards as a fortress and which had been converted later into something more picturesque, was impressive enough until one saw the slums behind the main streets of the town.

There might be modern cinemas, a racecourse, American bars, English tea shops and advertisements for Coca-Cola; but hidden away behind the neon lights there was starvation and a lack of the most elementary sanitation, which contrasted badly with the garish, gold-laced uniforms of the Palace guards.

There was something wrong with the country; and thinking of what she had seen already, Skye decided to use the most modern weapon available to combat such out-of-date evils—the Press.

She knew she would have no difficulty in getting anything she wrote published in America, for when she had in-

herited her grandfather's fortune and was the sole heir to
millions of dollars made in oil, the Press besieged her night
and day for interviews, for articles, her autobiography and
anything she cared to set down on paper.

She thought, for a short time, that she might take up
writing as a profession, but Jimmy had dissuaded her.

"Live and learn first and write about it afterwards," he
said. "You are too young to be sure of anything but your
own ignorance."

For once she had been in agreement with him; but
sometimes she had scribbled down stories and fragments
of her thoughts which, although she did not try to have
them published, she knew were worthy of print.

One day, perhaps, she would write well, but in the
meantime here was the chance to try her hand at doing
something worth while, helping and perhaps saving a
people who were obviously being misgoverned.

Excited by the idea, she found it hard to go to sleep;
and when she did, it seemed to her in her dreams that
she was haunted by two faces, that of the dead man and
that of the one who had killed him.

"El Diablo!" Even in her dreams she could hear his
hateful voice saying, "Don't interfere with things which
do not concern you!"

Once she awoke to hear her own voice say aloud:

"How dare you! . . . you devil!"

Now that morning had come, all that she intended to
do came flooding back to her and it was with an air of
determination that she began to dress. She had decided
not to ride until the afternoon. This morning she would
explore Jácara and made a few discreet equiries.

First, however, she sat down and wrote a letter to her
Aunt in England. Without telling a lie she deliberately
gave the impression that Jimmy was still with her. Poor
Aunt Hilda was always beset by endless, although name-
less, fears as to what might happen in "foreign parts."

Her correspondence finished, Skye went on deck and,
giving a man on the quay ten pesos, told him to take the
letter to the Post Office. He hurried off obediently, all
smiles at earning so much money for so little effort.

Skye gave a sigh of relief—her last duty was done! Now
she could begin to enjoy herself.

It was still early when she left the yacht. She was wearing a dress of thin white linen and she carried a sunshade
to keep the sun from her bare head. From the moment she

stepped ashore people stopped to stare at her as she went by.

The men, winking and whistling, made pointed remarks to each other about her beauty. Skye ignored them and was not in the least embarrassed.

She was not interested in the attention she created, especially where men were concerned, for she had spoken the truth to Jimmy when she told him she hated men. He had not really believed her, but there were young men both in America and England who could have told him things which would have surprised him.

"You say I am unkind," Skye said once to a young Guards Officer whom she had refused to marry. "Is it my fault that you fall in love with me? No-one could say that I encouraged you."

"No, that is true; but don't you understand that I can't help loving you—you are so beautiful? You make any man who sees you want you and yet . . ."

He stopped and Skye looked at him with a little smile on her lips.

"And yet?" she prompted.

"You are hard," he said finally. "There is something unfeminine about you."

-"You say that simply because I don't throw myself into your arms. As I have told you, I don't want to marry you or anyone else."

"Let me try to teach you to love me," the young man pleaded.

"Why waste time when I know it is impossible for you to succeed?" Skye asked.

"But I love you," he said miserably; "let me kiss you, Skye, if only to say good-bye."

She looked at him scornfully.

"I hate being kissed," she answered, "and I can imagine nothing I should dislike more than for you to touch me."

She saw the expression on his face as she spoke and knew that she was being brutal, then asked herself what else she could do. She despised him and all the other men who desired her because she was pretty, because she was rich, and not because they knew anything about her character or her real self.

Deep down in her heart there was, as Skye well knew, an unhealed wound which was responsible for her abnormal sensitiveness where men were concerned, but of that she would not think.

"What the men I meet call love is usually lust or greed," she said once to Aunt Hilda, who was extremely shocked.

But now at last she was free from the Society functions she had been forced to attend by her aunt, the dances in London, the races at Ascot, Hunt Balls in the winter and the ceaseless round of cocktail parties, luncheons, dinners and theatres.

What were they, she had often asked herself, but marriage markets, where a girl was sold to the highest bidder or in many cases laid a trap for him, her body the bait?

Skye had never enjoyed the social whirl, it had seemed so unexciting somehow. She wished for adventure, she longed to see the world—and now at last the opportunity to do both lay before her!

She wanted to run, jump and shout with the joy of it; instead, she walked sedately down the beautiful, narrow old Spanish street where all the best shops of Jácara were situated. High above the town were many flat-roofed white houses, usually shaded by the native ombu trees or surrounded by a trelliswork of vines and green figs.

Here the well-to-do inhabitants of Jácara lived, their windows barred with iron grilles so that, as had been traditional down the ages, their daughters were protected from the *caballeros* who courted them.

But there were many more houses, filthy mud huts and bamboo shacks without even the most primitive necessities of life, where the Indians, negroes and the poorest Mariposans lived.

Here children ran about naked, pitiably thin and emaciated, their little fingers clutching like claws for any fragments of food they could find in the gutters or the refuse dumps.

Oblivious to their sufferings, the Palace was silhouetted against the vivid Madonna blue of the sky, its flag flying, the sun glinting on its shining windows and gilded towers. Skye looked up at it and squared her chin so that for a moment she had a strong resemblance to her American grandfather who had come to Mariposa as a mining engineer over sixty years ago.

"Dictators and bandits, here I come!" she murmured.

Yet anyone else would have been discouraged when luncheon time found her back at the yacht little wiser than she had been when she left it. She had been greeted enthusiastically everywhere she went. The shops had welcomed her with open arms.

Tourists were comparative rarities in Mariposa owing to the unstable state of the government and the fact that there were very few amenities in the way of modern hotels.

But although the people of Jácara were anxious to sell her anything and everything in their stores, they were not prepared to supply her with information.

When she spoke of Alejo, they looked wary; and when she spoke of El Diablo, they shut up like clams. With regard to the latter there was no doubt that they knew exactly of whom she was speaking, but they were not going to admit it.

"*Excusa*, Señorita, but I do not understand."

It was the same answer over and over again, and yet she knew they understood her very well.

"I will find out more if it is the last thing I ever do!" Skye swore to herself.

When luncheon was finished, she changed her clothes, calling for Evans, the steward, to bring her the things she wanted. Despite Aunt Hilda's protests, she had refused to have a lady's maid or a woman of any sort aboard the yacht.

She knew what a nuisance they could be at sea with their eternal whining and grumbling and inevitable bouts of seasickness. Evans would look after her as skilfully as any woman could have done and with far less fuss.

By the time Skye was ready a taxi was waiting to take her to the stables where she had arranged to hire riding horses during her stay in Mariposa.

The owner, a wrinkled, middle-aged man who looked out of place unless he was astride a horse, was extremely voluble about his animals; but when Skye spoke to him of El Diablo, she saw the usual blank expression mask his face.

"*Mire*," she said impatiently, "I am not asking out of idle curiosity. I don't know whether your boys told you, but yesterday, when I was out riding with my cousin, we encountered the rude and arrogant person who, I understand, is nicknamed 'El Diablo'."

"So I hear, Señorita. It was indiscreet for you to go so far into the interior. I was very angry with my boys for disobeying my orders."

"But why should you give such orders?" Skye enquired. "I wish to see country and I have every intention of doing so. Do you mean to tell me that a few hours' ride from Jácara is as far as I am permitted to go?"

"No, Señorita. Yesterday was a mistake—today it will be different."

"Who is this man they call El Diablo?"

"*Excusa*, but I have no idea, Señorita. I do not even know that he exists. But it is always best that someone so young and so beautiful as the Señorita should not take risks."

Skye was up against a blank wall and she knew it. They were not going to tell her what she wanted to know, but she felt her temper rising at being so obviously circumvented.

She had been spoilt these last years since she had so much money; everything, except of course freedom, had been hers for the asking. She was certainly not used to people refusing her what she wanted to hear.

She let a groom help her up on the horse's back, and as she did so, two men came into the yard leading horses.

"Are these the guides who are to accompany me today?" she enquired of the owner. "Where are the boys I had yesterday?"

"I regret, Señorita, they are otherwise engaged. These men are experienced guides, they will take you a very pleasant ride."

Skye glanced at them. One was an Indian and the other had clear-cut, almost aristocratic features which are characteristic of Mariposans.

They had mounted their horses and sat there, staring at her impassively. She did not know why, but she had an absurd inclination to refuse their company.

"I would prefer to have the boys I had yesterday," she observed petulantly.

"*Perdone*, Señorita," the owner of the stables said, "tomorrow perhaps, but today it is impossible."

"Very well."

Skye turned her horse to lead the way from the stable yard. She was being fanciful, she thought. There was no reason why she would prefer the frightened boys who had run away yesterday when they thought there was a chance of danger.

The breeze was still blowing in from the sea. She put up her hand to steady the wide-brimmed hat she wore and was glad that the air was cooler than yesterday.

She had not made the mistake again of wearing tight riding-breeches. Instead she wore a loose riding-skirt of soft red-brown leather which had been made for her in

California. It was fringed Mexican-fashion and as she rode down the dusty path from the stables the eyes of the passers-by watching her from the roadside were full of admiration.

Her shirt of leafgreen silk was cool against her skin— she felt untrammelled and happy. For a moment she forgot her frustration and the irritations of the morning and thought only that the world was beautiful and that she was riding a horse which responded to her every wish almost instinctively.

The stables were a little way out of the town and off a main road, but as they came down the side-track she saw a long, low American car come speeding towards them in a cloud of dust.

She reined in her horse to let it pass, then realized that it was stopping and saw that its occupant was an officer wearing the blue and white uniform of the Mariposan Army. There was much saluting and clicking of heels and the flash of white teeth beneath an ingratiating smile.

"*Como esta,* Señorita Standish?" he asked. "I was afraid I might miss you. I went to the yacht in the harbour and was told that you had already left."

"I am sorry you have had the trouble of following me." Skye said. "Do you wish to see me about anything important?"

"Yes, indeed, Señorita, a message from El Supremo himself."

"I am honoured," Skye said, thinking that Jimmy would be proud of her diplomacy.

"El Supremo asks me to warn you, Señorita, not to ride too far away from the town. It is dangerous—you understand—for a young lady as beautiful as yourself to travel far without a proper escort."

"And what does El Supremo think might happen to me?" Skye asked.

The officer looked uncomfortable; then he made the familiar, characteristic gesture with his hands and shrugged his shoulders.

"There are many things which might happen," he said evasively. "El Supremo did not specify the risks, he only advised you not to take them."

"He must have something in mind," Skye insisted. "What does El Supremo expect me to find in the country-side—wild animals . . . savages . . . robbers?"

"No, no, Señorita, you are mistaken. Besides, how should I know what was in El Supremo's mind?"

It was the same old prevarication, Skye thought, and she smiled at the officer's discomfiture.

"Look, Señor, I have with me two stalwart men to protect me. I have here a very good friend." She looked down as she spoke and put her hand on the small revolver she carried in a leather holster slung from her waist. Then she raised her eyes again and looked straight at him.

"Will you tell El Supremo," she said coolly and clearly, "that I am honoured by his kindness in thinking of me; at the same time, I am, as an Englishwoman, completely unafraid and unalarmed by any twopenny-ha'penny bandit I might find hiding in the countryside of Mariposa."

Deliberately she used the same words she had used to Jimmy, translating them freely into Spanish in an idiom which made them even more insulting.

Then, as she finished speaking, she heard a little gasp and realized that not only had the officer heard her reply to El Supremo, but also quite a crowd of people who had gathered round, coming as crowds do from nowhere, attracted no doubt by the car from the Palace and by her own very European appearance.

"*Gracias, Señor,*" Skye said, bowing politely to the officer before he could reply; then, whipping up her horse, she rode away.

She was smiling as she went. That would give El Supremo and whatever other ridiculous titles he called himself something to think about. If there were dangers in the country, he should be vigilant and see they were removed so that tourists could travel without fear of interference.

She took the same road she had taken the day before. Sooner than she expected, one of the guides came forward and suggested another route branching away to the north. She hesitated for a moment, then agreed to the way they suggested.

For a long way they trotted along a road of hard caking red earth, passing mules panniered with bulbous bundles on which women sat patiently chewing their cigar stubs.

They met bullock waggons like small huts on wheels toiling in laborious procession towards the town, old peasants, dark-eyed and dark-faced, massive and tough as rocks, carrying their produce—eggs, fruit and chickens.

There were a few *estancias* while they were still near Jácara, but after a while the road ended and they were in the wild, lovely and apparently uninhabited countryside.

Soon they began to climb the low range of hills which sheltered the town from the interior.

It was the same range they had climbed the day before; and as Skye's bump of locality was good, she realized that they were not very far from the same track she had followed through the woods and fertile valley which had led, eventually, to the part of the country dominated by El Diablo.

As before, the beauty of the scenery with its flowers and tropical shrubs, its butterflies and brilliantly-plumaged birds, was enchanting.

At times Skye was sorry Jimmy was not with her so that they could have exclaimed together over the loveliness of periwinkles and arum lilies growing side by side, of the hedges of geraniums, the clumps of pink marguerites and the great banks of sweet-scented stock which spread themselves beneath the broad-leaved palms.

She rode on and on, neither tired nor thirsty, until suddenly she realized that the sun had lost some of its strength and the heat of the day was past.

She drew her broad-rimmed hat from her head and fastened it to her saddle. Then she looked at her wristwatch. For the first time for several hours she turned to speak to the men who were riding behind her.

"It is getting late. We must be turning for home."

To her surprise they did not immediately agree to her suggestion.

"If the Señorita will go a little further," the Mariposan suggested politely, "there is a very fine view—*sumamente bello*—only a little mile or two."

"Of course I would like to see it," Skye said, not wishing to appear ungracious.

She spurred her horse into a trot. The country here was wild and rough; but as they passed through a narrow belt of trees, they came to a broad valley and some grazing pasture.

"Is this the view you spoke of?" she asked.

It was lovely, but no lovelier than anything they had passed on the way.

"No, no, Señorita, it is a little further still."

He pointed ahead and Skye cantered forward, coming after another quarter of an hour's riding to another clump of trees. She wove her way slowly through them, the branches were low and she had to bend her head a dozen times.

The birds were singing and she caught a glimpse of some brilliant parakeets fluttering from branch to branch. Then the trees thinned and she saw, as she expected, another valley and beyond in the distance a range of rugged mountains, shimmering purple against the sky.

She reined in her horse.

"It is very lovely," she said approvingly, "but now I think we should turn back."

"Just a little further, Señorita," the Mariposan pleaded, "there is much beauty to be seen—a waterfall."

"Another day, I think," Skye said firmly.

She glanced up at the sun as she spoke. It had lost its heat and was sinking lower in the sky. They had been riding for hours and it would be dark before they got back to Jácara.

"Con permiso de Vd, Señorita, let me show you the waterfall."

It was the Indian who spoke now, a pleading look in his sorrowful dark eyes.

"Why are you so anxious for me to see this waterfall?" Skye enquired. "We can come this way another day."

"Perhaps I shall not be with the Señorita," the Indian replied in a low voice, his Spanish unexpectedly fluent. "It is a place with special association for me. Señorita, be gracious."

"Well, how far is it?" Skye asked grudingly.

Jimmy would not approve of this, she was sure, but somehow she hated to be unkind and churlish to the men who were so obviously anxious for her to enjoy herself.

"Just a few minutes only, Señorita, three . . . five . . . no more."

Skye laughed. She knew full well that time and mileage meant nothing to an Indian.

"Very well," she said, "I will go on for ten minutes and if we have not found your waterfall by then I shall turn back—you understand?"

"Si, si. Gracias, Señorita."

They were all smiles now. She rode ahead, keeping to the right where she could see some rocks. If the waterfall existed, it would be there. Ten minutes, fifteen, twenty passed, yet no waterfall could be seen; but still Skye did not have the heart to turn back.

It must be just ahead for there was a trickling stream running beneath the trees, banked by high ferns, many strange and exotic specimens she had never seen before.

On they went, until at last, as the stream grew no wider and no deeper and the rocks were left behind, they came into yet another valley of grass and flowers. Then Skye began to lose patience.

"It will be midnight before we get home at this rate," she said sharply; "we must turn back. We will come here another day and start early."

As she spoke, she looked at her two guides and for a moment she had a strange feeling that they were going to refuse to obey her; then, before they could speak, their faces cleared as if by magic and the Indian made a sound which was half an exclamation and half grunt.

"Is it there?" Skye asked, turning her head, expecting to see the waterfall.

Instead, over the horizon she saw that a posse of men on horseback was approaching. They were riding close together, a dark pattern against the flower-covered plain, just as she had seen them the day before.

For one moment her instinct was to turn and ride away. She wanted to find out everything she could about El Diablo, but somehow she did not want to meet him now, so late in the evening! And yet . . . surely that was absurd?

She had tried to make enquiries about him; she had planned to expose him; she had even thought that one day she would ferret out where he lived.

And when she came to think about it, to brave his insolence now was better than to encounter any more of those blank refusals to speak of him.

She glanced quickly at her two companions; if they were like the boys she had with her yesterday, this was when they should turn and run away, but they were sitting still and impassive, watching the men approach.

"Who is coming?" Skye enquired.

She wondered if for once she would hear the truth; but as usual, the blank stupidity of their expressions concealed everything but their guile.

"We do not know, Señorita," was the reply, "but it would be best to wait and see, not to run away."

"In which case," Skye said, "we will go and meet them."

She moved forward and knew, without looking back, that the two guides were following her. The men were coming nearer, but there were more of them than yesterday.

They were riding quicky with the ease which seemed characteristic of every *gaucho* in Mariposa so that he looked a part of his horse rather than a separate entity from it.

They came closer still. Skye could see now that these men were better dressed than those she had encountered yesterday.

They all wore the baggy *bombachas* and loose jackets, but their harnesses glittered with silver as did their saddles and stirrups, and several had swinging from their shoulders the short brightly coloured cloaks called *ponchos*. Red, blue and yellow, the colours gave them a picturesque attraction.

Then, as Skye looked among the approaching band, she realized that someone was missing, the man she had expected to see—the leader, with his hawk-like countenance and unmistakable broad shoulders.

He was not there! She felt unreasonably disappointed.

The men came galloping up to her, reined in their horses suddenly so that they reared dramatically, and the foremost rider, a middle-aged man with a weather-beaten face like old leather and heavy black moustaches, swept his hat from his head.

"*Buenos dias, Señorita.*"

"*Buenos dias, Señor,*" Skye replied.

He rode forward, his horse stirrup to stirrup with hers, and held out his right hand in greeting. She smiled and shook hands with him.

Only as the fingers of his right hand were on hers did she realize what he was about, for he bent forward and, with a swift gesture of his free hand, drew her revolver from its holster at her waist.

For a moment she tried to snatch her hand from his grasp and then, even as she began to struggle with him, she was still. Twelve men against her—or, remembering the quietness of her guides, was it fourteen? The man with the black moustaches wheeled his horse round.

"You will come with us, Señorita."

"Where to?" Skye enquired.

"I will show you the way."

The words were quiet and impassive, but Skye knew there was no possible chance to protest or refuse. She knew without glancing back that there would be no resistance from her two guides. She was right—there were fourteen men against her and she had not even a revolver to protect herself.

Proudly, with her head held high, she rode forward. There was nothing she could do, nothing she could say. The men did not talk to her or speak among themselves; they all rode in silence.

The pace they set was a quick one and it soon became obvious to Skye that they had a long way to go.

She had time to think, time to compose herself. She had wanted adventure and here it was. She guessed, without the need for being told, that it was El Diablo who had sent for her.

She was being kidnapped—for ransom, of course! It was annoying to think how easily she had walked into the trap. She remembered for a moment her premonition of danger when the two strange guides had come to escort her on her ride instead of the boys who had taken her yesterday.

She should have guessed then that something was about to happen. How Jimmy would laugh! She wondered how big a ransom El Diablo would dare to ask—two or three hundred pounds would seem a fortune to a man like that!

Thank goodness, it would mean nothing to her except the humiliation of admitting that it was dangerous to go about Mariposa alone.

She began to scheme in her mind how she could hand over the money without getting in touch with Jimmy. The Captain of her yacht could supply a certain amount and she could wire to New York for the rest.

It was too ignominious to think that the very day Jimmy left her she should be involved in a situation of this sort.

At the same time, what copy it would be! Already she could see the headlines in the newspaper, *"Oil Heiress Kidnapped by Bandits"*. This would show up the rotten state of affairs in Mariposa if nothing else did.

It would make Alejo look a fool, too. Of course, he had warned her—there was that to say in his favour; but they were only about four or five hours' ride from Jācara and he should have the power to keep such enemies of justice under control.

"Yes, it might turn out quite a good thing," Skye decided.

She began to plan to herself the very words in which she would inform the newspapers of what had happened to her. She remembered someone she knew on the *New York*

Times—she would send him a telegram as soon as she was free.

She was not in the slightest afraid as they galloped on. The men obviously had no intention of harming her, and though it might have been comforting to have her revolver bumping at her side, it could hardly be of much use against fourteen men, all of them armed.

On they went and Skye saw at last that they were making for the purple mountains which had once seemed a long way off but were now drawing nearer.

She made no effort to talk to her captors and they obviously had no intention of speaking to her.

On, on, the jingle of the harness an accompaniment to her thoughts. But the mountains were further off than she had thought, and as she grew tired, even the beauty of the scenery and the feeling of adventure began to pall.

She was hot, hungry and thirsty. It was a long time since she had eaten a light luncheon in the yacht. She wondered what Captain Maclean would do when she didn't return.

She supposed he would make enquiries locally and then telegraph to Jimmy.

Skye licked the dust from her lips and pushed back the wet curls from her forehead. She was on the verge of demanding a rest when they slowed down from a quick trot to walk the horses up a mountainous path.

It soon became only a track and they went in single file.

On, on, the dust rising in a cloud, the sun sinking lower in the sky.

"How much longer?" Skye asked herself wearily.

She felt as if she had been riding a whole lifetime. Then, suddenly, they came to a pass between two low peaks. At one point there was a drop on one side of them so sheer that for a moment Skye closed her eyes. She had never cared for heights.

When she opened them again, she gave a little gasp. They had come through the range of mountains to the other side.

Beyond them was a valley, lush and fertile, filled with cattle grazing the high grass. Immediately below was a camp of wooden huts and tents of rawhide. They were nestling under the shadow of the mountains, and a quick glance to the right showed Skye the long-disused and over-grown opening to a mine.

The horses were walking on a terrace cut out of the side of the rock and in astonishment Skye saw that, opening off it, were hundreds of caves rising in tiers from the ground, hewn out of the solid stone thousands of years ago, perhaps by some tribe of master builders like the Incas.

"Ola! Cómo va? Ola!"

There was no doubt now that the caves were inhabited. Men and women came hurrying to the open doorways to call a greeting as the little cavalcade passed. Mostly Indians, bronze-skinned and dark-haired, they stared with undisguised curiosity at Skye.

The terrace curved in a hairpin bend into the one below and again into the one below that until eventually, still running the gamut of those hundreds of dark, inquisitive eyes, they reached the camp. Here the man who had first greeted Skye dismounted and took the bridle of her horse in his hand.

She swung herself lightly to the ground.

"This way, Señorita, if you please."

Suddenly she wanted to laugh. He might have been a butler showing her into some smart Drawing-Room in Grosvernor Square or an apartment on Fifth Avenue.

He led the way to a flight of stone steps leading to another terrace, set apart by itself on a rock which jutted out from the mountain range and was divided from it by a deep gully. Its caves were fewer in number and from their outer appearance constructed on a grander scale than the others.

As she climbed, Skye heard the other men trot away shouting to the women waiting for them beside the huts and tents. The steps were clearly cut, but steep.

The man with the moustaches walked ahead, his silver spurs clinking as he moved.

The terrace came abruptly to an end; beyond was only a sheer drop over the mouth of the mine, its sides vivid with shrubs. They stopped at the opening of the last cave.

The man drew aside a leather curtain and stood waiting for Skye to pass him.

She walked through the aperture, her head held high. She expected to step into a place that was small and dark, but found herself in what appeared to be an enormous room. It was brilliant with light, for the setting sun, gold and crimson, was streaming through a high window, unglazed, but barred by a grille.

The floor was covered with the skins of wild animals and there was a big couch from which a man rose to his feet as she entered.

He was taller than she had expected and yet his face was just as she remembered it—hawk-like, handsome, unsmiling and somehow frighteningly menacing.

Here, waiting for her, was El Diablo!

3

For a moment they stood very still, neither of them speaking, just looking at each other, before something in the dark eyes which seemed to take in everything with their arrogant scrutiny made Skye's hand go instinctively to the low neck of her riding shirt.

She felt in that moment as she had never felt before, as if she stood naked while this stranger appraised her; then pride came to her rescue.

"I thought it must be on your orders, Señor, that I have been brought here," she said.

She took care not to speak aggressively, but quietly and with what she hoped appeared to be an unruffled self-possession. If El Diablo expected her to be frightened or disconcerted by his actions, then he should be disappointed.

It seemed to her that a glint of appreciation came to lighten the hardness of his expression.

"*Buenos dias*, Señorita Standish," he said "and you must be both tired and hungry. Would you not like to wash and tidy yourself before we dine?"

His words were courteous enough, but again, because he was looking at her, she was acutely conscious of her appearance. She had not given it a thought during the long hours she had been travelling here, but now she knew that her face was hot and dusty, her hair untidy.

With an effort, because somehow his eyes held hers magnetically, she looked down at her hands as she drew her riding-gloves from them.

"Thank you, I would like to wash."

"Let me show you the way."

He moved across the cave as he spoke and she followed him. A wooden floor had been laid in the cave and now she had time to see that there was other furniture besides the big couch—a writing desk, chairs and several tables.

Before she had time to take in more than a fleeting impression, El Diablo had pulled aside a curtain and she saw an opening behind it.

"I hope you will find everything you want, Señorita," he said courteously.

Then the curtain swung back behind her and she was alone in the strangest place she had ever seen in her life.

It was another cave, almost circular in shape, not as big as the one she had just left, but which nevertheless compared favourably with a medium-sized bedroom. The walls were hung with Indian blankets dyed the lovely clear blue of a periwinkle.

A wide low bed set against one wall was covered in the same shade, while on the floor were innumerable mats made from the skins of the puma.

Skye recognized the fur because in California her American grandfather had had one to which she was very attached. He had told her how he had killed it in the mountains of Mariposa and how the puma was often called the "American lion" chiefly on account of its colour.

In the cave there was a window through which the sun was shining, but it was heavily barred with a beautiful grille of sixteenth-century Spanish ironwork.

There was furniture of black and white urunday, a native rosewood, carved exquisitely, and a long table of quelracha on which stood a mirror in a frame of burnished silver.

The whole was so surprising and so unexpectedly beautiful that for some seconds Skye could only stand looking about her, astonished as she had never before been in her life.

Then she saw that there was a basin and jug of coarse earthenware, such as the Indians bake, waiting on a side table, and beside them a towel which had been made on a hand loom.

Quickly she slipped off her shirt and washed not only her face and hands, but to her waist, feeling the cool water refreshing and invigorating after the heat and dirt of the long ride.

Then she sat in front of the mirror to tidy her hair. She was thankful that she always carried a small comb in the pocket of her riding skirt, besides powder and lipstick.

As she began, she noticed that beside the dressing-table there were several pairs of slippers, cleverly fashioned from the soft skins of goat kids. They were ornamented with Indian designs and skilfully coloured with vegetable dyes. There were four pairs, all different in size, and Skye found herself smiling.

What perfect hospitality, she thought, and how considerate! After being all day in the saddle she longed to take off her boots.

She pulled them now with a little exclamation of relief and slipped her feet into the smallest pair of slippers. Only when she stood up and found the absence of heels made her seem shorter than usual did she feel apprehensive of the evening which lay ahead of her.

There was the ransom to be decided and doubtless argued about.

Then she shrugged her shoulders. There was no need to dread the discomfort of being kidnapped while her captor was so considerate as to think even of the tiredness of her feet.

At the same time, she realized that this was a quirk in El Diablo's character which was not going to fit in with the picture she was planning to present to the world of an arrogant, murderous barbarian, intent only on gaining money for himself.

How surprised Jimmy would be when she told him! She smiled a little at the prospect and for a moment her eyes twinkled back at her from her reflection in the mirror. But Jimmy would be angry, too.

He had expected something like this to happen; and although it would be maddening to hear him say "I told you so!" she still had the satisfaction of being in the thick of an adventure.

In the meantime she was hungry, and with a last glance

at her hair to see if it was tidy she turned and crossed the room to the leather curtain. She drew it back slowly and saw that El Diablo was waiting for her at the other side of the cave.

He had changed from the breeches he had been wearing when she arrived into a white silk shirt and long dark trousers, with a red *fada*—a tight wide sash—round his waist.

There was almost a social elegance about him and as Skye crossed the room she felt that this was all a dream and that she would wake up to find El Diablo was nothing more sinister than a charming young man who was going to take her out to dinner and on to a nightclub.

The idea persisted when she saw that the table in the centre of the room had been laid and that two Indians were bringing in through the open doorway attractive dishes made of earthenware.

There was a carved high-backed chair for El Diablo and another one less ornate but roomy and comfortable was provided for Skye. She seated herself on his right, while to her amazement the Indians proceeded to wait on them.

"I have a French cook," El Diablo said conversationally. "So I hope, Señorita, that you will enjoy this meal."

"I am hungry enough to eat anything," Skye replied, taking her tone from his and speaking as if they had known each other for some time. "But this dish is delicious."

The first course was of eggs, skilfully cooked with herbs. A golden wine was poured into glass goblets and afterwards they were served with young turkey, followed by peaches cooked in brandy.

Skye longed to ask questions, but she felt it might give El Diablo a tactical advantage if she showed her surprise or even admitted that anything was unusual.

As she ate and drank, her fatigue fell from her and she felt alive and alert, ready to pit her wits against this strange bandit, who lived, as the servants at home would have said, "like a lord."

While they were eating, they did not talk more than was necessary. The Indians were in the room and apart from the ordinary politeness of a host in asking Skye if she would have a second helping or another glass of wine, there was little said until the meal ended and El Diablo rose from the table.

As she also pushed back her chair, Skye felt a sense of excitement and apprehension—the moment was coming when she would learn the truth!

Coffee, such as only a Frenchman can make, was brought and set on a low table in front of the couch, where, with a courteous gesture of his hand, El Diablo invited her to sit.

While the Indians were busying themselves with removing the plates and dishes from the table, Skye, to hide a sudden shyness, pointed to a rug lying on the floor and remarked:

"What a beautiful skin! What animal is it?"

"Wild cat," El Diablo replied; "there are a great number of them in these mountains; but that, as you can see, is a remarkable specimen. They are not usually so big or so well marked. I was lucky to get a shot at him."

"You have made yourself very comfortable here," Skye smiled. "Have you been here long?"

"Nearly a year. It is my home, and, like the French and the Spanish, I find no virtue in discomfort; only the British enjoy it."

There was something in the tone of his voice which made Skye look at him quickly.

"You sound as if you are not a particular admirer of my countrymen," she said.

"I admire their women," he replied insolently.

She felt the colour rise in her cheeks as he bent his head to light a small cigar.

"I must thank you for an excellent dinner," Skye said hastily, and added, her voice hardening a little, "but I suggest we get down to business."

He raised his eyebrows.

"Business?"

"Yes," Skye replied steadily. "I am well aware why you brought me here, and there is no point in not being frank about it. The question is, how much do you intend to ask?"

El Diablo took a puff at his cigar before he answered, then, through a cloud of blue smoke, he said:

"You are an unexpected young woman."

"You are not used to directness, I think," Skye replied. "It is a heritage from my American mother which makes me ready to come to the point rather more quickly than is usual in your country."

"So without any preliminaries you ask me to state how much money I require!"

"But let me warn you first, before you say too much, that it would be a mistake to be greedy."

"And why?" Again his eyebrows went up.

"If you ask too much, it may not be paid," Skye suggested.

"You came here in a very expensive yacht," El Diablo suggested.

"Lent me by a friend," Skye said quickly.

He drew on his cigar before he replied.

"I must have been misinformed. I understood you paid a little over one hundred thousand dollars for her last January."

There was silence for a moment, then Skye exclaimed:

"How can you . . . how on earth do you know?"

"You would be surprised how much I do know," El Diablo said with a twist to his lips. "And I do not make my enquiries of strangers!"

"What do you mean?" Skye asked, feeling uncomfortable.

"The grocer, the baker, the butcher, or, as you say in England, 'Every Tom, Dick and Harry'."

"I still don't know what you mean."

"I think you do," El Diablo insisted. "The questions you asked this morning in Jácara, the conversations in the shops, a flower-seller in the market-place; they were all, if I am not conceited in saying so, about one person."

Skye put her coffee-cup down with a little bang on the table.

"How can you know this?" she asked.

"I have many ways of learning what I wish to know," El Diablo replied. "So you were curious about me, Señorita! Now you are here, why not ask me personally for information?"

Skye was speechless and she felt as if he had taken the power of thought from her so that for the moment she could only stare at him.

It was growing dark, the night had come with its usual swift transformation when, as the sun sets, the stars come out.

El Diablo clapped his hands together and the two Indians came back, each carrying a lighted taper which they applied to huge white candles, such as one sees in churches, set in heavy wrought-iron candelabra.

The great cave flared into a new beauty, as a curtain was

drawn over the window to shut out the many insects which
would have come fluttering in towards the light.

For the first time Skye saw that the roof was arched
and carved with strange devices. El Diablo saw her glance
up and said:

"No one knows when it was done, five hundred, perhaps
a thousand years ago when the Indians started mining here
and made these caves, every one of which has been hewn
out by hand, by a tribe, I suspect, from Peru, taught by
the Incas. Perhaps this was the Council Chamber, perhaps
the Chieftain's private apartments. Tomorrow you will see
how cleverly this cave and the next one are constructed on
the curve of a rock so that they can have windows."

Skye had thrown back her head to inspect the ceiling.
Now she was conscious that, as he spoke, El Diablo's eyes
were on the taut line of her white throat and that her small
breasts, thrown forward, showed clearly against the thin
silk of her shirt. Hastily she sat up.

The Indians had left the room and they were alone in
the candlelight.

"Is it surprising that I should have been curious about
you?" Skye asked, feeling that she must justify herself,
rather like a child who has been caught out in some mis-
demeanour.

"I am flattered," El Diablo said.

"I expected to find many strange things in Mariposa, but
nothing like this," Skye said. "When I saw you, I
knew . . ."

She stopped suddenly.

"Yes? What did you know?" he enquired.

"Why did you kill that man?" she asked impulsively.

As soon as she had said the words she remembered that
Jimmy had cautioned her to ask no questions. Opposite
her she saw El Diablo's lips tighten and his eyes narrow.

"He was a spy," he said briefly.

"A spy? Spying on you?" Skye enquired. "For any
particular reason, or just because he was curious?"

"If you are worried that I shall treat you in the same
manner," El Diablo said evasively, "you need not be afraid.
Your neck is too pretty for me to wish to put a rope
around it."

It was a compliment such as any South American might
have made to a woman, but somehow it was not the words
but the way they were said that made Skye feel embarrassed.

"You could not commit a crime like that in many other countries in the world today and get away with it."

"Far worse crimes are committed every day by Europeans, as you well know," El Diablo replied coolly. "The extermination of one rat more or less in Mariposa is of no great consequence."

"What this country wants is a competent government," Skye snapped.

"I am the first to agree with you," El Diablo said, "but until one is found I am content to take the law into my own hands and administer it as I think best."

"That makes you a murderer."

"Many times over, if that is how you regard it," El Diablo agreed; "but some must die miserably so that others can live well."

There was a note of bored indifference in his voice which incensed her and made her lose all sense of caution.

"One day you will get your just desserts."

"Are you threatening me or merely being prophetic?" El Diablo asked. "Surely you are making a very unreasonable fuss about one small hanging?

"How can you be so callous?" Skye stormed hotly; "he was a man just as you are one. He had feelings, ideals and aspirations; he wanted to live just as you want to live; and yet, because you have the power, you killed him, just as you might stand on a black-beetle and think nothing of it."

"And what does this all prove?" El Diablo enquired.

"It proves you are a——" She stopped suddenly.

In her anger she had been about to say the unforgivable words, but he spoke them for her.

"Go on," he said teasingly, "you were about to say that I am a devil. Well, this is what I am called. Can a leopard change his spots?"

Skye choked and looked away from him. After a moment she said in a low voice:

"Forgive me, I was rude and I am well aware that what you do is no business of mine, not where it does not concern me. Let us return to what is my concern—the reason why I have been brought here."

"The reason for which I understand, Señorita, you have already made up your mind."

"If you mean by that that I think you have kidnapped me for the purpose of extracting a ransom, yes, I am well aware that this is why I have been brought here; so let us get down to brass tacks, Señor . . .?" Skye stopped. "What is your name?" she asked. "You know mine. Surely it is only fair that you should give me yours?"

"But you already know I am called El Diablo!"

"I can hardly write a cheque 'pay to El Diablo . . .' "

"I do not require a cheque."

"I did not expect that you would really take one," Skye smiled. "I understand that all transactions such as this are made in cash; but you still have not answered by questions."

"As to my name? I am afraid you will have to be satisfied with 'El Diablo' or else what my servants call me, 'El Cabeza', which means their head or leader."

"And what do your friends call you?"

"I have no friends."

"And if you had?"

He frowned a moment at her persistence and then reluctantly said:

"I assume they would call me Guido, for that is my name."

"And your surname?"

"That is my business!"

Skye swallowed and tried not to look as if she was being rude. With an effort she said:

"Well, Señor, we are now introduced, so perhaps it will be easier for us to talk frankly. You have, of course, some fixed idea in your mind as to how much you require to set me free?"

El Diablo rose to his feet and walked across the room.

"Come here," he said.

Wonderingly, Skye followed him. Against the wall she saw a big iron chest, such as the Spaniards of the sixteenth century used to carry on their ships to hold the money with which they paid the crews. There were two strong padlocks on it and El Diablo, drawing a key from his pocket, unlocked them and opened the chest. Full of curiosity, Skye stared into it.

She had a moment of disappointment. She did not know what she expected, but certainly not that the chest should be half full of small white, half-transparent stones, little different, as far as she could see, from the pebbles one could pick up anywhere on a beach in England or along the roadside in California.

"What do you imagine these are?" El Diablo enquired.

"I haven't the slightest idea," Skye replied.

Then the fact that they were locked away seemed to stir a memory of something someone once said to her after they had visited Johannesburg and her eyes were wide as she looked up at him.

"They . . . are not diamonds?" she asked.

"Yes, diamonds," he said. "They are found in the bed of a river about ten miles north of here. What, at a glance, do you imagine that little pile is worth?"

"I have no idea," Skye replied.

"They are not such fine diamonds as those found in Brazil and certainly not the same quality as those which come from the South African mines; but they are diamonds, and even if every one of these is found to be flawed or a bad colour, this pile would still be worth something like two or three hundred thousand pounds sterling."

He looked down at her astonished face and said quietly:

"Would you like me to give you some?"

"No, no, thank you!" Skye replied.

He smiled at the positiveness of her tone and, bending down, opened a little compartment at the top of the chest.

"Diamonds are not very attractive until they are cut," he said; "these should appeal to you more."

He took out a little canvas bag and, opening his hands, poured a stream of flashing, glistening gems on to his palm. There were perhaps thirty or forty diamonds sparkling in the candlelight, shining against the brown of his skin.

"Take two or three," he said, "or a dozen, if you wish."

Instinctively Skye drew away from him.

"It is kind of you," she said coldly, "but I do not like diamonds."

"Then you are indeed different from the majority of your sex," El Diablo said grimly. He held out his hand again. "Won't you change your mind? They would make pretty ear-rings or a bracelet for your wrist."

"Thank you, no!"

Skye walked back towards the couch. What did this mean? she was wondering to herself. He had brought her here for ransom and now, having shown her a stupendous fortune in uncut jewels, he offered her jewels as a present!

She felt bewildered and at a loss. This was something else she had certainly not expected.

Without hurrying himself, El Diablo replaced the cut diamonds in their canvas bag, put them back in their separate compartment and, closing the top of the chest, locked the two padlocks and put the key in his pocket.

Then he turned towards Skye.

"It's getting late," he said, "my people all go to bed early here. They work hard during the daytime."

They did not sound as though they were tired, Skye thought. During dinner there had been a background of sound and noise which she had hardly noticed, but which had been an accompaniment to everything they said and did.

The lowing of the cattle, the bleating of the goats, the barking of dogs, the shrill cry of children, and always and incessantly the thrumming of a guitar. The sounds had come wafting up through the windows; and now with the fall of darkness it appeared to have been intensified. The music particularly was louder and had a wild gaiety about it. However, she answered him gravely.

"I, too, would like to go to bed, Señor, and therefore, because you will be busy tomorrow and because I would not wish to trespass upon your hospitality too long, let us get this matter settled. If you have not brought me here for ransom, what is it that you want?"

"I should not have thought the truth would have eluded you for so long," El Diablo replied.

"I don't know what you mean. You obviously require a ransom of some sort, but if it is not money, what is it?"

"Doesn't your womanly intuition tell you what it is?" El Diablo enquired.

He did not look at her as he spoke, but bent to put out his cigar; then as he straightened himself, she realized how tall he was, how broad-shouldered, how strong and for the first time since she had set eyes on him she realized, too, that he was a young man.

Somehow she had thought of him as middle-aged, or rather ageless, a power rather a person, inhuman rather than human. Skye's lips were suddenly dry.

"I . . . do not . . . understand," she stammered; perhaps I am being stupid. . . . Perhaps it is because we speak a different language."

"Then let us speak the same," he answered in English.

She gave a cry of sheer amazement.

"You speak English!"

"Most certainly, even as you speak Spanish."

"But . . . it sounds so rude to say it is something I never expected . . . but you know what I mean."

"Can no one have any talents but the British—or, of course, the inestimable Americans?" he remarked.

"But you speak so well."

"I am flattered that you should think so."

"Then as we are talking in my own language, perhaps it will be easier for you to make me understand. You brought me here by force. Although I did not try to escape from your men, it was obvious that I should not have the slightest hope of being able to do so. You know that I have money, that I have a yacht, so it's obvious, isn't it, that the reason you are holding me here is for ransom?"

"That is your idea, not mine."

"Well, then, what else? Why go on prevaricating? Let me know once and for all what it is you want, for I have not the slightest idea what it can be."

"You are very modest," El Diablo said. "Have all the social wastrels in London and New York lost their eyesight?"

"I . . . I don't . . . understand."

"I think you do!"

Skye felt her heart give a frightened leap.

"If you mean what I think you mean . . ." and despite every resolution her voice trembled, ". . . then you must be mad."

"No, I am not mad—merely appreciative of beauty when I see it.'

"I think this conversation is becoming ridiculous," Skye said with an effort. "If you are trying to frighten me, you are not succeeding. I am a British subject. Have you forgotten?"

There was a faint smile on the lips of El Diablo as he moved across the room towards her.

"A British subject in the middle of Mariposa," he said slowly, "and the nearest Ambassador is perhaps three hundred miles away. What shall we do about it?'

His irony was somehow more difficult to combat than anything she had yet encountered, but with a supreme effort she threw back her head to look up at him.

"If you are so conceited as to think yourself attractive, let me tell you the truth. I hated you from the first moment that I saw you; you are cruel, brutal and bestial . . . and a murderer!"

"Is that all?" he asked, seemingly quite unperturbed by the words she almost spat at him.

"Isn't that enough? And now this farce has gone on

long enough. You will give me a horse and let me return to Jácara. I want no escort, I want no guides; I will find my own way home. You will let me go this moment, do you hear?"

"And do you think you would get far alone?" El Diablo asked. "I have many young and virile men out there."

"Perhaps I should be safer with them than with you," Skye retorted. "They at least may have some semblance of decency left."

He smiled at that and putting out his hand slipped it under her chin and turned her face up to his.

"So little and so fiery," he said. "I had forgotten that a woman could have so much spirit and be—utterly desirable."

His voice caressed the last words before, with a swift movement, she struck his hand away from her.

"Don't you dare to touch me!" she cried. "If I had a gun, I would kill you for so much as laying a finger on me; and now I am going, whatever you may say."

She ran towards the doorway, but with a swiftness she did not believe possible, he was there before her. Moving too swiftly to stop herself, she collided against him.

In a moment, his arms were around her. She had known he would be strong, but she had not imagined for one moment that his strength would envelop her so that she was helpless, completely and absolutely helpless, within the steel of his arms.

"Let me go!" she cried furiously. "Let me go!"

She was not pleading but commanding, and she knew that he was laughing as he held her against him so that she could not do anything but throw back her head and cry abuse at him.

"You brute! You devil! I will kill you for this!" she cried, and then her voice was still.

His lips were on hers, hard and passionate. They seemed to draw the very breath from her body and with the sickness of a dark despair she knew her own helplessness, knew that she was utterly powerless againt him.

Then, as quickly as he had taken her in his arms, El Diablo set her free. She would have fallen if she had not held on to the back of a chair.

She stood there palpitating, her breath coming gaspingly from between her lips, her eyes wide with terror.

"And now," El Diablo said suavely, "we must not keep the priest waiting any longer."

"The priest?" Skye managed to whisper.

". . . who is to marry us! It was, perhaps, remiss of me not to have explained that sooner."

Perhaps Skye's white, bewildered face evoked some sort of compassion in him for El Diablo went on:

"I owe you an explanation which must, of necessity, be brief. I am in command of certain forces here. Who and what they are need not concern you—it is sufficient for me to say that amongst them are two large groups of Indians, both of whom wish to present me with one of their most prized squaws. To take one would be to bitterly offend the other; to take neither would be to declare myself but half a man. The solution is very obvious—I must have a wife! As the woman who bears my name must be a credit to me I have chosen you."

"You are mad!" Skye exclaimed.

"So you have already told me."

"Do you think that for one moment I would agree to go through with such a ceremony with you? Nothing and nobody would make me say yes."

"You prefer to stay here with me without the blessing of the Church?"

For a moment there was silence, then, to avoid a direct answer, Skye said quickly:

"Anyway, the marriage would not be legal; there has to be a civil ceremony."

"Which has already taken place."

"What do you mean?"

In reply El Diablo took a document from his desk and held it out to Skye. She took it with a trembling hand.

For a moment the paper swam before her eyes and then she saw it was indeed a Certificate of Marriage between *"Guido, known as El Diablo, and Skye Standish"*.

"How did you get this?" Her voice was harsh with anger.

"We were married by proxy," El Diablo smiled. "The Registrar in Jácara required very little persuasion."

Skye threw the document on the floor.

"There are no depths to which you will not sink," she said. "But even you cannot make a priest marry a woman who tells him she is unwilling."

"If he understands her," El Diablo answered softly. "Unfortunately, in the rush in which these arrangements had to be made I could only procure the services of a travelling priest who is on his way back to Brazil. I regret, for your sake, he only speaks Portuguese."

There was nothing Skye could say, and as she stared at him wordlessly El Diablo turned toward the doorway and drew back the curtain.

"Come," he commanded. "You will marry me—there is no alternative."

Almost as if she was mesmerized, Skye stepped forward. For a moment she could think of nothing save that she must obey the order she had been given and then, as she reached El Diablo's side and looked out across the terrace and down into the camp below, wild thoughts of screaming, running, fighting, ran through her mind. Only to be checked by some solid common sense at the back of her brain which told her it would be useless.

The place seemed transformed from when she last saw it. Along the terrace, down the steps and all round a clearing in the centre of the camp, men stood with flaming torches which cast a weird, barbaric light over the sea of faces which Skye could see turned towards her and El Diablo as they appeared.

For a moment there was a hush before, almost with one voice, the waiting people gave a shout of welcome.

Skye felt El Diablo take her hand, and as if in a dream she found herself descending the steps and walking between the rows of lighted torches to where, before a roughly improvised altar, the priest stood waiting.

"I won't do it, I won't!" She tried to speak the words aloud but she could not force them through the dryness of her lips.

El Diablo's hand was relentless, inexorable, and she knew that to struggle or to fight against him would be utterly useless. Besides, suddenly she was afraid—not only of him but of all these strange unknown people.

It was difficult to see any of them clearly and yet she had the impression that she had moved backwards in the centuries and this was some barbaric ceremony taking place in the Middle Ages. If she refused to do what they wanted what might not these people do to her?

The whole thing was unreal and it was if his voice came from a very great distance when she heard El Diablo speak to her.

"The ceremony will be very short," he said, "for you are not a Catholic."

They had reached the priest by now. Skye realized that the crowd had closed in behind them, encircling them completely so that she was a prisoner not only of one man but also of his followers.

The priest had opened his book. He was wearing the brown habit of a travelling friar. He was a middle-aged man with a husky travel-tired voice, and even when he spoke in Latin he had a strange accent. She did not know what was being said.

As if she was an automaton, she obeyed the commands El Diablo gave her from time to time.

"Say *si*," he commanded her. And then again, "*si*."

The priest took her left hand and gave it to El Diablo. She felt the ring encircle her finger and then they both knelt to receive the blessing. By this time Skye was past praying, past feeling anything save a strange, almost terrifying numbness.

Suddenly El Diablo's hand was beneath her elbow. He helped her to her feet, and half-lifted, half-assisted her on to the platform on which the priest had been standing, and turning towards the people grouped beneath them he shouted in Spanish:

"My friends, let me present my wife!"

A great roar of cheering was echoed and re-echoed by the caves behind them.

"There will be wine for all of you," El Diablo said when he could make himself heard, "and music, too. Let there be music on such an auspicious occasion."

He looked down at Skye as he spoke the last words and she saw the laughter in his eyes, the twist on his lips.

Then, as the guitars started to strum, still drowned by the cheering and shouts of the people, El Diablo led her back the way they had come.

They climbed the stone steps to the terrace; as they reached the entrance to the cave El Diablo stopped for a moment so that Skye could look back.

Men and women were dancing wildly, wine was being brought in great barrels into the arena in the centre of which a fire was being lighted so that the torches should no longer be necessary.

There was something very beautiful about the whole scene. It was like nothing Skye had even seen before in her life and yet, with some part of her critical faculties, she could not fail to appreciate the great shadowy darkness of the caves beneath the starlit sky, the scarlet tongues of flame already leaping from the wood-piled fire.

But before she could see more, El Diablo guided her in through the doorway of the cave and drew the leather curtain across it.

The candles were lit and for a moment the room seemed almost dazzling in contrast to the darkness outside.

Then she saw him turn towards her, a light in his eyes, a smile on his lips, and she remembered that she was alone with El Diablo and that he was now her husband.

4

Skye stirred and opened her eyes with a feeling that she had slept for a very long time—the dreamless, heavy sleep which comes from utter exhaustion.

The sunshine was percolating into the room making the Indian blankets which covered the walls glow with a soft radiance as if they were made of seventeenth-century velvet.

Skye shut her eyes against the light and buried her face deeper in the pillow. She had not lain down on her bed until the dawn had broken and the camp below had begun to stir into life.

Then, as the dogs began to bark, the children tumbled from the tents and wooden huts, the men emerged yawning and unshaven while the women hurried to the river for water for their ablutions and for cooking, she had known that she could sleep.

But by that time she had been so tired, so completely exhausted, she could only drag her shirt and riding-skirt from her to leave them tumbled on the floor, and fall into bed to be unconscious from the very moment her head touched the pillow.

It had been a night of fear and terror such as she had never experienced in the whole of her soft, sheltered life. And yet nothing had happened.

She had remained alone in her room—alone with the darkness and the terror of her own thoughts.

She had rushed first to the window to see if there was any chance of escaping, but when she had pulled back the curtain she saw that the beautiful iron grille, painstakingly wrought by a sixteenth-century ironsmith, had been made to keep out importunate lovers.

A hand might flutter between the bars to receive the ardent kisses of some serenading gallant, but nothing more substantial could get through, and Skye saw there was not even a pathway outside but that the side of the mountain fell steep and precipitous to the camp below.

She had drawn back the curtain and waited, listening, but she had heard nothing, only the noise from the camp.

The music grew wilder and faster, the shouts and laughter of the dancers rose to a shrill crescendo.

Then that, too, had ceased and there had been only silence and the frightened thumping of her own heart.

She could not believe even then that he would not suddenly surprise her, would not come into her room and proclaim her his wife. She had not believed him when he had said goodnight.

He had crossed the cave to where she stood, every muscle tense, her hands clenched so that the nails bit into the soft flesh of her palms. But when he reached her he said:

"You have had a long day; go to bed now."

She had not known how to answer him. She had been ready to fight, to struggle, to battle against his kisses, even though she knew how helpless she was against his great strength.

She could still feel the fierce possessiveness of his lips on her mouth and she had thought then that if he kissed her again she must die from the very horror of it.

Instead he had merely smiled at her, lifted the curtain which divided her bedroom from the main cave and, with a gesture, invited her to pass through. She had gone towards him warily, afraid, as an animal might be afraid of some inviting trap.

Then, as she reached him, she had looked up to see a strange expression on his face which somehow belied the sudden fire within his eyes.

She wanted to run away, but an innate pride prevented her from doing so. And as if he guessed at the effort with which she held herself in check there was a sudden twist to his lips as he reached out and took her hand in his.

"You came through that with flying colours," he said. "Let me assure you that the ceremony was most necessary from my point of view."

He bent his head as he spoke and kissed her fingers. She snatched them away from him.

"It is too late now to tell you what I think of you," she cried. "Besides, you know already."

He laughed at that.

"Still so fiery?" he questioned. "I thought perhaps you were too tired to be angry with me any more."

"Angry!" she retorted in a low voice. "I am past anger —I loathe you. I hate and despise you. You are everything that is low and despicable. No, you are right—I am not angry!"

He laughed again and before she was aware of what he was about, bent forward and kissed her lightly on the lips.

He took her by surprise and before she had time to cry out or try to struggle against him he was gone; the curtain that he had released fell forward and Skye found herself alone in her bedroom.

It was then she looked round wildly, wondering for a moment how she could barricade herself in, realizing even as she thought of it that the idea was ridiculous.

There was nothing in the room that El Diablo could not push aside with the greatest of ease. There was nothing, indeed, with which she could protect herself.

So she had waited, standing first by the window and then moving restlessly backwards and forwards across the fur rugs.

Still he had not come! Why had he spared her? Skye asked herself now. For what reason?

She could not find an answer, she could only lie back against her pillows and go over the events of yesterday as they had taken place, one by one, and know herself to be utterly bewildered and even more frightened than she had been before.

How right Jimmy had been in warning her that she had no idea of the dangers she might encounter in Mariposa! Never in her wildest imaginings had she thought that something like this might occur. She had felt utterly sure and complacent of her own inviolability.

Her British nationality and her American dollars had always seemed to safeguard her against any contingency, and yet neither had been the slightest use in grappling with El Diablo.

A sudden sound now made Skye hold her breath with an agonizing fear. It was a footfall she had heard, the soft rattle of the rings as a hand drew aside the curtain which covered the opening into the outer cave.

She did not raise her face, she did not move! She could only lie there unable to breathe from the terror which seemed to paralyse her very thoughts.

Someone had come into the room!

And then she knew it was not the person she feared. The footfall was softer, more gentle. Skye opened her eyes. An Indian girl stood there, her jet-black hair carefully braided on either side of her bronze-skinned young face with slanting sloe-like eyes which dropped shyly before the enquiry in Skye's.

"I will bring food, Señora," she said in the soft, slurring Spanish to which the Indians manage to give a lilting pronunciation all their own.

"Señora"; the word stabbed Skye like a physical wound. She was a married woman now and no longer addressed as "Señorita". It made her shudder as if at some new horror.

"I don't want any," she tried to say, but the Indian girl had left the room.

Skye sat up in bed and looked at her watch. To her astonishment she saw that the hands pointed to nearly three o'clock; she must have slept from dawn until now.

A long time, and yet it was not surprising that she had been exhausted for not only had the physical exertions of the day before been extremely strenuous but the emotions she had experienced had also taken their toll.

Then, as she looked at her wrist-watch her eyes travelled to another piece of jewellry on the same hand—the ring on her third finger, the ring which El Diablo had put there.

For a moment Skye stared at it, then she pulled it from her finger and flung it with all her strength away from her. It hit one of the blue hangings and fell tinkling on to the wooden floor to lie there where she could still see it, glinting in the sunshine.

As she stared at it, hating all that it stood for and the

man who had put it on her finger, she remembered how often she had sworn that she would never get married.

"I hate men!" She had said that not once but dozens of times. She had vowed to herself that she would remain single, subservient to no man, a law unto herself—and yet now she had a husband! And he was El Diablo, a murderer, a revolutionary—a devil!

Skye put her hands up to her face and even as she did so she heard the Indian girl coming from the outer cave. She brought a tray and set it down beside the bed.

Skye wanted to refuse to eat anything and then she realized that she would need all her strength and all her intelligence to cope with the ordeals which lay ahead of her.

With an effort she forced herself to drink a little of the soup that was flavoured with a fresh green vegetable not unlike asparagus. She could not face another dish, but sipped the yerba maté, which was biting hot on the tongue.

She had already got a taste for the roasted crushed leaves of the yerba plant which is the national drink of the South Americans. Skye liked the little tube with a bulbous end through which the yerba was sucked from the ground leaves.

The tube was usually of silver, but the maté the Indian girl had brought her had one of gold. She felt the drink stimulate and invigorate her so that it was not too difficult to say graciously:

"Thank you, that has made me feel better! What is your name?"

"Neengai, Señora."

"What a pretty name! Will you bring some water so that I can wash, Neengai?"

The Indian girl brought a big earthenware jug full of warm water, and while Skye washed she moved around the room picking up her riding clothes from the floor and tidying her things.

"Now my clothes, Neengai!" Skye said when she had dried herself.

The Indian girl nodded her head.

"Your clothes, Señora; yes, they come; I bring to you."

She ran from the room and Skye looked towards the window. How was she to escape?

The words seemed to repeat themselves over and over again in her mind! Or would he let her go? That was another question.

"I hate him! God, how I hate him!"

She said the words out loud, yet they gave her no relief, no satisfaction. They only sounded empty and weak.

"Your clothes, Señora."

The Indian girl spoke from the doorway, then came staggering into the room carrying a heavy suitcase.

Skye gave an exclamation which seemed to come like a pistol-shot from between her lips. She recognized the case —and why not? She had bought it on Fifth Avenue only six months ago, with a dozen others to match it.

"Where did that come from?" Her voice, in her surprise, sounded high and querulous.

"There are more, Señora—two more."

The Indian girl made two more journeys. Skye heard her speak in Indian to someone in the outer room who obviously handed her the cases, then she pulled the curtain to and turned to Skye with an eagerness that was very feminine.

"I unpack for the Senora?"

"How did these get there?" Skye strove to speak calmly.

"Men bring them just two . . . three minutes ago," the Indian girl answered.

"And where did they get them from?" Skye enquired and then she knew that she had no hope of an answer even if she asked the question.

What would this girl know of what was happening? She shut her eyes for a moment, willing herself to remain calm. She had a sudden feeling that she wanted to shriek, to yell out her fears and her hatred so that all the world could hear them.

Then, as she thought of screaming, she saw how ridiculous she would appear—caged high above the people down below, who might hear her voice, but would not be able to see her.

"Open the cases," she said curtly to the Indian girl. "I will choose something to wear."

There would be time later, she thought, to speculate how the things got there and why they had been packed and sent.

Had El Diablo stolen them, or had he raided her yacht and taken her crew prisoner? There were so many possibilities. One thing only mattered at the moment—that she should be decently clothed before she saw him again.

Skye dragged things out at random, refusing everything that was bright or attractive, choosing finally a white silk riding-shirt buttoned high at the neck and secured with a plain mannish-looking tie, a severely tailored pair of yachting trousers and a tailored jacket which made her figure appear flat and thin and almost as sexless as a young boy's.

With her hair-brush that had come in her dressing-case with other articles of toilet, Skye tried to force her hair to lie demurely against her head; but the golden curls defeated her, curling riotously round her small ears and slipping back rebelliously against her white forehead as soon as the brush left them.

A pair of low-heeled walking shoes and thick silk stockings completed her outfit and when at last she was ready, she walked from the bedroom. She had a moment's apprehension as she drew back the curtain.

The outer cave was even bigger than she remembered and she saw that on the other side of the room was an opening similar to the one which led to her bedroom, and she guessed that this was where El Diablo slept.

She had no time, however, to speculate on anything save that the room was empty.

Softly she crossed it and only as she reached the open doorway which led on to the terrace outside did she see that a man stood there. He was leaning against the wall, but there was a rifle at his side.

With a revolver in a holster, a knife in his belt, he was smoking and watching the business of the camp below him, and yet he was on guard!

Skye waited a moment and drew a deep breath. She had to be sure. With an effort she walked to the doorway.

"*Buenos dias,*" she said to the man, who swept his sombrero from his head.

"*Buenos dias, Señora.*"

Twisting her lips into the semblance of a smile, Skye tried to walk past him, but raising his rifle he barred her way.

"*Excusa,* Señora, El Cabeza commands that you remain inside."

"But I would like to go for a walk to get the air."

"*Excusa,* Señora, it is not permitted."

The words were inflexible and there could be no arguing about them. Skye turned with a little flounce and went back into the cave.

She had expected it and yet it was humiliating to know

she was publicly branded as prisoner, guarded by men who must, amongst themselves, smile on her helplessness.

She felt her anger rising within her so that it was with difficulty that she restrained herself from rushing past the man and striving to escape. If only she had a revolver!

She looked round the big cave with its exquisitely carved ceiling, at the granite walls which had been chiselled smooth with infinite labour.

There was a big open fireplace in one wall, against another was a carved cabinet. Anxiously, hoping that the man at the door would not hear her movements, Skye tried to open it—it was locked!

There remained the chest which contained the diamonds and a desk under the window. There were several drawers in the latter and yet even without trying them Skye felt certain they would be locked.

She was up against something more subtle than the type of man who would leave a revolver waiting for her to pick it up. If she were to gain anything, she would have to be cunning; if her plans to escape were to succeed, she would have to make them calmly and unemotionally.

She tried to remember if El Diablo had worn a revolver when she arrived the night before, but somehow she could remember only the great height of him as he had risen from the couch on her entrance and the expression in his eyes which made her hand creep to the neck of her riding-shirt.

She should have known then—no, she should have known even sooner—that time she had spoken to him about the man hanged from the tree. She had seen then an expression on his face that she did not understand.

She had encountered love in her life, she had encountered admiration, she had even been aware that men desired her; but never before had she known a man who could look at her with a disdain that seemed almost to be akin to hatred and yet desire to kiss her at the same time.

She put her hands up to her eyes as she thought of it!

The hours passed slowly; Skye walked from cave to cave and back again. The Indian girl finished unpacking her clothes, hanging the dresses in an alcove behind one of the blankets, which made a natural wardrobe, and filling the chest with diaphanous nightgowns and lace-trimmed underclothes.

"Will not the Señora rest?" she asked at length, seeing

Skye's strained white face and disturbed by the restlessness of her movements.

"No . . . no . . . I am not tired."

"I will fetch you some fresh maté," Neengai said softly, offering the only panacea she knew for a troubled mind, and she hurried away before Skye could tell her that she wanted nothing.

She dreaded El Diablo's return and yet at the same time she wanted to see him, the suspense was intolerable, beset by her fears and her terror.

She sipped the maté when the Indian girl brought it, but it seemed to stick in her throat. Hour after hour went by and then at length there came a sudden shout from below.

Skye ran to the window to see El Diablo and six of his followers come riding into the camp.

The setting sun shone on the silver of his harness and saddle as he swung himself off his horse. It glinted, too, on his spurs. He stopped to speak to several men who had obviously been waiting for his return, and then at length he left them and started in an unhurried manner to climb the steep stone stairway which led to the caves.

Skye drew back from the window.

Now that he was coming she could feel her heart beating in a manner which made her feel sick, and she gripped her hands together in an effort to force herself to think calmly of what she must say and what she must do.

But it was impossible for her to stop the trembling of her knees.

She heard his footsteps ring out on the wooden floor of the sitting-room, heard his voice, low and deep, as he gave an order to someone to bring him a glass of wine—and then there was silence.

She expected him to come to the door of her bedroom, she expected him to send for her, but nothing happened. She stood plucking with nervous fingers at the iron grille, waiting, waiting!

She could have gone to him, but she could not force herself to do so. She could only wait and wonder if this was a worse humiliation than those she had suffered already.

Five minutes went by, ten, twenty—Skye glanced at her watch—it was nearly eight o'clock. She supposed that he would send for her when dinner was ready.

In this supposition she was right. Skye had not heard the Indian girl leave the room, but now she returned.

"Dinner is ready, Señora." She bowed and vanished.

And at last Skye must force herself from the window and cross the bedroom towards the outer cave.

She walked slowly, striving for dignity and a pride which had seemed to come so easily to her only yesterday. She drew back the curtain.

He was standing with his back to the empty fireplace, facing her, and she saw that he had changed into clothes he had worn the night before—the white shirt, vivid red sash, the long dark trousers which made him seem even taller than when he wore riding-breeches.

He was smoking a cigar and as she entered the room he took it from his mouth, holding it between his fingers so that the smoke from it rose towards his face as if it were incense before some heathen god.

"So your clothes have arrived!"

He spoke abruptly in English and, because they were not the words she expected him to say, she started a little nervously.

"I would like an explanation . . ." she began, only to be interrupted.

"That can wait," he said. "At the moment there is another matter—the way you are dressed! A very unattractive get-up and decidedly masculine. I think you have forgotten that the reason I brought you here is because you are a woman. I have a fancy to see you in evening dress. Dinner will wait while you change."

The colour came flooding in a crimson tide into Skye's pale cheeks.

"How dare you!"

He raised his eyebrows at that.

"Surely that is an old-fashioned retort?"

"I refuse to change. Do you hear me?" Skye said. "I refuse."

He looked down at his cigar. For a moment there was a faint smile on his lips.

"Must I play lady's maid?" he enquired.

There was no mistaking the threat underlying the quietness of his words, for he raised his eyes as he spoke and Skye saw the determination in them.

For a moment she defied him, her chin high, her breath coming quickly; then with a little sound that was neither a sob nor a groan, she fled behind the curtain which screened her bedroom.

The Indian girl was not there to help her.

Hurriedly, and in a fever lest he should follow her and

put his threat into operation, she dragged off the jacket and trousers, flung off the walking shoes and heavy silk stockings and took from behind the blue hangings the first dress her hand encountered.

It was only when she had put it on, and caught a glimpse of herself in the mirror as she bent down to fasten her evening sandals, that she realized she was wearing a ball gown.

A frock of pale green tulle, embroidered with diamanté, it had a great cluster of coral-coloured flowers trailing over one shoulder and down the side of the skirt.

It was a dress she had only worn once before at a ball in New York, and now she wondered if anything could be more incongruous than its billowing, sparkling skirts in a cave fashioned by Incas and inhabited by a modern bandit.

She tidied her hair, had a glimpse of her white face, her eyes wide and frightened. Then she turned from the mirror towards the outer cave. As she came in, he was still standing where she had left him.

His cigar was finished, but now he held a glass in his hand. He looked at her for a moment without speaking.

She was vividly conscious of the nakedness of her shoulders, of the low-cut bodice revealing the soft curves of her breasts, moving tumultuously now from the violence of her emotions.

"That is better," he said.

His approval seemed even harder to bear than when he had found fault with her.

"I hate you!" she said in a low voice fraught with anger. "I hate you!"

"In that case you will continue to amuse me," he said. "It is the mawkish sentimentality which most women call love which I find intolerable. Hatred is healthy and extremely stimulating."

Skye gripped the back of a chair. Afterwards she wondered what she would have answered if the Indians had not entered that moment with dinner.

The meal was even more delicious than the night before, with wines of a subtle bouquet that might have graced a banquet in any great capital of Europe. But Skye found it hard to make even a pretence of eating.

She sipped a little of the wine, waiting until coffee was served before she asked the questions which had been trembling on her lips all evening.

"How long are you going to keep me here?"

He looked at her appraisingly; his eyes flickered over her face, vivid and lovely even in its strained anxiety, and travelled over the rest of her body from her shining, golden head to her silver sandals.

"Until you bore me," he answered. "Even the novelty of being married will not survive *ennui*."

Skye sprang to her feet.

"How can you be so preposterous? Do you imagine that I shall not be missed? Why, by now the Captain of my yacht will have telegraphed to my cousin in Chile. Search parties will be sent to find me. You will suffer for this outrage."

"I think not," El Diablo said quietly; "you see, I have taken every precaution to ensure that you should see undisturbed the country in which you are so interested."

"What do you mean by that?"

"Exactly what I say. Even a 'twopenny-ha'penny bandit' can have brains, if he cares to use them."

"Who told you I had said that? This is a nightmare. No one could be so omnipotent as you pretend to be."

"I pretend nothing," El Diablo said. "To set your mind at rest and to assure you that your inestimable cousin is not being disturbed, I will, if you wish, explain what I have arranged."

El Diablo rose as he spoke and walked across the room to his desk. He took a letter from the blotter and brought it to Skye, holding it out for her to take.

"This is a copy of the letter that the Captain of your yacht received early this morning."

Skye took the writing paper from him and then stood staring. One glance was enough to make her open her eyes wide in astonishment and her lips parted in perplexity.

It was a letter in her own handwriting, a letter so cleverly inscribed that she could hardly believe that she had not indeed writtten it.

She read in amazement:

Dear Captain Maclean,

    I have had the good fortune to meet some friends and they have asked me to stay with them. I feel this is a great opportunity to see the interior of the country and I would be grateful, therefore, if you would have packed and sent by the bearers of this letter a sufficient amount of my clothes to last me two or three weeks. Evans will know what I require; and ask him also to include my evening dresses. I hope you and the crew will enjoy your stay in Jácara.

One of my host's servants will call every few days in case there are any letters for me which require attention.

With best wishes,

Yours sincerely,
Skye Standish.

Skye stared at her own signature and then ejaculated: "But how . . . where? . . . I can't believe it!"

"I'm afraid a letter to your aunt in England has been delayed for a day," El Diablo said, smiling at her bewilderment.

For a moment Skye did not understand what he meant. Then she remembered the letter she had written early yesterday morning and handed to a man on the quay to post.

He must have been one of El Diablo's men and her letter had provided the bandit with a specimen of her handwriting.

In what she hoped was a stinging manner, Skye said scornfully:

"So you are a forger as well as a murderer!"

"Unfortunately I cannot claim such an outstanding talent as that," El Diablo replied; "but there is a man in the camp here who is undoubtedly an artist in such matters. I think, if we knew the truth about him, we would find that he had left Argentina for some very good reason, connected with his genius for being able to copy other people's signatures! But here we ask very few questions about a man's past. We are more concerned with his future."

"As I am concerned with mine," Skye said. "You cannot seriously mean that you intend to keep me here for . . . for so long."

"It may be long, it may be short," El Diablo said. "I have told you what governs the time factor of your visit."

"You insult me."

"So you have told me several times already. It begins to be wearisome."

"Good. If I weary you perhaps you will let me go."

El Diablo smiled.

"Not when you look like that," he said. "Come here."

He was standing with his back to the fireplace, to which he had moved as Skye read the letter. She was some paces from him and now instinctively she took a step further back.

"Perhaps you didn't hear me," El Diablo said, not raising his voice, but speaking still in the quiet, even tone that he had used all through dinner. "I told you to come here."

"No!"

It was a defiant monosyllable, but not a very steady one.

"You will learn that here I am used to getting my own way," El Diablo said. "I expect to be obeyed . . . especially by my wife."

Skye did not move. She was staring at him, her eyes very dark against the whiteness of her face, her hands pressed against the bodice of her tulle gown where it met her naked skin.

There was a silence so poignant that it seemed to Skye that he must hear the frightened throb of her heart, and then he said softly:

"It would be a pity to spoil that pretty dress."

Slowly then, one foot dragging after another, she went towards him.

5

Neengai's soft Indian voice awoke Skye from a deep sleep.

"El Cabeza say you go riding with him, Señora. He ready in twenty minutes."

Skye sat up in bed, her tiredness gone, a sense of excitement rising within her. If she was free of the imprisoning walls, there was always a chance of her finding some opportunity of escape.

She had not slept for a long time the night before but had lain awake, her mind running through the whole gamut of human emotions starting with anger so fierce and so murderous that she almost frightened herself.

Yet, once again he had left her at the door of her own room, once again she had waited fearfully as the hours had passed slowly—once again she had been left undisturbed.

When dinner was over he had kissed her. She writhed now as she thought of his kisses, long, fierce, passionate and possessive, which had seemed in their very ruthlessness to force her to acknowledge him her master.

He had made love to her as she had imagined the conquerors in the Spanish Invasion had made love to the women they had acquired through conquest.

He had flattered her and paid her compliments; he had talked of love, choosing exquisite words and exquisite phrases as only a South American could spin out one subject hour upon hour and never manage to repeat himself.

He had teased her and made her angry and then when she would have abused him had stopped her mouth with his kisses so that she had been unable to say anything.

It was a humiliation such as she had never imagined could happen to her, or to any woman, and all the time she had felt that there was something behind the manner in which he played with her.

She could not put it into words, could not explain even to herself that strange feeling she had—and yet it was there.

He desired her, she knew that. There was no pretence about the fire in his eyes or the demanding passion of his kisses. She excited him and yet he had kissed her goodnight at the door of her bed-chamber and let her enter it alone. What did it mean? Why was he so forbearing?

Skye asked the question and could find no answer. She did not understand; she could not pretend to do so.

He was an enigma; a man so different, so utterly the opposite in every way to the men she had met before in her life, that she could only feel completely at a loss to account for anything she said or did.

"I hate him! I hate him!" She said the words over and over again to herself.

Now there was a kind of sick helplessness in the very repetition of them. She might hate him but there was nothing she could do about it.

When he took her in his arms she might as well struggle against the walls of the cave or the vastness of the mountains beyond.

"When will you cease to fight me?" he asked once, as his hand caressed the softness of her white shoulder and she twisted fruitlessly to evade his touch.

"When I am dead," she flashed, "and at times I wish that could be soon."

He laughed at her.

"Like the flowers of the field you were made for the delight of man. Why else should you be so beautiful?"

"I wish I was hideous, deformed, mutilated, and then perhaps you would leave me alone."

"But because you are none of those things I want to touch you, to kiss you," he said. "My beautiful wife! All men who see you will envy me."

She knew by the tone of his voice that he was trying to provoke her and yet she could not forbear to cry wildly:

"Give me a knife or a gun and I will show those other men how much you are to be envied."

But now that Neengai had told her that she could go riding she was ready to rush to El Diablo's side rather than spend the day alone.

More than anything else she had dreaded the long day ahead, when there would be nothing for her to do but to sit thinking and waiting for the evening to come and for El Diablo to return.

Now she was reprieved, and without wasting any time in talking she started to wash in cold water.

"Wait, wait, Señora," Neengai cried; "I will bring you hot water while you eat breakfast."

"I can manage with cold," Skye replied.

She was certain that El Diablo would not wait for her if she were even a few seconds late. In his egotism and arrogance he would consider no one but himself and if she were not ready at the moment appointed, he would, she was sure, ride away without giving her so much as a second thought.

Only when she was dressed, her gloves and riding-whip in her hand, did she cross the room to the breakfast tray beside her bed to sip a cup of hot coffee and pick at the fruit which the Indian girl had brought her as well as a more substantial dish of eggs.

"The Señora will be hungry," Neengai wailed as Skye turned towards the door after biting into a fresh apricot and leaving everything else untouched.

"Don't worry about me," Skye said with a smile, perhaps

the first which had parted her lips since she came to the camp.

There was no one in the sitting-room and Skye went quickly to the open door, but the guard was outside. He gave her a look out of his dark eyes which told her without words that she was not yet permitted to pass, so she withdrew to the window and looked down on the camp.

She could see horses being saddled and men hurrying to and fro in their wide sombreros, while women stood at the doors of the huts watching them.

The sun was rising in the heavens but had not yet come to its full strength; the breeze was cool and Skye felt a longing to be out in the open, away from the horror and disgust that these strange caves had for her.

She was so intent on watching the scene below that she did not hear El Diablo arrive and started when his voice behind her asked:

"Are you ready?"

She turned quickly, the sun streaming through the window turning her curls to living gold and making them a halo for her small face.

Anger and sleeplessness had left dark lines under her eyes and made them seem even bigger than usual. She was lovely and even in her riding-clothes, exquisitely and provocatively feminine.

El Diablo stood looking at her and she saw the smouldering fire behind his eyes. He took a step towards her and instinctively Skye shrank away, backing until she could go no further, her shoulders against the iron grille of the window.

"You look like spring itself," he said softly.

When she did not answer, he put his hand under her chin and, tipping back her head, looked down at her face which was suddenly drained of all colour.

"I am only going to kiss you," he said reassuringly and added, as he saw her swallow convulsively, "do you hate my kisses as much as all that?"

"Yes, I hate them," Skye cried passionately, "and you, too!"

For a moment he held her prisoner, his hand against her chin as inflexible as a steel bar; then with a little laugh he set her free.

"You are certainly frank," he said, "if not complimentary."

"Are you so vain as to imagine that contact with you could do anything but increase my hatred of you?"

"In that you are at least original," El Diablo replied, taking a cigar from the box on his desk.

"What do you mean by that?" Skye asked, not quite understanding.

He lit his cigar slowly.

"I mean that I believe you when you say you hate me," he answered. "Women do not always mean what they say."

"It is true enough as far as I am concerned," Skye said bitterly; then, turning towards him on a sudden impulse, she cried, "Why don't you let me go? There may be women who would like to be here, who could even care for you—though God help them if they did!—but I loathe and detest every second that I must be in your company. Surely that cannot be amusing for you?"

"The unexpected never bores me," El Diablo replied.

"If only I could become fond of you, I might be able to bore you!" Skye cried bitterly; "but as it is, you are inflicting a life sentence on me!" Her tone was one of despair.

As if he were suddenly tired of the conversation, El Diablo flicked the ash from his cigar and picked up his riding-whip.

"Come," he commanded, "it is too early for dramatics."

Skye felt herself quiver with rage at the manner in which her feelings could be dismissed so lightly and so callously; but she knew that to rage and storm would get her no further.

Biting back the words that rose to her lips, she took her hat from the table, where she had laid it on entering the room, and put it on her head.

"I am ready," she said flatly.

Courteously he indicated that she would leave the cave before him and with her chin held high, not looking at him, she stepped out into the sunshine.

She had been too tired and too worried on the night she arrived to take more than a cursory glance at the caves, but now in the bright morning sunlight she saw that they were indeed amazing.

There were hundreds of them opening off the narrow pathways which had been carved out of the solid rock. They had a beauty of their own, and the loveliness of their surroundings was almost beyond words.

The sides of the mountains were covered in flowering

shrubs and beyond the camp was the cattle pasture, rich grassland gay with scarlet and white verbena.

The river in the distance was as vividly blue as the Mediterranean as it reflected the sky above. And the people moving in this strange, secret encampment were as colourful as their surroundings.

The Indian women wore gaily patterned dresses of cotton or wool woven on their primitive hand-looms. Their bronze skins were in vivid contrast to the warm darkness of their eyes.

Mingling with them were white skins and black, the parchment yellow of the Japanese, the oriental saffron of the Chinese. But among the mixture of races the true Mariposans stood out unmistakably.

They were easily recognizable by their height and their clear complexions; their dark eyes, inherited from some Spanish forbear, were offset by finely cut features which gave them a proud, almost aristocratic, air, while many of their women had a regal loveliness which would have made them outstanding in any European ballroom.

After her first quick appreciation of the scene around her, Skye felt a sudden embarrassment. She realized that she was the cynosure of all eyes.

She was being watched from the caves, from the huts on the encampment, by the men sitting on the horses, by the guards posted at advantageous points, rifles in their hands.

Even the children seemed to have stopped their play for the moment as she came down the long flight of stone steps to where the horses were waiting at the foot of them. In spite of her every resolution to show only complete indifference, she felt the colour rising in her cheeks so that, when El Diablo drew level with her as the steps ended, she said to him:

"Have your people never seen a white woman before?"

"Many," he answered, "but they are always incurably inquisitive about those who honour me by their presence, and especially the one who is unique in that she bears my name."

It was not his irony that made her angry but the realization, though perhaps she had been stupid not to guess it before, that she was but one of many women whom El Diablo brought to the camp.

It came to her with something of a shock and then she

remembered those four pairs of moccasins laid out the night she had arrived.

For a moment the humiliation of it made her feel like screaming; her fingers tightened on her riding-whip and it was only with difficulty that she prevented herself from striking him in the face.

With an almost superhuman effort of self-control she said nothing, but the fury vibrating through her must have communicated itself to him, for he looked down at her with a faint smile and repeated:

"It is still too early for dramatics."

"One day you will go too far."

She spoke in a low voice between clenched teeth.

He laughed and turned away from her to inspect the horses which were being held with difficulty by the two Indian grooms. They were both magnificent specimens of horseflesh and though Skye might hate many things about Mariposa she could never resist the pleasure which a fine horse gave her.

Prancing and capering, the animal which had been brought for her to ride was an almost black mare.

"Will she be too much for you?" El Diablo enquired.

Skye realized that for once his question was serious and that, if her reply was in the affirmative, he would find her a less spirited animal.

"I have ridden since I could walk," Skye answered proudly, "I have also helped to break in horses on my grandfather's ranch in California."

He said no more and with a brief gesture of his hand he indicated to the Indian standing by that he should help her to mount, while he swung himself into the saddle. Both horses reared, took a few prancing steps sideways and reared again.

Then Skye felt her mare respond to the touch of the rein, and as she moved forward beside El Diablo the horses quickly settled into a brisk trot.

The *gauchos* waiting in a group a little way ahead spurred their horses forward and in a minute the whole cavalcade passed out of the camp and on to the grassy plain.

There were six men in their escort, Skye counted; and now some of her anger began to pass from her and with it the tension under which she had been suffering ever since she awoke.

It was impossible not to smell the fragrance of the wild

flowers and notice the flamingoes and white herons flying down to the river.

There were clouds of humming-birds over the pampas, their swiftness of flight an enchantment even apart from the beauty of their plumage.

Several times Skye saw an ostrich hurrying away from their path and once, as they rode past the solitary majesty of an ombu tree, she caught a glimpse of a vividly coloured toucan, its enormous beak open to emit its raucous voice, which seemed strangely discordant amidst so much beauty.

They rode in silence, the clatter of hoofs, the jingle of harness seeming to make a music of their own.

Now Skye had a chance to note that every man was armed not only with a revolver, some of them the old, heavy brass-handled type, but also with the *cuchillo*, an enormous silver-hilted knife, without which any *gaucho* would feel undressed.

She longed to ask El Diablo where they were going, but she would not bring herself to speak to him, vowing with suddenly tightened lips that she would not even address him more than was necessary.

She glanced at him as they rode forward side by side and despite her hatred she could not help but admit that he rode well. His horse, a dark chestnut, was bigger than the average mount and it carried him proudly, his height and breadth of shoulder in perfect proportion to the spirited animal beneath him. Yet in spite of his height he had a lithe grace about him and a wiry inflexibility.

Even to think of him added fuel to Skye's anger and hatred until, forcing herself to look ahead, she kept her eyes away from the man riding beside her.

They rode on for perhaps an hour, then came to a low *hacienda* shielded by a clump of eucalyptus trees.

Two men came running out to talk with El Diablo. Skye gathered that they were the owners of the farm and she was surprised to note the deference and eagerness with which they greeted him.

They spoke of their stock; and then with a friendly "*Beunos dias*" they were riding on again, over the rolling country to the next *hacienda*.

They visited half a dozen, El Diablo listening to the troubles of the owners, giving advice and sometimes issuing orders.

At times Skye noticed, when the farm was a very poor

one, that he gave the owner money—heavy silver pesos which he carried in his saddle-bag.

They were moving inland all the time, keeping north of the river, the mountains on their right. Skye had a good bump of locality and while they were riding she kept her eyes open for possible landmarks which might one day be of use to her.

Jácara lay behind them, south as they were heading at the moment, but due east of the camp.

It was about noon when they stopped at a *hacienda* where their coming was anticipated and a meal was laid for them.

It was a primitive, rough meal, very unlike the good food El Diablo had prepared for him in his own camp; but he ate with apparent enjoyment while Skye had to force herself to swallow even a few mouthfuls of the *puchero*—a stew of tough, newly-killed meat which had been cooked over a wood fire.

There was also home-baked maize bread with goat's-milk cheese and for the *gauchos* quantities of a local rough red wine and, of course, the inevitable yerba maté. The only sweet was a spoonful of quince jelly, very sweet and sticky, which made the *gauchos* suck their lips appreciatively.

All the time they were eating, waited on by the women-folk of the farm, the owner talked, grumbling in long, monotonous undertones of his troubles. He was an unprepossessing sight, with a greasy shirt bulging over greasy *bombachas,* his dirty, naked feet thrust into ragged, rope-soled slippers.

"Misery, misery!" he seemed to be saying, and he looked the personification of it.

He complained that the cattle had done well, but now there was no market for them. What was to become of him and of the farmers like him if they could not find a market? El Diablo said nothing until the meal was finished.

Then he rose to his feet and put a handful of silver pesos down on the table.

"Markets will be found," he said. "For the moment you have got to be patient. If we hurry things now, we are likely to lose everything."

"*Si, si,* Señor, I understand that. We know you are fighting for us, but still I have my livelihood to consider—and my family, my wife, my four daughters."

"You must have patience, my friend."

El Diablo turned away abruptly and the farewells were not so good humoured this time as they rode away from the *hacienda*.

"Why can't he find a market for his cattle?" Skye asked.

She had not meant to question El Diablo, but somehow her curiosity was too much for her. Despite her own problems, she found herself becoming interested in those of other people.

This farmer in an isolated *hacienda*, miles from any-where—how could he live there if he was prevented from taking his cattle to Jácara? What was happening that things were worse apparently than they had been in the past?

"Are you really interested?"

She saw a twinkle in El Diablo's eyes as if he had known that she had deliberately refrained from speaking to him until now.

"Yes, I am," Skye answered truthfully.

They were having to go a little more slowly at this moment as they were passing over a small, rocky ridge where the shrubs were so thick that it was impossible for the horses to move except at a walk. The *gauchos* were behind them, well out of earshot, and anyhow, they spoke in English.

"Very well, then, I will tell you," El Diablo said, "and it can be put in one word—Alejo!"

"Just him or his government, too?" Skye enquired.

"There is no government apart from Alejo," El Diablo replied. "He is surrounded by a small company of 'yes men' who call him 'El Supremo'—is any other description necessary?"

"Go on!" Skye said.

"A few months ago, Alejo decreed that the land north of Jácara was government property—it was to be what you call in England nationalized. Men who have had their farms here for hundreds of years were to be dispossessed of their land overnight for no reason at all that they could understand. This decree only concerned the north of the country, the country between Jácara and Brazil."

"But why?" Skye asked.

"That is exactly what most people asked," El Diablo said. "The answer lies in those mountains."

"Why?" Skye enquired again.

El Diablo looked at her and looked away.

"I am telling you just as much as it is advisable for you to know," he said. "It is sufficient for me to say that El

Supremo had his reasons—and very good ones at that. Unfortunately he reckoned without the opposition of the Indians who for years have made this part of the country their own. An Indian always wants land.

"Perhaps the greatest sin the white conquerors of South America have committed has been to dispossess the Indian of his native soil. In Mariposa no one has troubled about them for generations and they have staked their claim as it were—not on the plains where the Mariposan farmers have their herds, but on the shrub ground and on the sides of the mountains which no one else wanted. Yet now they are told that they have no real claim to it. It is General Alejo's!"

"Has he tried to turn them out?"

"Not yet," El Diablo said grimly. "The standing army of Mariposa is about seven hundred strong. Counting every trained and semi-trained man, they could, I imagine, bring their strength up to about two thousand. There are already over four thousand men here in the north, the majority of them Indians, who are ready to fight with the farmers for what they believe to be their birthright."

"So that is why you are afraid of spies!"

"I am not afraid of them," El Diablo answered; "I merely eliminate them."

Skye felt herself shiver. There was a hard note of cruelty in his tone which made her remember again the man who had hung from the tree with his staring eyes and open mouth.

For a moment she was almost sorry for the Dictator; then she remembered she had heard only one side of the story.

It was plausible enough as told her by El Diablo, but she wondered what the official government of Mariposa would say about a man who defied their laws and hanged those they employed.

They were over the ridge now and were cantering again. On they went, all through the afternoon, stopping only to water their horses and visit the *haciendas* and to talk with various small companies of Indians whom they found camped on the hillside.

Once El Diablo pointed out to her the river where the diamonds were found and she could see men working in the river bed.

"The stones are larger near the source," he said briefly.

"May I see what is happening?"

"Not today."

She had another glimpse of men at the mouth of a mine. There were huts and tents not far away, looking in the distance very like El Diablo's own camp. But again she was not allowed close enough to see what was happening and they rode on to another *hacienda*.

It was going to be late before they turned for home. The evening was drawing on, the heat of the day was past. Skye bent forward to pat her horse's neck. The mare seemed as fresh as when they had set out.

As if El Diablo guessed her thoughts, he said:

"These animals are bred for long distances. Have you never heard of the Creole horses?"

"No."

"Unfortunately they are dying out, but the Americas owe them much."

"What are they?"

"Descendants of the Arab stock brought here by the Spaniards at the time of the conquest. It has been proved that no horses existed in the continent before then."

"Arab stock! That accounts for so much!"

Skye patted her horse's head again.

"You ride well," El Diablo said, watching her.

Skye stiffened at the compliment. She had forgotten her hatred of him while they talked of horses. Now, like an animal, she shied away from the admiration in his eyes.

He laughed softly.

"No Englishwoman knows how to receive a compliment gracefully."

"We are particular as to who pays them to us."

"And mine are not acceptable?"

"No! That should be obvious."

She stared at him with a disdain which would have made an Englishman or an American shrivel into silence, but El Diablo only laughed again.

"Aren't you tired of fighting me?"

"No. I will fight you to the last breath I draw!"

"Inevitably a losing battle!"

"Perhaps an opportunity will come, or fate will be kind. And in victory I shall be merciless."

Skye spoke passionately. El Diablo swept his broad-brimmed hat from his head.

"A challenge from my most beautiful wife!" he smiled. "And I accept it."

He was mocking her, and Skye could have killed him at that moment had she carried a gun. She turned her face away and with her chin held high she rode on quickly.

Every nerve in her body was vibrant with her loathing of this man who held her in his power and played with her as a cat plays cruelly with the mouse it has captured.

One more *hacienda* and then they rode east towards the camp. Skye had been observant all the afternoon of where they were going, watching for any opportunity which might present itself for her to escape, but never for one moment had she been left unguarded.

Six men and El Diablo himself were a formidable escort. She felt her spirits sink. She was haunted with the thought of what night could bring in its train; and now with a sickening sense of desperation she found herself praying that something might happen to save her.

Wildly she thought of dragging the revolver from the holster of one of the men riding beside her and holding them up before they could draw against her. But she knew that such ideas exist only in story books.

The gun would scarcely be in her hand before someone might shoot it from her fingers, or, worse still, overpower her from behind.

She had no illusions about her cleverness in being able to out-shoot men who used revolvers with the habitual ease with which she used a knife and fork.

No, she had to think of something better than that—but what?

They were growing nearer and nearer to the camp—another mile or so and they would be back. Skye felt her heart begin to throb at the thought of climbing up the stone stairs to the caves.

They were like the web of some monstrous spider, she thought a little hysterically. She remembered the fire in El Diablo's eyes as he had come towards her that morning, intending to kiss her.

She had saved herself then by the bitterness of her attack upon him, but she would not be able to save herself that evening, when she must put on one of her low-cut gowns for his delight and delectation.

She might be a slave in some Eastern market, she had no more choice of freedom than those poor black negroes who, less than a century ago, had been brought here in the slave ships from their homes in Africa.

She remembered what fate had been waiting for the

younger and better-looking women and the thought made her quiver with a sudden horror.

At that moment a shout interrupted their jogging, homeward trot.

"*Ja-guá! Ja-guá!*"

It was a man who yelled to them. El Diablo turned the head of their small column to ride towards him.

As they drew nearer, they saw that he was an Indian and apparently known to them, for one man riding at the back spoke his name. He waved his arms, talking volubly in his own language which Skye did not understand, and they followed him towards some rocks.

Skye had a quick glimpse of a man lying there mauled and bleeding as if from the claws of a large animal.

Then, as the men all dismounted, El Diablo amongst them, she realized that her chance had come. They all had their backs to her, hurrying towards the fallen man.

She wheeled her horse, but was wise enough not to gallop away immediately. Instead she moved quietly for a short way over the soft grass and then, bringing her whip down sharply on the mare's flank, started her off into a wild gallop.

She was quite an appreciable way from the dismounted *gauchos* before she heard a shout. Glancing back over her shoulder, she saw that someone had seen her and the men were all staring after her.

Headlong she galloped wildly, crouching low in the saddle, the wind blowing away her hat, whistling riotously through her hair.

The entrance to the camp lay ahead, but Skye turned south, knowing that she must keep to the plain, hoping to cross the range lower down when she had thrown off her pursuers.

She did not look back again, and yet she was sure they were coming after her. On she went, keeping beside the river for a little while, then plunging across it when she saw a shallow place where cows must have crossed habitually.

It was only as her horse clambered up the bank on the other side that she looked back. The men were about a mile away from her, galloping hard.

One figure was nearer, half-way between her and them and coming on towards her with speed which she dared not underestimate. His horse was the better of the two.

Her only chance was to take advantage of the start she had and to keep it.

Grassland stretched away ahead, mile upon mile of it, the mountains, their sides thick with shrubs, were on her left. There was nothing she could do but go straight on.

Then she realized that he was gaining on her. Now she could hear his horse's hoofs and then the jingle of his silver harness.

She was gasping for breath and she used her whip mercilessly in her desperation to get away.

It was like a nightmare to realize that El Diablo was growing nearer and nearer. She thought of turning her horse up the mountain-side, but she knew that even a little check would give him the chance to catch up.

Then she determined that if he did, she must run for it. She was lighter than he and perhaps if she took to the mountains she might find a place to hide somewhere amongst the rocks where he might not be able to find her until the darkness came.

Wildly the thoughts went through Skye's mind and with them a terror of being pursued, of being hunted, such as an animal might feel.

He was growing nearer and nearer, the thunder of his horse's hoofs was as loud now as the beat of her heart. In a moment he would catch hold of her horse's bridle and then she must fling herself to the ground and run— run as she had never run before.

The pounding of the horses' hoofs thundered in her ears; she was almost blinded by the speed, her breath coming in choking sobs from between her parted lips.

He was drawing nearer and nearer, his horse was level with hers; then she felt his arm encircle her and she screamed a cry of sheer and abject terror.

He swung her out of the saddle with a skill which requires almost superhuman strength.

He lifted her in full gallop from her own horse on to his.

As she felt herself travel through the air and land roughly in front of him on his saddle, Skye, for a moment, lost consciousness.

It was only a second of merciful oblivion and she came back to reality to know that her chest felt as if someone had hit her with a sledge-hammer.

Her face was buried against El Diablo's coat. She knew then that the arms that held her tightly to him were a prison bar she was unable to break or evade.

She wanted to fight him, she raised her hand weakly to batter against his chest, but she was too exhausted and could only lie limp and impotent in his arms, struggling for breath.

Only gradually abating the speed of his horse, El Diablo galloped some way before he turned, and then as he slowed down he spoke.

He looked down at Skye's half-hidden face, the dark lashes over closed eyes, the parted lips, the quivering nostrils, the tumultuous rise and fall of her tortured breasts.

"You little fool," he said softly, "did you think you could escape me?"

She hardly heard him. There was only the black misery of knowing that she had failed.

The sun, crimson and large, was sinking into a great green sea of grass and all around rose the sweet fluting notes of the partridges, bird answering bird.

Skye heard them as if in a trance.

Then she heard, too, the *gauchos* as they caught up with them, cheering a brilliant feat of horsemanship on the part of their leader—cheering, too, the capture of a fugitive!

6

Skye spread out the American dollar notes in her hand as if they were a pack of cards, shuffled them together and spread them out again, adding several more notes of high denomination which had lain at her side on the couch.

The Indian was watching her movements, she was sure of that, although his lean face, which might have come to life from an Egyptian frieze, was expressionless.

She added up the notes which she held, three dollars short of a hundred—it was a fortune to a native of Mariposa!

The Indian set the glasses carefully on the table, yet before he turned to fetch the cutlery she saw his eyes, under his thick eyelashes, flicker towards the money.

His skin was the colour of ripe tobacco leaves and his jet-black hair hung down on to the collar of his shirt. He was young, he was handsome, he was greedy.

Skye was certain of it, so certain that she spread out the notes again, and then deliberately let one flutter away to fall on the floor between her couch and the Indian.

He bent to pick it up and hand it back to her, and as he did so she smiled.

"Thank you. What is your name?"

"I am called Yokseyi, Señora," he replied, his voice making new music of the Spanish tongue, quelling its excitement, slowing its hurry to a lazy drone.

"Have you been here long?"

"Only a few weeks, Señora."

That was what she wanted to know, for it would be no use attempting to bribe one of the men who had been with El Diablo a long time; strange though it may seem, they were devoted to him and almost fanatical loyalty showed in their faces.

They treated him, she thought scornfully, as if he were a god rather than a man.

But Yokseyi was new! One of the Indians whom El Diablo had chosen as his personal servants was sick with a touch of fever and his place had been taken while he was away by this younger man, chosen, Skye learned, from dozens of eager volunteers, because he had been trained to wait at one of the hotels in Jácara.

She rose to her feet and, walking to the very back of the cave, beckoned him.

He did not hesitate, but came across the wooden floor softly and almost silently to wait beside her enquiringly, his dark eyes on hers.

She spread out the dollars in her hand.

"Will you take a message to Jácara for me?" she asked.

The words were hardly above a whisper so that the guards outside the door should not hear.

The Indian looked down at the dollar bills. There was no mistaking the longing in his eyes although he did not speak.

"Ninety-seven dollars," Skye said softly.

As in many South American countries, the currency of any nation was acceptable, but American dollars were more coveted than any other money. Translated into pesos such a sum would make a poor Indian rich for life.

"No Señora, I dare not."

The words were almost hissed between his tobacco-stained teeth.

"Do not say 'no'," Skye pleaded. "It is such a little thing to do. Look, here is the note; I want you to take it to the white yacht in the harbour called the *Liberty*—anyone will tell you which she is. That is all you have to do. Leave the note and come away. See, I will give you the dollars now and . . ." She thought wildly of what else would tempt him; then she unclasped from her wrist her gold wrist-watch set with rubies and diamonds. She placed it in the dark fingers, which seemed to quiver.

"I will go, Señora."

He had only begun to speak the words when suddenly his hand moved with incredible swiftness, the money, wrist-watch and note to Captain Maclean disappeared as if by magic. Picking up an ash-tray which stood on an adjacent table, he walked quickly across the room towards the door.

Then Skye realized that the Indian with his naturally acute sense of hearing had heard someone coming.

It was only Neengai, but even so Skye drew a deep breath of relief. She had not really been afraid that they might be interrupted by El Diablo himself.

He had gone this morning to inspect the mine, telling her that he would be back for the midday meal and that afterwards, if nothing unexpected turned up, they would go riding.

After being over a week in the camp, Skye had learned of the immense amount of work that was done every day.

There were not only the *haciendas* to visit and the grazing fields to patrol and a watch to be kept on the roads from Jácara, but there was also the mine to be inspected and the gold, which was still brought to the surface by the primitive, wasteful methods which had altered very little down the centuries, taken every other day or so to a safe place.

Both gold and diamonds were found in such small quantities that Skye had begun to wonder if the effort was really worth while or if El Diablo had ulterior reasons for keeping his men at work.

Indians were also employed in weaving and making pottery and furniture. Skye noticed that El Diablo paid for their work and the finished articles were stored in some of the uninhabited caves, where she had seen stools carved from solid blocks of beautiful hardwood and tables and chairs fashioned from the red quebracho or black and white urunday.

She supposed that one day El Diablo intended to sell these things, but in the meantime the people who followed him were fully employed. The fingers of the Indian women especially were never still of their spinning.

There was poetry in their movements as with their brown breasts naked, their wide skirts, layer upon layer of them, swinging, they made the bobbins dance in their hands.

And always, whatever was being done, there would be the thrumming of the guitar, its music becoming so much a part of her existence that after a time Skye paid no more attention to it than to the buzzing of the bees and the songs of the birds.

Yet, while she had time to look around her, to listen and rest, El Diablo was constantly and incessantly busy.

There was always someone waiting to see him, bringing him news from Jăcara or the south of the country. And as Skye knew only too well, his faculty for knowing everything was phenomenal.

She found it easy to understand now how everything she had done had been reported to El Diablo.

He must have known of her arrival as soon as her yacht nosed its way into the harbour; and the particulars given to the Authorities on the quay would have been relayed to him within the hour.

His followers were everywhere—in the offices, in the shops, among the beggars, in the Palace. There was nothing too small or too big to be brought to the ears of El Diablo.

There was a telephone system in operation, Skye discovered, to one of the *haciendas*, but much more important was El Diablo's human contact with his people.

They came to see him at all hours of the day and often there were conferences long into the night. Then he would send Skye to bed. She would lie in the darkness, listening to the murmur of voices, until she fell asleep.

She had given up lying tense and wakeful for fear El Diablo should come to her room. He always said goodnight to her in the doorway and she knew that once the curtain fell between them he would not disturb her again.

Why he should behave in such a manner she still had not the slightest idea. Every evening he would make love to her on the couch—kissing her, fondling her, whispering words of passion in her ear.

Doing everything, it seemed, to gratify his own desires save that of making her his wife in the full sense of the word.

She had given up fighting against his kisses because she knew how utterly useless it was; wasting her strength and energy, leaving her only angry and exhausted while she ignited in him a sense of elation and triumph which she was well aware only increased his desire for her.

What made everything harder to bear was the realization that her feelings meant nothing to him.

She was just a woman—one who attracted him, it was true—but he had no interest in her apart from the beauty of her body and the loveliness of her face.

"Women are for love—what else?" he said to her once, and she knew he meant it in all seriousness.

When he took her with him on his rides, Skye suspected it was not for any real desire for her company, for when he was with his men he had companionship enough, but simply because he felt it safer to keep her under his eye, his interest entirely selfish, supremely self-centred.

Skye would shut her eyes and wonder if this could really be happening.

She remembered the fuss that had been made about her in New York, the men who had danced attendance on her in London, appearing to find a delight in just being with her, in listening to her conversation, in deferring to her views.

All day and most of the night she thought of how to escape, her ideas going round and round as if they were in a squirrel's cage.

She had been thankful when she found how much money she had with her. Fortunately on the day on which she had been captured she had decided to pay daily for the horses she hired and also to tip the guides who rode with her.

She had determined to be generous about this, for she had learned long ago that the English habit of tipping when one left a place or when one had finished what one was doing was not conducive to receiving the best services.

"Always tip generously when you arrive," her grandfather had said to her once, when she was quite young, and Skye had never forgotten.

Apart from this sum of money carried in the pocket of her riding-skirt, she had found various odd sums stored away in the handbags which had been sent to her with her clothes from the yacht.

Altogether it had come to ninety-seven dollars and Skye could only pray that with her wrist-watch it was enough to tempt the young Indian to brave the wrath of El Diablo and to compensate him for being exiled from the camp.

There was no chance of further conversation with him for El Diablo's other servant, an older man who had been with him many years, came into the room and, when he left, the younger Indian went with him.

If only this plan could succeed! Skye moved restlessly about the cave and was wondering if she had made her instructions clear enough to Captain Maclean.

He was to wireless to Jimmy and to go in person to the Police and speak to General Alejo. She drew a quick breath of excitement. What it would mean to be free again, to be safe in her own yacht, to be able to sail away from Mariposa and from El Diablo!

She had looked at herself in the mirror that morning and wondered why all that she was experiencing had left so little mark on her face.

She was, it was true, thinner, but that enhanced her beauty rather than detracted from it. She was also, though she hated to admit it, extremely well in health.

The long hours in the saddle, far from tiring her, seemed only to sweep away the softness of over-luxuriant living.

She had thought, for one wild moment, of going on a hunger strike; but when food was put before her she was so hungry that she knew she had not the strength of will to refuse the delicious dishes which the French chef managed to cook on an oil stove with the skill of an artist.

"Why has such an exceptional cook come here?" Skye asked El Diablo one evening after a dinner which seemed to her to excel everything she had ever eaten in Paris.

"Alphonse had to leave Jácara in a hurry," El Diablo replied. "He was chef to a rich and distinguished family, but one evening, after too much wine, he used his carving-knife on one of his fellow servants."

"And killed him?" Skye enquired.

"I am afraid so. A murderer like myself. There are a number of them in the camp."

He was deliberately baiting her, but Skye had grown wiser.

"I cannot believe that a man who can make a *soufflé* like this could murder anyone except accidentally," she said.

"Your kind heart does you credit," El Diablo said sarcastically.

She had learned to be silent when he was rude to her. Sometimes she wondered if she could indeed be Skye Standish who would hear in silence an insult and let it pass.

How quick-tempered she had been, how easily roused!—and now she must force herself to an unwilling control which checked words as they rose to her lips and forced her at times even to lower her eyes so that he should not see the blazing hatred in them and be moved to retaliate.

He would tease her as a child might tease a kitten, making her wild with rage so that he could laugh and pull her down beside him to kiss the angry words from her lips.

This was harder to endure than the effort of forcing herself into silence, and Skye was learning to be subtle.

But at times he took her unawares. The previous day had been a Sunday and as the men did not work El Diablo spent a quiet morning at his desk. When luncheon was over, he told Skye they were going riding and they set off alone without their usual escort of *gauchos*.

About six miles from the camp they came to a thick wood. They dismounted and El Diablo led the way through the trees to where at the foot of the mountains a stream cascaded down the rocks then widened out into a deep, clear pool.

It was encircled with tropical ferns and the hot sunshine glinting through the overhanging branches speckled it with gold, while the vividly-coloured butterflies hovering above the still water were reflected on its surface.

It was a hidden, secret place so exotically beautiful that Skye gave a cry of delight.

"A perfect swimming pool!" she exclaimed; "what a pity we didn't bring our bathing clothes with us!"

She looked at El Diablo quickly as she spoke and saw the smile on his lips. . . .

It had been foolish to run away from him among the tree trunks, for he caught her easily, with little effort to himself, while she was breathless with haste and anger.

"I thought modesty was out of date!" he said softly. "I

must be out of date, too, for I find it unexpectedly exciting."

He looked down at her quivering, frightened face.

"You will find two bathing dresses—one for you and one for me—in my saddle-bag. I'm sorry I can't provide a bathing tent as a sop to your Victorian prudery, but if you take the bushes on one side of the pool and I the other, doubtless the conventions will not be outraged."

As the shamed colour came flooding into Skye's cheeks he laughed.

"To the pure all things be impure!" he said.

She knew then he had deliberately enticed her into making a fool of herself!

"I hate you, I hate you!" she stormed, but he only laughed and her voice sounded weak and ineffective even to herself.

Skye heard him coming now along the terrace to the caves and forced herself to sit negligently on the couch in an affectation of ease and with what she hoped was a bored expression on her face.

He came striding into the room, seeming to fill it with the breadth of his shoulders and his great height. In his hand he had a small canvas bag which he flung on to the desk.

"More diamonds?" Skye asked pleasantly.

"Very few," he replied, "and not of good quality."

"How sad," she mocked. "You will soon be poor if you are not careful."

"I?" he enquired and laughed. "I had forgotten that you believed all that nonsense I told you the first night you were here. The diamonds are not mine, they belong to the country, and Alejo is not going to have them if I can help it."

"So you have stolen them?" Skye enquired.

"On the contrary, I have taken them into protective custody until such time as they can be utilized for the good of the people."

"By you?"

"By someone who, if he has no other virtue, is at least loyal to Mariposa."

"Which I assume Alejo is not?"

El Diablo poured himself a glass of wine from a carafe which stood on a side table and, walking across to where Skye sat, stood beside her, sipping his glass and scowling a little as if with the effort of concentration.

"I am worried," he said.

Skye looked surprised. In all the time she had known him she had never before heard him admit of any weakness.

"Why?" she asked quietly.

"I will tell you if you like. I don't suppose it can do any harm. Alejo will have to make a move within the next few days, and then the secret will be out of the bag."

"What secret?"

"The secret of what lies here," El Diablo said with a sweeping gesture of his hand.

"Gold and diamond mines?" Skye enquired.

"More—much more than that," El Diablo said. "There is no secret about them. They have been worked since long before the Spanish Conquest. They are as good or as bad as the mines in many other countries. They can bring in a little money to the revenue each year, but they are not of any real use; that is why Alejo has not got his hands on them before now. But his Communist friends told him something which altered everything and made him frantic to gain control of these mountains."

"I had no idea Alejo was a Communist," Skye commented.

"He isn't. He is a dictator. He has only one creed, one religion, one thought—Alejo! But democracy is going to be no help to him, so he must rely on Communism for the money and power to control these mountains."

"But what is in them that is so vitally important?" Skye enquired.

"Pitch-blende," El Diablo said.

Then he laughed as he saw the blank expression on Skye's face.

"You don't know what it is, of course; nor did I when I first heard about it, but it is uranimite, which makes uranium! The mineral the whole world is seeking, the mineral which is worth more than a hundred thousand gold mines put together!"

There was an excitement in his voice that was somehow catching.

"Can you be sure of this?" Skye asked.

"Alejo is sure of it," El Diablo said; "I only wish I was more experienced. I have worked in a mine, but that does not make one expert. If the uranimite is here, it has got to be worked by the Mariposans for the good of the country. I am not going to let it be handed over to a Communist organization who I hear are planning to bring in their own labour and give Mariposa only the smallest participating share."

"Why did Alejo agree to this?" Skye asked.

"They made it very worth his while."

"How did you find out?"

"Nothing is secret for very long in Mariposa. I have my people in the Palace."

"And in the shops and on the roads!" Skye ejaculated. "Can you be certain that those in Jácara will support you?"

He shrugged his shoulders.

"That is one of the things which is worrying me. Let us hope that it is worrying Alejo as well. He is not quite a fool when it comes to strategy."

"How can you fight—are you armed?"

"We have guns brought in from Brazil. They are coming over all the time. But do you think I want to fight? I would give my life to prevent civil war in Mariposa— brother against brother, father against son!"

El Diablo spoke with a sudden sincerity which astonished Skye, and then with a quick change of mood he walked across to the table.

"I am hungry. I have work to do this afternoon," he said.

"Tell me more," Skye pleaded.

"There is no more to tell," he said briefly, "and now that you know so much you will not be allowed to escape from here alive until Alejo has shown his hand."

"Perhaps that is why you told me!"

The expression on his face was inscrutable and for a moment she was afraid that he knew of her attempt to bribe the Indian. She felt suddenly frightened; but when he started to eat his luncheon quite calmly she was sure it was only coincidence which made him speak of such things at this particular moment.

They ate quickly, and when they had finished they went down to where the horses were waiting. The jaguar which had killed the man eight days earlier had taken toll of another victim the night before.

News had been brought to El Diablo that a child from one of the *haciendas* was missing when nightfall came. A search had been made, but it had been fruitless till dawn, when they had found him mauled and dead about half a mile from his home.

It was rare, Skye learned, to find a man-eating jaguar; they usually preyed on horses, dogs or cattle, and often fed on fresh-water turtles. But occasionally, after having tasted human flesh, the jaguar became a confirmed man-eater.

The night before, Skye had been awakened by a strange sound, deep and hoarse and frightening, which came from outside.

"Pu, pu—pu, pu."

It was repeated again and again. Skye jumped out of bed and slipping on her dressing-gown ran into the outer cave just as El Diablo came from his bedroom already dressed, a gun in his hand.

"What is that noise?" Skye asked, frightened and yet not certain what she had to fear.

"It is a jaguar," El Diablo answered.

She heard him call the guards as he ran out to the terrace; but the great cat was not heard again and they had no chance of a shot at it.

El Diablo had come back into the outer cave while Skye was still there peeping through the iron grid to see if she could see anything. In her desire for a glimpse of the jaguar she had forgotten how she was dressed until El El Diablo returned and lit one of the candles.

Then she saw the expression in his eyes as they took in every detail of her cheeks flushed with sleep, her hair curling riotously against her forehead, the lines of her slim figure hardly concealed by the soft folds of her chiffon nightgown and silk wrapper.

"I must go back to bed," Skye said nervously.

"Why hurry?" he enquired. "In London the night-clubs will still be full."

"I only wish I was in one," Skye flashed at him.

"Listening to pretty compliments, no doubt! Well, I can pay them too if that is what you want! You look very alluring, Madame!"

Skye pulled the laces of the dressing-gown closer.

"You know that I do not want to listen to that sort of nonsense," she said.

"Perhaps deeds, not words, are preferable—the kisses you would doubtless give without protest in the taxi which carried you home."

"I have never been kissed in a taxi," Skye retorted. "I have told you before that I hate being kissed; I hate all men and I loathe you."

He laughed softly at her anger, then walked towards her.

She was suddenly silent, backing away from him in a quickly rising terror. But he had only put out his hand to ruffle her already untidy head.

"You look like a cross choir-boy," he said. "Go to bed."

Grateful for what she felt was a reprieve, Skye went quickly into her own room, but somehow she could not sleep and she knew that for some hours after she had left him El Diablo sat in the outer cave, smoking.

Skye went with him now to visit the mother of the child who had been killed. She was wailing pathetically at her loss; but as she had seven children already and another on the way, it was impossible, however sympathetic one might be, not to feel that she had some consolations left.

The ride that afternoon did not take so long as usual and they were back at the camp while the sun was still high. Skye went up to her room and asked Neengai to bring her bath immediately so that she would have time to linger in it.

She had learned that El Diablo had a special contraption erected in another cave off his bedroom which made it easy for him to have a shower at any time he wished.

It was only a primitive construction, the sort often found among planters in the East—a bucket was fixed on the top of bamboo poles and manipulated by the simple expedient of tipping it over as one stood beneath it.

But for Skye, washing facilities were not so easy.

A flat-bottomed tin bath, such as she had seen preserved in the attics of her home in England, and which Aunt Hilda said she used as a girl, was carried into her room and set on the floor, where it was filled with jugs of water brought by a slow procession of Indians up the steep steeps into the caves.

Hot water for the hands and face could be heated in the kitchen; but the bath water was always cold, although often by the end of the day, when the heat of the sun had blazed on the stream from which the Indians filled their pots, it was warmer than one really desired.

Horrified at first at the amount of labour such a simple action as bathing required, Skye had learned to enjoy it without thinking of the trouble it caused.

After riding, the cool freshness of the water swept away all fatigue and she was at ease and almost happy when she forgot for a moment her fear of El Diablo and the thought of being his prisoner did not irritate her almost to madness.

As soon as Skye had finished bathing, Neengai collected the water in pots and it was carried away, usually, Skye knew, by the occupants of the other caves, who were thankful to have it with so little exertion for themselves.

Tonight, when Skye had rubbed herself dry, she put on a dressing-gown of blue satin, trimmed round the wide hem and open sleeves with frills of lace and tiny bows of pink velvet ribbon.

Then she went to the dressing-table to sit brushing the dust from her hair, making the curls dance, electric and vibrant with each stroke of the brush.

Through the open window she could hear the music of the guitar, the shrill shouts of the children and the bleating of a goat which had lost its kid. In New York, Skye thought suddenly, her friends would be going to cocktail parties; perhaps lifting a dry martini to their lips, they would think of her and wonder where she was at this moment.

Some of them would be envious. There are always those who are ready to dislike anybody richer than themselves, to find something caustic to say about someone who has inherited a great fortune, no matter how little harm she may have done them personally. Yet perhaps there were some who were genuinely fond of her.

"I wonder what Skye Standish is doing?" they would say to each other.

If only they knew! Skye suddenly covered her face with her hands. How could she go on like this? And yet, what else could she do?

There was a sudden sound, the noise of footsteps coming across the wooden floor in the outer room and then the leather curtain was drawn back with impetuous abruptness.

Skye turned round, startled. El Diablo had never come to her room before; and then one glance at him brought her to her feet, palpitating with fright such as she had never known in her whole life.

She saw Neengai slip behind him and disappear, and then she could only stand, frozen into an immobility which seemed to sap her brain, as she saw the expression on his face. It was the face of a devil.

His eyes were blazing with anger, his lips taut with a fury which could not be disguised.

For a moment he stood looking at her and then he

walked across to seize her by the wrist and drag her across the room.

"What is the matter? What has happened? Where are you taking me?" Skye asked.

He did not answer, only dragged her along, the high heels of her satin mules slipping beneath her feet as she strove to keep her balance.

"Where are we going? I am not dressed," she cried, conscious suddenly of her nakedness beneath the thin satin of her dressing-gown; and then, while she still protested, they reached the door of the outer cave and he pulled her out on to the terrace.

Then she could question him no more and the words on her lips died away. Down below, directly at the bottom of the stone steps leading up to the caves, a man lay spread-eagled, pinioned by his arms and legs, his shirt stripped from his back.

Only for a second did Skye have to look at that bronze-tinted skin before she knew who lay there.

There was no need to see his face, no need to ask why she had been brought here to look down on him.

Then as the breath seemed to be squeezed from her body at the sight below, El Diablo made a gesture with the riding-whip he carried in one hand. The silver on it flashed in the rays of the setting sun.

As he moved, another whip was raised, a whip with a long flat thong, held in the hand of a man standing beside the pinioned Indian.

It whistled through the air and fell with a sickening sound against the smooth flesh. The Indian screamed and the whip fell again and again.

Twenty strokes, each one of them seeming like a pistol-shot in the silence.

There was a crowd watching, a great crowd of men, women and children. None of them moved, none of them spoke. Only the whip cut through the hazy golden air to leave a long crimson weal on a defenceless back.

Then it was over. A sudden sound, half a groan, half a grunt, seemed to come from the crowd. The Indian was silent, the screams had died before the last stroke and Skye knew that he was unconscious. And she knew that she, too, could bear no more.

She put up her hands to her face and, finding her way by instinct, ran from the terrace back through the sitting-room and into her own bedroom.

Only as she reached the dressing-table, to stand trembling beside it, did she see in the mirror that El Diablo had followed her.

Slowly he came across the room and she did not dare to look at his face and see again the fury of it. He stopped beside her and drew from the pocket of his coat first her letter, then the American dollars and lastly her watch.

"A good man deliberately tempted into disloyalty and treachery," he said, his tone raw with anger.

He flung her things down on the wooden surface of the table and then turned towards her. Skye was too numbed and stupefied by what she had seen to have the slightest anticipation of what he might be about to do. In a daze, she saw the flash of his *rebenque* as he raised it high in the air.

She fell against the bed and knew a pain which seemed to sear its way like a dagger across her shoulders. The whip fell on her again and yet again.

The thin silk of her dressing-gown was no protection and she heard herself scream before the pain became too intense to be endured. As the last blow fell she was half-unconscious.

Far away, as if she was separated from reality by a fog, she heard his footsteps going away from her, leaving her alone. She prayed for oblivion then, but it did not come to her.

Instead she was conscious of the agony of her back, but worse still of the agony in her mind. She had thought already that she had suffered humiliation at his hands, yet this was worse than anything she had ever anticipated.

Like an injured animal that wants only to hide, she crawled under the bedclothes, where she lay utterly still, hardly breathing, hardly thinking, only suffering the tortures of the damned in the depths of a personal hell.

It grew dark and still she did not stir. Neengai lit one candle then tip-toed from the cave.

Then at last, when there were only the shadows and the crucifixion of her own thoughts, Skye heard him come to the bedside.

"Skye!"

He spoke her name, his voice deep and resonant, and somehow, it seemed to her, that there was a note of pleading in it. She did not answer and after a little while he blew out the candle and left her.

His footsteps died away in the distance and she was alone in the darkness.

7

"Why did you come here?" Skye asked Neengai.

The Indian girl looked up from where she was sitting crosslegged on the floor and a smile lit her sad, sloe-like eyes.

"Very happy here, Señora," she said. "My father and I came many miles from Peru. We starved when we arrive. No one want us until we find El Cabeza."

"How did you find him?" Skye asked.

"People tell us to come here. We come and El Cabeza say, "Welcome, I have work for you." He great and good man, Señora."

There was no disguising the earnestness or the sincerity in Neengai's voice.

"You think El Cabeza good because he gives your father work. Would you think the same of anyone who found you employment?"

This was too hard for Neengai to understand.

"*Excusa, Señora?*" she asked uncertainly.

Skye laughed.

"Don't worry," she said. "El Cabeza is good as far as you are concerned."

"*Si, si, Señora.* Very good. El Cabeza very great chief— my father say so."

There was nothing to say in the face of such blind devotion, and Skye, rising from the couch, walked across the room to stand looking out through the window as she had done a dozen times already that day.

She had not believed that time could pass so slowly. How often had she wanted to be alone, how often had she sought solitude!

Yet now she had it she felt the hours dragging wearily

and she was, if she were frank, exceedingly bored with her own company.

Enforced solitude was not the same when one had planned it oneself; and although she always dreaded El Diablo's return, she was beginning to feel it was preferable to the boredom of being imprisoned with no one to talk to except Neengai.

She had not seen El Diablo since the night he had beaten her. Mentally as well as physically exhausted, Skye had made no effort to get up the next morning. Her body ached, and worse still was the suffering inflicted on her pride.

She lay in bed, drinking the maté Neengai brought her, but refusing all food until late in the afternoon she learnt from the Indian girl that El Diablo had gone off on a hunt for the man-eating jaguar.

When she realized that he would not be back that evening, Skye fell into a deep, dreamless sleep and awoke to find it morning.

With the elasticity of youth the dark despair of the day before was forgotten. Her shoulders were still very sore, a hasty movement made her wince with pain, but the colour had come back into her face and the dullness had gone from her eyes.

Even if she had been tortured and beaten, she was still alive and the sun was still shining. There was always the chance that she might get away another time.

She dressed in her riding things although she realized that, unless El Diablo returned, she would be kept a close prisoner inside the caves.

There were two guards outside and, to Skye's astonishment, a door had been placed in the opening which until now had been veiled only by a curtain of hide.

There were bolts inside and out, made of iron, the handles ornamented with a curious little pattern which told her they had been fashioned by the Indians. Always the craftsmen in them came out in whatever they did.

To Skye the door at the mouth of the cave was in some ways a greater menace to her hopes of freedom than anything else. She remembered now that, as she had lain in a kind of half-unconscious stupor the day before, she had heard the sound of hammering.

It had only seemed part and parcel of the noise which always came flooding in through the windows from the camp below.

Now she realized that El Diablo was taking no chances —two guards outside, a bolted door, two men to serve her meals who came in together and left together—and finally Neengai to sleep across the threshold of her bedroom.

"You will get cold lying there," Skye said sharply when she found the Indian girl. "Go to your own quarters."

"No, Señora, I cannot do that. El Cabeza said I was to stay here."

"But does he imagine I would try to escape with a door to bar my way and two men with guns outside?" Skye asked scornfully.

Neengai looked serious.

"I think, Señora," she said slowly, "El Cabeza told me to stay here not to keep you a prisoner but to guard you."

Her hand went to her side as she spoke and Skye saw with astonishment that she carried the long, sharp *cuchillo* from which no *gaucho* is ever separated.

"To guard me?" she repeated in a different tone.

She remembered then the looks she had seen directed at her when she moved about the camp. She was used to ignoring the unwelcome attentions of men, and yet the expression in those dark eyes, strange and varied as might be their faces, was always the same.

She would have been a fool not to realize that her fair skin and golden hair made her beauty all the more obvious in a land where women owed their hair and eyes to their Spanish ancestors and the darkness of their skins to the heat of the sun.

For a moment Skye felt herself shiver. She had laughed at Jimmy for being nervous as to what dangers might beset her, but now she understood a little of her own foolhardiness. This was a country of hot-blooded men and in their eyes she was desirable.

"Let me have a knife, too," she suggested to Neengai, but the Indian girl shook her head.

"No, no Señora. I will guard you well. I promise El Cabeza that if anything happened to you I would pay forfeit with my life."

Skye put her hands up to her cheeks. "The cleverness of him!" she thought. It was almost unbearable that she must find the cunning workings of his mind at every turn.

She hated him, hated him so much that the pain of the weals of her back seemed part of the aching hatred within her heart.

And yet it was possible to be bored without him.

"My watch must have stopped," she said to Neengai half a dozen times during the day, only to find that the minutes were ticking by punctuated by yawns.

"I want to go out. Why should I stay here to stifle without air?" she stormed once, stamping her foot like a child who has been thwarted.

"El Cabeza will be home soon, Señora," Neengai said soothingly, an answer which brought no solace, only a feeling of horror that she must see him again.

How could she look him in the eyes after he had humiliated her in the very dust. How could she speak to him naturally when her hands were itching to strike him in the face for what he had done to her?

"God! the helplessness of being a woman," Skye said aloud.

"Excusa, Señora?" Neengai asked.

"Never mind, you would not understand." Skye said, then added, "Haven't you ever wanted to be a man rather than a woman?"

"Me wish to be a man?" Neengai asked, touching her brown breast to emphasize the point.

"Yes, a man," Skye repeated.

Neengai gave a little gurgling laugh.

"Oh, no, Señora. I happy to be woman. One day I wife and mother, have babies, many, many babies."

There was a softness in her eyes and a tenderness about her lips. Skye turned away from her. How could she make anyone as stupid as this understand what she felt? "Many, many babies" that was the extent of Neengai's ambition.

She laid her head against the cool bar of the window. There were babies in the camp below, playing outside in the dust or being carried Indian-fashion on their mothers' backs.

Outside one tent an Indian girl with long hair which rippled over her shoulders was feeding a child, her head bent over it in the protective gesture of universal motherhood.

Skye watched her and suddenly the idea came to her that perhaps after all there were compensations in being a woman.

For a man there could never be that ultimate moment of possession, of knowing that the flesh of one's flesh lay beneath one's heart. And then there came to her the thought that perhaps one day she might bear a child. She had thought of it before. What girl hadn't?

But always she had avoided thinking of the man who must father it—her husband. She had vowed never to marry but now, with what was almost a sob, she remembered she was married, a wife in name if not in fact— the wife of El Diablo!

Because she was afraid of her own thoughts, Skye ran from the window to throw herself down on the couch, saying as she did so:

"Talk to me, Neengai. Tell me about yourself, tell me about your tribe! What happened to your mother? Tell me anything, but only talk, quickly . . . quickly!"

Obediently Neengai tried to do as she was told, breaking often into her own language, stumbling over words, finding it impossible to express herself and yet managing to keep Skye's interest concentrated so that another hour of the afternoon passed by.

The sun was sinking when they heard a cheer break out, followed by another and yet another. Both Skye and Neengai hurried to the window, to see a dozen men come riding into the camp, El Diablo at their head.

There was no need to wonder if they had been successful, a jaguar skin was flung over the back of one of the horses and the *gaucho* riding it was grinning from ear to ear.

There was a shrill cry of excitement as everyone came running from the huts, tents and the terraces.

"El Cabeza is back," Neengai's eyes were shining with excitement.

"Why not go and meet him?" Skye suggested.

The Indian girl needed no second bidding. She pulled open the heavy door and sped from it, leaving it ajar, while Skye crossed the room to sit on the couch, determined that he should not think she was interested in his return.

She felt an almost suffocating sense of embarrassment now that the moment of meeting was near; yet her own pride prevented her from retiring into the bedroom.

She was not afraid, she told herself; it was only that it was hard to feel calm and steady with her heart fluttering like a captive butterfly within her breast and the sudden difficulty she had in swallowing.

He came striding into the room. There was no mistaking the triumph in his face. He was a man elated, thrilled with the spoils of the chase.

He walked across the room to Skye and lifting her to

her feet, kissed her affectionately and without passion as a man might kiss his wife on his return home from the office.

"We got the jaguar," he said simply.

"That is good," Skye answered.

He looked down at her and smiled.

"You are safe—and well?"

There was just a little pause before the last words, and despising herself because she could not be calm in his presence, Skye forced herself to answer coldly:

"I am here, as you see."

His eyes flickered over her, at the exciting redness of her lips, at the golden curls soft against the fairness of her skin. He stood for a moment just looking and then abruptly he turned away.

"I must go and have a shower," he said. "There will be a *fiesta* tonight, so put on one of your prettiest dresses."

He had gone into his room before she could answer or ask him when the *fiesta* would be; but when Neengai came hurrying back, full of excitement and descriptions of the jaguar, Skye questioned her.

"What will the *fiesta* be like?" she asked.

"I do not know," Neengai answered, "but everyone very excited. Men go out and kill young bullock. El Cabeza give permission."

That was all Skye could learn, and though she told herself that she was dreading the evening because she must spend it in El Diablo's company, she was nevertheless curious. Her grandmother had spoken to her of *fiestas* in Mariposa, but they had mostly been of a religious nature. This was a camp celebration and she wondered what sort of entertainment would be provided.

This was the sort of thing she had come to Mariposa to see, she thought to herself; and if only the circumstances under which it was taking place were different, how interested she would be!

El Diablo was back! She felt herself tremble at the thought of it, yet she told herself that to show weakness or fear of him was to surrender herself even further than she had done already to his tyranny.

It was a command that she should look her prettiest tonight, and she knew that to refuse was only to invite a repetition of what had happened on the first night when he had sent her back to change her clothes.

But she could not wear an evening dress that was low at the back, for the weals on her white skin were as a tiger's stripes. No longer crimson, they were turning black and blue, branding her, she thought bitterly, as the property of El Diablo, as the cattle cropping the grass round the *haciendas* were branded with their owner's mark.

Finally she chose a short evening dress of flame-coloured lace which fell away from the narrowness of her waist into a full ballet-length skirt supported by stiffened petticoats which gave it a gay fullness.

The bodice was cut low in the front, but had a lace-covered back and little short sleeves. Over it, to be quite certain the weals were hidden and in case the evening was cool, Skye draped a scarf of purple chiffon embroidered with stars.

She dressed slowly, for she hoped that by the time she returned to the sitting-room the Indian servants would be waiting to serve dinner.

But though she combed her hair unnecessarily and took a long time choosing a handkerchief to match her dress, when finally she came into the sitting room there was no one there save El Diablo standing with his back to the empty fireplace, a glass of wine in his hand.

Skye came through the leather curtain and looked at the table with a glance of enquiry.

"Isn't dinner ready?" she asked.

"It will be brought when we are ready for it," he replied. "Let me look at you."

Obediently she stood still where she was, half-way across the floor towards him, silhouetted in her flame and purple against the darkness of the walls.

The last dying brilliance of the sun coming through the window shone on her hair and on the transparent purity of her skin.

"You are very lovely."

There was no mockery in El Diablo's voice this evening, only a new depth—or was it her imagination?

"I have told you I hate compliments,' she said coldly.

"I was just stating a fact," he replied. "Surely you cannot resent the truth?"

"I think all personal remarks are odious."

He smiled at that.

"I am inclined to agree with you. Those you have directed at me certainly deserve that adjective."

Skye shrugged her shoulders.

"Forgive me, I was forgetting that you have had nothing to drink," El Diablo said.

He poured out a glass of the light wine not unlike a Spanish sherry which he took as an *apéritif* before meals. Skye usually refused to drink more than half a glass of wine at dinner.

Tonight she felt the need of some sustenance. She felt curiously weak. It was the result, she knew, of being physically so utterly helpless at his hands.

"Have you missed me?"

She was so astonished by the question that she found herself answering hastily and without thought.

"No . . . no, of course not!"

"Why so vehement? I think perhaps you have been a little lonely in my absence."

"If there was a chance of being happy in prison, I should have been happy these last forty-eight hours," Skye said sharply.

El Diablo drank off his wine and put down the glass.

"If I was really as ruthless and as brutal as you insist," he remarked, "I should behave as the Spanish conquerors of this country behaved to the Mariposan women who defied them."

"How was that?" Skye enquired, seeing that he waited for her comment.

"They cut out their tongues."

"So that is what is going to happen to me next." Skye threw back her head with a little air of defiance.

"Perhaps," he agreed, "or perhaps, instead, I shall stop your mouth with kisses."

He saw the sudden flash of her eyes and laughed softly.

"You haven't greeted me as a successful hunter should be greeted on his return home. Come and kiss me!"

"No . . . no, I won't!"

Instinctively Skye backed away from him, putting the table between them, but El Diablo did not move.

"Still disobedient?" he asked. "I should have thought that by now you would have learned to do as you were told."

"I won't!" Skye spoke through clenched teeth; and then, as he did not speak, she knew with a sense of utter helplessness that he was waiting.

He would wait all night if necessary, or if it pleased him he could, with two strides, be at her side, and she would be helpless against his strength.

"I . . . I . . . won't," she repeated, but her voice was no longer defiant.

Still he did not speak, there was only that terrifying magnetism about him, the will to be obeyed that was almost physical in its intensity. Almost as if she were hypnotized Skye felt herself walking towards him.

She came nearer, each footstep an agony, until she stopped before him, her fingers twisted together until the knuckles showed white, her lips a tight line.

Then she stood irresolute until after what seemed a very long time he said quietly:

"A kiss of welcome."

She moved forward then and abruptly, with a gaucheness which was foreign to her nature, laid her cheek against his in the conventional greeting of woman to woman, a social gesture meaning little, as commonplace in modern times as the shaking of hands.

She had laid her hands against his chest to reach up to him and now, when she would have drawn away, he put both his hands over hers, holding her captive.

"Have I not taught you how to kiss better than that?" he asked. Her eyes fell before his. "I want you to kiss me for once as if you meant it—forget your hatred."

"How can I do anything so impossible?" Skye asked. "I hate you, you know that. Kisses are for those who love."

"And what do you know about love?" he asked.

"Nothing, and thank God for it," Skye replied.

"Shall I teach you to love me?" His fingers seemed to tighten on hers.

"That is the one thing you can never do."

"Is it? Are you quite sure of that?"

Skye's lips curled scornfully.

"You must be confusing me with your other women, the women who were eager to stay here after you had tired of them."

"And if I never grow tired of you?"

"You will—you must. Think how much more pleasant it would be to have someone here who loved you, who wanted to kiss you."

"More pleasant?"

Skye's voice had broken with the intensity of her pleading; but when she looked up into El Diablo's eyes she could say no more.

There was the fire of which she was so afraid, and then

he released one of her hands and took instead her chin between his fingers.

"Could anything be more pleasant than this?" he asked, and kissed her.

His lips, fierce and compelling, held her mouth captive and then his other arm went round her and he drew her slim body close against him. The passion of his kisses left Skye breathless. Then suddenly with a strength that surprised him, she fought herself free.

"I am hungry," she said in a tone which seemed suddenly to rasp like the cry of a toucan in the forest.

For a moment he did not answer; then, as she stood on the other side of the room trembling for fear of him, he walked to the door and opened it.

"Dinner," he commanded to the man outside; and before he could return to his place on the hearthrug the Indian servants came hurrying into the room.

If there was to be a feast for the camp, the French chef had obviously decreed there should be one for his master also. Skye had eaten many delicious meals since she had been an unwilling guest of El Diablo's, but tonight's repast exceeded all others.

There was fresh fish from the river and baby chickens young and tender, very unlike the gristly, long-legged monsters they became as they grew older. There was lamb cooked in some special way with cream and vegetables, and there were small pineapples which grew locally, soaked in wine and served with limes to which a strange liqueur had been added.

Two wines were served during dinner, a white one, light and golden as the sunshine itself, and a red one which seemed to have been distilled from the warmth and crimson of the sunset.

As they ate, El Diablo told Skye of their hunt for the jaguar, how the Indians had tracked it up the hillside, and when finally they had found its lair they had discovered the dead body of its mate. It might have been grief that had driven it berserk, making it seek to kill, not for food but for revenge.

"How will you cure its skin?" Skye asked.

"The Indians will cure it," El Diablo replied. "It is a long and laborious process for they have no modern tools, but their skill makes it just as permanent and effective as if it was done by Rowland Ward."

"Rowland Ward?" Skye repeated, remembering the taxidermist in Piccadilly where her father had sent the first ptarmigan he shot to be set up and where some sealskins from the Orkneys had been made into a rug for her aunt.

"So you do know London?"

"I know enough to know that I never wish to see it again," El Diablo said harshly. "Let us talk of something else."

He pushed back his chair from the table as he spoke and Skye had the sudden conviction that he had made a slip. He had not meant to refer to Rowland Ward; it was a mistake on his part; and suddenly she was very curious, longing to know more, yet knowing that she would gain nothing by asking questions.

El Diablo went to his desk, where he picked up something wrapped in paper.

"I have a present for you," he said.

"A present?" Skye also got to her feet. "I don't want any presents."

"I am afraid you will have to have this one," El Diablo said. "It has been made for you while I have been away."

He crossed the room to her side. He opened a piece of bark such as the Indians use for wrapping-paper and she saw what was lying in it flash in the light of the candles. Ear-rings, fashioned of twin aquamarines, were set around with big diamonds.

They were lovely and yet at the same time it was easy to see the Indian craftsmanship in the arrangement of the stones in the gold setting and in the strangely-fashioned clips which held the ear.

"Did the aquamarines come from these mines?" Skye asked.

"No, but from one in the furthest west of the country, right on the Paraguayan border," El Diablo answered. "I worked there some years ago and I mined these myself and also the diamonds, so, unlike those I offered you before and which you refused, they are mine to give."

"I won't take presents from you."

"I am leaving you no choice in the matter," El Diablo replied. "They are a present for my wife."

He took one ear-ring in the palm of his hand and held it out to her.

"Will you put it on yourself or must I do it for you?" he said. "I might hurt you."

"That will be nothing new," Skye flashed at him.

"I am very thick-skinned," he retorted quietly, "and also very obstinate."

She took the ear-ring from him and clipped it on to her ear. It was heavy but quite comfortable. She put on the other; then she stood pouting a little because once again he had asserted his authority.

"They suit you," he said approvingly, and added with a sudden gleam of humour, "You needn't thank me."

"I will wear these because you make me," Skye replied, "but one day I shall be in a position to give them back to you."

"On the day that I am tired of you and you get your divorce?" he queried. "It is a long way off, so we need not trouble about it."

Skye suddenly stamped her foot.

"Why, oh why," she cried miserably, "must you be so bestial? It gives you pleasure to torture me, and I know I am a fool to mind, but I cannot stay here for ever—how can I?"

The last words were spoken pleadingly, the cry of a child frightened of the dark. Suddenly El Diablo reached out and took her hands in his.

"So you can feel something besides a murderous hatred!" he said. "You amuse me when you are angry, but perhaps I like you best when you forget you are an Amazon and became a little girl who has been frightened. Then your eyes plead with me and your lips are no longer bitter. My present was meant to make you happy because there is a *fiesta* tonight and we are going to enjoy ourselves. Listen! the music is beginning. Shall we go down to it?"

He was suddenly surprisingly human. There was no arrogance in his voice now; instead, he was trying to charm her into a good humour, tempting her with a treat, perhaps in his own way apologizing for his cruelty.

Slowly Skye drew her hands from his.

"Yes, let us go to the *fiesta*," she said and smiled.

8

Skye walked ahead of El Diablo through the open door, but as she reached the terrace she found she must wait a moment so that her eyes could grow accustomed to the darkness. The moon had not yet risen; and when El Diablo joined her she was glad to find that he held in one hand an electric torch. It cast a yellow circle of light before them; but when they reached the steps, he slipped his arm through hers.

The camp was deserted. They walked through it, passing the empty huts and the tents, coming out on to the rough grass of the grazing ground.

It was then that Skye saw the first signs of the *fiesta*. A huge bonfire was throwing its flames up towards the sky and there was the gay, throbbing melody of several guitars and concertinas and with them the curious rhythm of the *cabaca*—only beans rattling in a gourd, but wielded with a skill which made exciting harmony of every movement.

They walked towards the flames and as they grew nearer Skye saw that a great crowd of people was sitting round the fire.

It lit their faces—white, bronze and black, giving a strange impression of glinting eyes and flashing teeth and of a people ecstatically happy.

They had evidently already eaten, for the bones of the bullock, which had been cooked in its hide over a wood fire, still swung above the red ashes.

The wine was passing from hand to hand and it was obvious that the entertainments of the evening were now to begin, for people were being pushed back further from the fire, leaving a big sandy space in front of them.

Two chairs had been set facing the improvised stage and

covered with Indian blankets. They looked like thrones, and as she and El Diablo walked towards them, Skye had a sudden desire to laugh. There was no doubt that his people looked on him, as Neengai had said, as a great Chief, and she was his squaw.

On their arrival there was a great murmur of approval and pleasure as if the people had been waiting for this moment, and it was clear that El Diablo's presence was the signal for the entertainment to begin.

Boys threw some more wood on the fire—the flames leapt higher and there was colour everywhere. For now, Skye could see that everyone was wearing their best.

The Indian women's wide skirts over voluminous petti-coats were trimmed with gold and tinsel, with ribbons and embroidery. Many of the *gauchos* were wearing the loose, flowing white *bombachas* with wide pleated seams known as *brasileños*, and their boots were of soft brown calf hide.

They wore leather belts with massive silver buckles round their waists and their short capes were every colour of the rainbow—yellow, purple, blue, green, orange and, of course, in every known shade of red from the dark, rich ruby which came from a small crocus-like plant to the vivid pink of the flamingo's breast.

"Danza! danza!" the crowd began to cry, beating their hands together.

And before Skye had time to absorb more, an Indian sprang into the centre of the cleared space and started to dance.

There was music such as Skye had never heard before, strange, wailing notes which seemed in their weirdness exactly what was needed for the strange pattern of the dance steps, advancing and retreating, the body turning and twisting like some wild animal, yet seeming to tell a story in every gesture and every movement.

The Indian was watched in a breathless silence. It was as if all were trying to understand what he wished to convey. Then as swiftly as he had come the dancer disappeared and the discordant notes of music died away.

There was riotous applause and, as soon as she could make herself heard, Skye asked of El Diablo:

"What did that dance mean?"

"So many people have asked what the Indians mean in their ceremonial dances," he replied. "There are a thousand theories and no-one knows for certain. This one may have been the worship of the sun, the invoking of the spirits, a prayer for fertility—who knows? Least of all the man who has just danced it. The origin is lost even as much of their craftsmanship has been lost through injustice and indifference."

Skye was silent; and then, because there had been a sadness in his voice as if the Indians' plight affected him, she enquired speaking with an impersonal pleasantness:

"What are the people drinking?"

"The Indians are drinking their own wine," he answered, "which is a fermentation of sweet potatoes, corn, yama and manioc. It is very potent, as you will see presently. Most of the Mariposans are drinking something called *"refresco de vino"*. It is red wine mixed with orange juice and sugar."

He smiled as he spoke and Skye suddenly thought how wonderful it would be if she had just met this man as an ordinary acquaintance.

He knew all the things she wanted to know about the country. If only they could have met and talked without being involved in so many tremendous overpowering and terrifying emotions!

Impulsively she bent forward.

"Tell me more!" she said.

He turned to look at her. Her eyes were alight with interest, and her face animated and exquisite in the light from the fire.

In her expensive dress and glittering ear-rings she might have been a creature from another world; and as if the thought of this aroused some dark memory within him, El Diablo's eyes were hard as he said:

"Why? So that you can jeer at their simplicity?"

"No, of course not; how could you think such a thing?" Skye replied indignantly, surprised into being hurt at such a suggestion.

"Why, then?"

"Because this is what I've always wanted to see, to learn about, to know. If these people are simple, it is because they do not pretend; their enjoyment is real; and this is so very, very different from the empty dullness of social parties and the boredom of social people."

Skye's voice throbbed with sincerity and it seemed that the hardness in El Diablo's eyes softened.

"Now we have the Fandango," he said. "I will tell you about it afterwards."

The Indian was followed by another dancer. There was no need for the guitars and concertina to begin a Spanish

tune to know his origin. The olive skin, the deep-fringed
eyes and thick lips were as characteristic as the grace of
his body and the slim strength of his hips.

He was a handsome young man and undoubtedly proud
of his appearance, for his suit was of spotless black cloth,
the tight braided trousers widening from the knee. He
wore a wide, red *fada* and his short *bolero* swung high
above his narrow waist.

Then, as he waited, his partner swept on to the soft
floor to meet him. Her full, many-tiered skirts raised a
little cloud of dust as she moved, and the flames rising high
from the fire showed the warm voluptuousness of her
heavy-lidded eyes and the sensuality of her generously-
curved body.

They began to dance, the ageless story of a man's
pursuit of woman told in the terms of the dance.

The Fandango began slowly and tenderly, the rhythm
marked by the click of castanets, the snapping of fingers,
the stamping of feet; then the speed gradually increased.

The dancers teased, entreated and pursued each other
until their subtle swaying began to fill the spectators with
ecstasy and the strange throbbing notes of the music were
curiously intoxicating.

There was the rustle of silk, the sparkle of dark eyes
flashing, dropping, flashing up again, until quivering with
passion the dance came to an end on a note of exaltation.

"That was wonderful!" Skye cried aloud, the breath coming quickly through her parted lips.

El Diablo smiled; the Fandango had done what it was
intended to do. Skye no longer asked him for explanations
or for facts and figures; she was feeling, she was living,
and she was one with the people and their *fiesta*.

And now, as dancer succeeded dancer, the music grew
wilder and not only Skye but the whole audience was lost
to everything but their own emotions.

Wine was passing continuously from hand to hand; but
there was a magic in the air which seemed to come from
the twinkling stars above and from the warm red earth
beneath.

There was something passionate and primitive and
spiritual and lovely in it, all rolled into one.

The dancers were whirling, twisting, bending, a pattern
of movement against the gold and scarlet of the flames;
the colours of their costumes and the colours of those who
watched seemed to become intermingled.

It was an unforgettable picture—a picture which Skye seemed to feel with her heart rather than see with her eyes.

The music with its low thrumming and deep underlying rhythm was awakening a response in her to which her blood responded.

She knew that every nerve in her body was beating time to the sweetness of a melody which could suddenly pluck on the heartstrings and bring one near to tears and then crash wildly into a crescendo of rising exhilaration, dragging one high towards the sky in its triumphal ecstasy.

How long she sat there in the blanket-covered chair she had no idea; so intent that she did not notice the couples creeping away into the shadows to lie mouth to mouth and breast to breast in the soft grass.

She did not understand either that the dances had grown not only wilder, but more erotic until the last thin veneer of civilization was being shed as one might throw away a superfluous cloak and beneath find only the primitive, natural desire of a man for a woman and a woman for a man.

"I think we should go." El Diablo spoke quietly and Skye started at his words.

For a moment she looked at him, hardly comprehending what he said; her eyes were wide and shining, her lips parted and her cheeks flushed with the light of the fire.

"I said we should go now," El Diablo repeated.

She felt as if he dragged her back to earth from some enchanted heaven.

"No! No, not yet!" Skye pleaded.

Then, as El Diablo looked round, she followed his gaze and saw for the first time the couples lying in the shadows, the abandonment of those who still sat round the fire, the frenzy of the dancers, a dozen or more of them now, twisting their bodies, silhouetted in the wildest contortions against the leaping flames.

Almost mechanically Skye rose to her feet; El Diablo's hand was on her arm and he was leading her away along the path which led back to the camp.

There was no one to bid them goodnight; and indeed as they went it seemed to Skye that the music and noise of the merry-makers grew louder and less restrained.

In the moonlight it was easy to see the outline of the huts, the pointed tops of the tents and the still emptiness of the camp.

The opening of the caves above looked like great dark

eyes peering out of the solid rock. A dog barked at their approach, otherwise there was only silence; and, looking up at the rocky cliffs, Skye thought for the first time that they resembled the burial-places of the dead that she had seen in Egypt.

She felt herself shiver at the thought. There was something eerie tonight in remembering that these caves had been there for centuries, that men had come and gone while the caves remained. And yet some singing within her heart, beating there because it had been aroused by the passion of the music, told Skye that such thoughts need not be sad.

She did not know why, but tonight, if at no other time, she was convinced of immortality.

Almost without thinking where she went she climbed the stone stairs, walked along the terrace and entered through the door which El Diablo held open for her; but while he lit the candles, she went to the window and stood looking out into the night and listening still to the throb of the music.

"I am glad to have seen that," she said at length, in a low voice, forgetting for a moment to whom she spoke, conscious only of the pounding of her pulses and the strange sensation she had never felt before vibrating through her.

"A glass of wine?" El Diablo suggested, holding one towards her.

She took it from him, her ear-rings glittering in the candlelight as she moved, her eyes still preoccupied with the darkness beyond the grille.

"We must close the curtains," he said, "or the insects will come flying in towards the light."

He drew them as he spoke.

Then it seemed to Skye as if she woke for the first time from the trance which had held her spellbound. She was alone again with El Diablo.

She drank a few sips of her wine and set down the glass. She did not look at him. She knew he was watching her. She moved across the room, the silk petticoats beneath the lace rustling as she did so.

"It is late," she said at length, in a voice which strove to be natural.

"Are you afraid?" The voice of El Diablo mocked her and instinctively her chin rose.

"No!" The monosyllable was sharp.

"I think you enjoyed yourself tonight," he said quietly.

"It is perhaps the first time that I have seen you look warm and animated—a woman instead of a human icicle."

Skye tried to freeze at his words, but the spell of the dance was still upon her. Instead she sat down on the couch and pulled the ear-rings from her ears. The diamonds twinkled beside the soft blue of the aquamarines that were like an English sky in spring.

"Shall I light the candles in your room?"

She heard in his voice the deep note which had frightened her before, and she knew, if she looked up, she would see the fire behind his eyes.

Was tonight to be different from all those other nights when he had kissed her and then left her alone? She felt her heart beat agonizingly against her breast.

He had not waited for her answer, but was feeling in his trouser pockets.

"Where did I put those matches?" he asked.

He glanced round and could not see them. There was a jingle of coins and then he drew a small revolver from one pocket and set it on the table with a bunch of keys and a silk handkerchief.

"Not there," he said, still speaking as if to himself. "Ah, there they are!"

They were on the arm of a chair where he had laid them down; and as impatiently he turned towards them, Skye moved too. She sprang from the couch with a swiftness born of desperation and as El Diablo's hand went out towards the box of matches, she grasped his revolver in hers.

He turned swiftly but he was too late.

Skye placed the table between him and her.

"Keep back!" she panted.

He put his hands in his pockets and leaned back against the stone of the fireplace.

"That was careless of me," he said.

"Very," Skye agreed drily, "and now I am going to kill you."

"Let me warn you, that gun pulls a little to the left. If you want to make a good job of it, you must aim a foot lower than your target, allowing for the kick."

"I have used a revolver before," Skye retorted.

"Good. I should dislike to be mangled." He made himself a little more comfortable and asked mockingly, "Am I allowed time to say my prayers?"

"Did you give the man you hanged time to say his?"

"Who? Alejo's spy? As a matter of fact, I did. He swore he was a Catholic, though I very much doubted it, but we gave him five minutes to make his peace with God."

"Then I will give you five minutes and you had better start praying."

"You wouldn't like to hear my last Confession?"

"No!"

"Why? Afraid of being shocked?"

"Not in the slightest, and you don't seem to be taking this seriously—I intend to kill you!"

"I believe you. You are very ferocious. Look how long you have managed to fight me as it is."

"Flattery won't save you."

"I never thought it would, but if a man can't speak the truth in the last moments of his life, when can he? Shall I tell you something—you are very different from what I expected."

"What did you expect?" Skye asked, curious in spite of herself.

"I will tell you. A pretty, but boring English girl, full of clichés, tiresome enthusiasms and repressed sex."

Skye could not help smiling.

"I am sorry you were disappointed."

"On the contrary, I have enjoyed myself more than I have enjoyed anything for a long time. Shall I tell you something else that surprised me?"

"If you wish—your time is getting short."

"Taking into consideration the social background and the vast dollar resources of the rich, spoiled Miss Standish, I have been astonished into believing that she has never—like so many of her contemporaries—indulged in any serious love affairs."

Steadily Skye kept her eyes on El Diablo's face; but try as she would, she could not help the colour creeping up her cheeks, deepening the flush that was already there, the blush rising till it touched the curls shining against her forehead.

To hide her embarrassment she said in a voice that was suddenly gruff:

"You have two minutes more."

"What else shall I tell you?" El Diablo enquired. "That you are very lovely? That one day you will fall in love! And now, tell me how you intend to get away."

"I don't imagine anyone will expect me to be leaving camp at this time of night," Skye replied.

"There is a guard at the pass," El Diablo said. "You may be able to shoot first if you are quick, but a shot will undoubtedly bring other guards to his assistance. Besides, I don't suppose you intend to return to Jácara on foot."

"You need not worry about me," Skye said proudly. "I am perfectly capable of looking after myself; and if your men kill me for having shot you, you can rest assured that I am not afraid to die."

El Diablo smiled at that.

"My dear child, they won't shoot you," he said. "The Mariposans have a better use for a pretty woman, as you must have already seen this evening."

"You are trying to frighten me," Skye replied, "but . . . I . . . I have thought of . . . a better plan. You shall come with me, you shall command one of the men outside to saddle two horses. We will ride together through the pass and when I am safely on the road to Jácara you can return here alone."

"And if I refuse?" El Diablo asked.

"If you refuse, I shall shoot you and take the consequences. If you betray me to the men outside, I shall also shoot you. This revolver will be at your back the whole time."

"Do you really believe I would allow you to bully me into doing such things? Funny little Skye, I should have thought you knew me better than that! Shoot me! Like you, I am not afraid to die. It comes to all of us sooner or later."

"How can you be so childish?" Skye cried. "You don't mean it, because I know that your death will destroy all those plans you have made for these people who trust you and who follow your leadership. What do you think will happen to them if you are killed? Alejo will be able to avenge himself on them for their defiance and many of them, perhaps all, will suffer in consequence."

"Are you now asking me to live?" El Diablo enquired. "I thought you were about to kill me?"

"I want to kill you," Skye said. "It would give me the greatest pleasure to see you die at my feet. At the same time, many innocent people might suffer, if what you have told me is true and Alejo is prepared to give away the land and all the precious minerals it contains. But that is the trouble, can I believe you?"

"It is the truth," El Diablo answered lightly, "but don't let it stop you from killing me. What is Mariposa to you?

When you go back to your playgrounds in England and America you will forget that the place so much as exists."

"If you think I shall ever forget what I have suffered here at your hands, then you are mistaken," Skye said.

"And what have I done? Married you before a priest and then left you untouched and unharmed, unless you count a few stolen kisses. Perhaps that is really why you are angry with me—for the sins I have not committed."

He was taunting her but Skye refused to reply, only lifting her head a little higher with what she hoped was a disdainful expression on her face. El Diablo laughed and shrugged his shoulders.

"Well, why not take your revenge? The gun is in your hand. You have only to pull the trigger."

"That is what I meant to do a few minutes ago," Skye said, "but now I am prepared to spare your life if you will help me to get free."

"Why should I let you go when I like having you here? Think what that admission means! There is someone in the world who really wants you, who appreciates your company—someone who isn't interested in your dollars, but in you. Besides, you should be grateful to me for teaching you how to kiss!"

Again he was, Skye realized, deliberately provoking her.

"I warn you that you can go too far," she said sharply. "You have a temper, but so have I."

"Had it been as quick as mine, I should be dead by now," El Diablo said with a faint smile. "I have always struck first and thought afterwards. You are more balanced, you have thought first and now you will not kill me."

"Don't be too sure of that. If I cannot escape any other way, I shall."

"I am beginning to think we are here for the night," El Diablo said. "May I smoke?"

"No!"

He shifted his shoulders again and crossed his feet. There was something about his negligent attitude and the faint smile on his lips which annoyed Skye beyond endurance.

"Go to the door and call a man," she commanded. "Tell him to saddle two horses. I shall be aiming at your back, so don't try any tricks."

He did not move, and after a second she said:

"At once!"

"No!"

The word was spoken softly and now El Diablo took his hands out of his pockets and walked forward towards the table.

"Keep back. I swear I will shoot if you come any nearer."

"Wasn't it a murderer that you called me?" he asked softly. "Yet I had nothing to gain by a man's death. He died through no act of personal vengeance. But you are not the stuff, Skye, of which murderers are made."

"When people are desperate, they do many strange things," Skye replied, "and I am desperate now. Your five minutes is up. Either you help me escape or I shoot you and risk getting away by myself."

He was standing now against the table, while she had backed away from him until the big writing desk prevented her from going any further. He had lit only the candles on either side of the fireplace and now that his back was towards them it was difficult for her to see the expression on his face, while the light was on hers.

"Are you sure that you want to leave me?" El Diablo asked.

The unexpectedness of the question made her suddenly angry.

"Have you not insulted me enough," she asked, "without suggesting that I wish to stay here, forced against my will to become your wife—the wife of a murderer, a revolutionary . . . a . . . a devil?"

"Then if you are determined . . ." El Diablo said with a sudden shrug of his shoulders.

As he spoke, he half-turned towards the door.

Skye drew a deep breath of relief and then gave a sudden cry, for with a movement so swift and unexpected that she was completely unprepared for it, El Diablo turned over the table and, as it crashed to the floor, leapt over it and flung her arm into the air.

The report of the pistol vibrated deafeningly around the cave. El Diablo took the revolver from Skye's hand and then she felt his arms go round her and his mouth was close to hers!

"You were made for love, my little one—not for hate," he said.

With her ears ringing, she tried to thrust him away, but he was too strong for her.

"I should have killed you! I should have killed you!" she wailed as his arms went around her.

He was smiling, but his eyes were afire as his mouth found hers and her voice was silenced beneath the fierce passionate demands of his kisses.

9

The early dawn, brilliantly golden, came seeping through the curtained window before El Diablo said:

"I must let you go to bed."

He looked down at her as she lay on the couch. Her face was very pale, her lips like the crushed petals of a flower, while her hair against the cushions was even in the half light as golden as the sun outside.

El Diablo put out his hand to touch the curls, smoothing them backwards from the oval of her white forehead. Restlessly she turned her head away from him.

"I should have killed you," she said, speaking without violence in a low voice husky with tiredness.

"You need fire in your veins to hate, as well as to love," El Diablo replied.

His hand slipped lower to the white roundness of her throat.

"Fire, not ice," he went on, speaking quietly with what might almost have passed for gentleness. "I seem to remember a fairy story about an ice maiden whose heart never beat until the thaws came."

His hand rested over her heart and then, unexpectedly, he lifted her up in his arms and carried her into her own cave. He set her down gently on the bed and as she looked up at him, too weary even to feel afraid, he bent his head and kissed her lightly on the forehead.

"Sleep well, Ice Maiden," he said, and left her.

Skye slept late to wake with that querulous, irritating feeling that something had gone wrong. As she opened her eyes to find Neengai waiting patiently in the corner, she remembered what had happened the night before.

She wanted in that moment to wail aloud as the Indian women would wail when they were bereaved or upset.

How, she asked herself, could she have been so stupid, so weak and so futile as to have victory within her grasp and let it escape her?

She could hardly credit her own foolishness. To think at this moment she might have been safely in Jācara having breakfast aboard the yacht!

Then she remembered the other alternatives—of being shot down by El Diablo's guards or, worse still, captured.

She shook herself mentally. He had played on her feelings; he had outwitted her with a cunning and a cleverness which it shamed her to remember.

Then, when she was once again his prisoner and in his power, he had made love to her with a mixture of passion, charm and self-control which left her utterly and completely bewildered. Why didn't he force himself upon her and make her completely his?

He desired her, she was sure of that, and yet he denied himself what was his right by law and conquest.

When Neengai brought in her breakfast tray, the first thing Skye saw were two letters lying on it.

For a moment she stared at them as if they were ghosts, and then she remembered that in the forged letter El Diablo had sent in her name to Captain Maclean he had said that letters would be called for at regular intervals.

Excitedly Skye opened the first envelope, which was addressed to her in Captain Maclean's writing. He wrote:

Dear Miss Standish,

I am delighted to hear that you are enjoying your stay up country. Everything is going on well here. The crew have been cleaning the ship and everything is in good order for your return.

I am sending with this a letter which arrived for you this morning; and if there is anything else you require, will you let me know?

Hoping we shall be seeing you soon,

I remain,

Yours faithfully,

Angus Maclean.

Skye's lips tightened as she read through the letter twice. It was obvious that Captain Maclean had received a second letter or a message from her, telling him that all was well.

"The impertinence of the man!" she said aloud, speaking of El Diablo, not of the Captain.

Then she felt weakly that it was no use getting annoyed over trifles when there were so many other things to arouse her anger.

She picked up the second letter. It was from Jimmy. He wrote glowingly of the delights of Valparaiso and she knew that this was intentional and that he was still hoping to lure her away from Mariposa. He ended his letter with the words:

I have hoped against hope that I might get a letter from you, but I suppose the Mariposan countryside is proving too attractive a rival for your time. Try to keep out of mischief. I continue to worry despite the fact that I am sure it is quite unnecessary.

If only he knew! Skye thought; yet somehow she found it difficult not to see the humour of the situation.

Jimmy, in Valparaiso, afraid that she might be getting into trouble, yet forcing himself to believe that no news was good news, while she had been married, imprisoned and insulted by a bandit who, as far as she could see, had no intention of setting her free.

"There must be an end to it sometime," she said aloud.

Neengai, coming into the room, thought she was addressing her.

"*Excusa, Señora?*" she said politely.

"It is all right, Neengai, I was talking to myself," Skye said. "What time is it?"

"Near to noon, Señora, and El Cabeza went away early with many men, Señora. He say you tired, no-one to disturb."

Skye stretched her arms above her head.

"I will get up," she said. "It is too hot to stay in bed."

Neengai brought her water and she had a bath and dressed herself in a cool cotton dress. If El Diablo had gone out, she knew she would not be allowed to leave the cave.

Another day she might have chafed at the restriction, but today she was almost glad. She felt languid and a little sleepy.

By the time she was dressed it was time for the mid-day meal, but she was not hungry and the Indians carried away again most of what Alphonse had spent so much care and trouble in preparing.

When they had gone, Skye stretched herself on the couch and was half asleep when she heard a voice outside.

"A message for the Señora from El Cabeza," she heard someone say.

The guards appeared to be arguing for the moment, then the door was opened and a *gaucho* came in, carrying a bunch of flowers. Skye recognized him as one of the regular band which accompanied El Diablo on his rides and with an effort she remembered, too, that his name was Pedro.

"*Buenos dias, Señora,*" Pedro said, bowing from the doorway; then as Skye returned his greeting he came across the room to present her with the flowers.

"El Cabeza's compliments, Señora, and he asks, if you are not tired, for you to join him on his ride. He waits for you a few miles away. I can take you there."

He spoke loudly, and then added in a low whisper.

"If you wish to escape, Señora, I will help you now."

Skye had taken the flowers automatically. But, at the man's whisper, she stared at him, suddenly tense as the meaning of his words came to her.

"Say something, Señora," he breathed; "the guards are listening."

With her brain racing with the effort of grasping what was happening, Skye said:

"It is very kind of El Cabeza to send me these flowers, and you say that he suggests my joining him? What is the day like? Is it very hot?"

"It is hot, yes," Pedro answered, "but there is a cool wind. Come to the window, Señora, and see for yourself."

At the window they were behind the open doorway and the guards could not see them and they were also a little more out of earshot.

"You must act quickly, Señora," Pedro murmured. "El Cabeza sent me home because I felt ill. He is a long way from here. It will be nightfall before he returns. By that time we can have reached Jácara."

"Yes, it is a nice day," Skye said, "even though the sun is hot"; and then in a whisper, "How much do you want for doing this?"

"It will get cooler later, Señora," Pedro replied. "Five hundred American dollars."

There was no time to argue even if she had wished to.

"I agree," Skye whispered and added aloud, "I will ride out to join El Cabeza. Have a horse saddled for me and wait below."

"*Gracias, Señora.*"

Pedro bowed and she turned and ran into the inner cave. It took her only a few minutes to change into her riding clothes. She stuffed all the money she possessed into the pockets of her riding breeches, and then, picking up her whip and gloves, she took one last glance around the cave.

This was the last time she would see it, this strangely beautiful place which she still felt, even after living here, had an unreality about it. The prison door was opening.

If El Diablo had been the victor last night, today the tables were turned. It would, she was sure, be nearly dark before he returned, for he had not made his usual tour of inspection for some days.

She had grown to know his routine—the calls at the *haciendas,* his visits to the mines and the diamond washers. Unless something untoward happened, as the day before yesterday when he had gone out to kill the jaguar, his programme was as regular as clockwork.

Skye looked at her watch. With any luck they should be within reach of Jācara by the time El Diablo returned home—far, far too late for him to follow them.

She smiled at the guards as she came out on to the terrace and they swept their hats from their heads and greeted her with a flash of their tobacco-stained teeth.

"It is a nice day for riding," she said, and they agreed with her; then they stood back to watch her slim figure appreciatively as she descended the stone steps to where Pedro was waiting with the horses.

He had brought her the black mare which she had ridden before and of whom she was particularly fond. The mare pranced and reared a little with excitement and then settled down to an easy trot as they moved from the camp and out into the open plain.

They turned north and Skye understood without questioning that it was obviously the way they must go while they were within sight of the guards.

As they rode away, deliberately without hurry, she studied her companion, for the first time asking herself if she could trust him.

It was hard to assess his character by his appearance. He had thick black hair, carefully greased, a plump face tanned by the sun to a golden brown, a thin black moustache above full smiling lips and bold eyes which seemed to Skye surprisingly unafraid considering the risks he was running.

She was so on edge that even a yellow *bien-te-veo* bird with its whistling "I spy you" call made her jump as it glided past. When they were over a mile from the camp she reined in her horse.

"We have to take to the mountains a little further on, Señora," Pedro answered. "There are El Cabeza's men on the pass to the camp and on the other roadway to the east."

"Is it a hard ride?" Skye asked.

"Very difficult for anyone who does not know it; but for me, not impossible," Pedro boasted. "I have the way several times, that is why I thought to myself, 'I, Pedro, will help the Señora escape, for there is no-one else who can assist her.'"

"It was kind of you," Skye said gratefully. "What made you think I wanted to escape?"

Pedro smiled the knowing smirk of a man who values highly his own intelligence.

"El Cabeza sent me with Juan to get the Señora's letters. I see the beautiful ship that belongs to the Señora, I talk with the Captain. He very nice man. He ask many questions about where the Señora stay. It is a big *estancia*, owned by nice people, and is the Señora happy? El Cabeza told Juan what to reply and the Captain, he delighted with what he hear; but as we come home I think about it. I remember Yokseyi, how he was whipped for taking the Señora's money—but he was a fool. He try to slip past the guards. I, Pedro, am much too clever to do anything like that."

"Yes, yes. I understand, let us hurry," Skye said, impatient of Pedro's volubility, realizing that the precious time was slipping by.

She spurred her horse into a gallop as she spoke and there was no time for further conversation until, far away from the camp, they left the plains for the mountains.

Skye had noted before when she was riding with El Diablo the curious formation of these mountains. The camp was situated where they crossed the country from north to south, a very narrow ridge, not high, and trailing away eventually into nothingness.

The main chain made a barrier between Mariposa and Brazil. Reaching rugged, barren and independent of law and order like some stupendous stairway to heaven, the mountains glowed in every colour from warm red to deep purple under the burning sun.

Pedro led the way through the great bushes of heliotrope, yellow calceolaria and prickly cactus which covered the foothills until, climbing higher, they came to a narrow, rocky path, so steep at times as to make Skye cling to her saddle lest she should slip off her horse's back, and at other times twisting round deep gulleys so sheer as to make her afraid to look down into them. The flowering shrubs were soon left behind.

These mountains, Skye knew, were the homes of the wild animals of Mariposa and she looked around, wondering if she might see a puma hurrying away into the shadows or even have a sight of the wolves and foxes which she knew abounded. Only the jaguar would be dangerous, the rest would slink out of sight at the first sound of a human being invading their solitude.

But if Skye looked around her, she also looked behind, not once but a thousand times. Supposing they had been followed, supposing El Diablo was already on their track!

It was impossible for her to pretend even to herself that she was not afraid of being overtaken.

The path twisted and turned; sometimes a landslide or a new gully caused by the winter rains seemed to have obliterated the track so that Pedro hesitated and searched around before going on.

Sometimes, too, the path separated and they had to make a choice of taking one to the right or the left.

"We should be heading further south by this time, surely?" Skye said once, her voice sharp with anxiety.

"Pedro knows the way and the Señora need not worry," he answered; and rather than offend him she did not ask any more questions than were necessary.

He had a jolly disposition, there was no doubt about that. Most of the time he whistled through his teeth, occasionally bursting into song.

After several hours, when the path was particularly steep, Skye suggested that they walk to give their horses a rest, and she noticed Pedro, striding ahead, moved with a swagger, boldly revealing the breadth and depth of his chest and the lissomeness of his narrow hips.

He was a vain fellow, and Skye guessed that the hard life at the camp and the work which El Diablo insisted that all his men should do was not particularly to his liking.

When they stopped at the top of the ridge to let their horses breathe and to tighten their saddle girths before they mounted, she said to him:

"It is brave of you to help me in this way. Are you planning to marry on the money I shall give you?"

"Marry? No, Señora!" He laughed heartily at that. "I was married many years ago when I was only a boy; but I left my wife—she was very jealous, always finding fault, always asking for money. One day I could stand no more and I left her. We lived in Seña, a town in the south. I came north to get work in Jácara."

"And you found it?"

"Si, si, there is always work for Pedro and there are always pretty women who are kind to him, so I am happy! But if I stay anywhere too long I get bored; so I join El Cabeza; and now, again, I go. Why not? The world is a big place."

"And where will you go after this?" Skye enquired, more to be pleasant than because she was interested.

He shrugged his shoulders.

"Rio . . . Buenos Aires . . . Montevideo . . . ? Perhaps the Señora take me with her to New York?"

"I think you would make a mistake to leave South America," Skye said hastily.

She did not want to be saddled with this man. Besides, already she was planning that, once she had paid him his money and sailed away from Jácara, she would obliterate the whole episode from her mind, she would go back to civilization and forget! No, that was not true, she told herself—she would never be able to forget; but no-one—except her lawyers who must set her free—should know about it, no-one else should ever learn of her shame and humiliation, no-one, no-one!

She looked back down the steep, difficult track they had just traversed. They must get on—supposing they were being followed, supposing she was recaptured!

Pedro was wiping the sweat from his forehead and Skye, putting up her fingers, realized that her face, too, was caked with dust and sweat, but this was not the time to worry about appearances.

"Let us hurry,' she said; surely by now it would be safe to come down from the mountains and on to the plain?"

"*Si, si* Señora, that is what I plan to do," Pedro answered.

His answer had a smoothness about it which aroused Skye's suspicions.

She had already mounted while he was standing by his horse's head and now she looked down at him and said accusingly:

"Have you lost your way?"

"No, of course not, Señora. You can trust Pedro, but the track changes after the rains—it is not always easy to find."

Skye looked up at the sun. It was still brilliant, but sinking lower in the sky. She began to feel apprehensive.

They should have been away from the mountains by now and yet here they were with nothing ahead but rocks and gullies difficult to traverse and often meaning a tiring climb up and down before they could get their horses over them.

"Do you think you have missed the right path?" Skye asked in a voice that she strove to keep calm. "Shall we retrace our steps a little?"

"No, no, Señora. Pedro will find the way. You can trust Pedro."

He smiled at her ingratiatingly as he spoke, then swung himself into the saddle. They started off again, moving as quickly as their horses could manage and heading, as far as Skye could ascertain, towards the south, yet she could not be sure.

She tried to determine from the position of the sun exactly where they might be; but they had to twist and turn so often that after a time she became confused.

There was no doubt now that Pedro, too, was worried. He no longer whistled and sang. Some of his self-assurance had gone, too, and he mopped his face more frequently.

At length, the path on which they were riding came abruptly to an end. The remains of what must have been a small avalanche lay ahead of them.

"We shall have to go back," Skye said firmly.

She tried to keep the note of despair out of her tone. She had been so confident earlier in the afternoon. She had been so sure that this time she would get away and escape that it was doubly bitter to think that her triumph must be so short-lived. But she was not yet defeated.

There was no doubt that there was a path over the mountains and if they had gone wrong it might be only a question of going back for a mile or so and turning left instead of right, or *vice versa*.

They rode back in silence and when finally they came to a fork in the path, Pedro's spirits revived with surprising suddenness.

"Here is the right track," he said. "It was easy to overlook, but Pedro does not often make mistakes. See, it is better, less stony. We can hurry and soon we shall be in Jácara."

"I certainly hope so," Skye retorted.

"I think you give Pedro just a little more than five hundred dollars—yes?"

"We will talk about that when we get to Jácara," Skye answered.

"Perhaps you will give him eight hundred dollars?"

"As I said, we will wait until we get there before we discuss that," Skye said.

"I, Pedro, would prefer the Señora to promise me now eight hundred and fifty dollars."

There was something in his voice and a glint in his eyes which made Skye agree without further prevarication.

"Very well," she said, "eight hundred and fifty dollars. But remember, you only get it when we arrive in Jácara."

She was being blackmailed, but she did not care. She was obsessed with the one idea—to get free, to make certain of her escape.

She thought of El Diablo's face when he came back to the camp and found how cleverly he had been outwitted by one of his own men. She wished she could be there to see his anger. She could imagine the questions he would fire at the guards, the rising fury in his eyes, the tightness of his lips.

Yes, he would be angry, very angry, but she would not be there to suffer from it.

A sudden burst of cursing from Pedro brought her thoughts back to the present.

She was not yet free of El Diablo and here they had come to yet another dead end. Pedro burst into a blasphemous tirade against the mountains, against the winter rain, the country, climate, in fact against everything except himself.

"We must go back," Skye said wearily.

She felt very tired. Her head was aching and so was her body. She was thirsty and she knew that, though she did not feel hungry, she was also in need of nourishment.

Pedro turned his horse.

"It is very hard to find the way to Jácara. When we get there, the Señora pay Pedro one . . . no, two thousand dollars?"

Skye looked at him. Why had she not noticed before that his eyes were too close? She must have been mad to trust herself to this incompetent braggart whose only achievement was to extort money from her.

"I refuse to promise you any more than what has already been agreed," she said coldly.

"I think the Señora change her mind," he answered quietly; and suddenly Skye was afraid.

She didn't know why; he did nothing but look at her, but there was something in his expression or perhaps in the stillness of his hands, surprisingly small and covered with dark hairs, which made her feel cold with fear.

She wanted to run away; she wished, with all her heart, that she had never left the camp, that she was safe in the cave, with the guards outside, and El Diablo returning at the end of the day.

Pedro was waiting for her to speak.

"All right—two thousands dollars," she said weakly; "but we aren't in Jácara yet."

"Pedro find the way," he said, cheerful again, and starting to whistle as he rode off.

Again they retraced their steps, again they found the path, and this one took them some way before Skye realized that the sun was disappearing behind the mountains.

It had grown cooler and now the gullies beneath them were deep in shadow and in a sudden terror she realized that they would find themselves in complete darkness when night came.

"It is going to be dark in twenty minutes," she said to Pedro. "What are we going to do about it?"

"We are going downhill," he answered hopefully.

Ten minutes later they were climbing again. The crimson glory of the sunset was the red flag of danger.

"We shall have to find a cave or something in which to spend the night," Skye said.

"Si, si, we shall have to do that," he agreed, and now they no longer hurried forward but looked from side to side to see some form of shelter.

It was Pedro who saw the stream cascading down the mountainside.

"We can follow it," he cried excitedly, "it will lead us down to the plains."

"It is too late," Skye replied. "Look, it will be dark in a few minutes. We shall have to stop somewhere about here. We can't go on until the moon rises."

They dismounted and led their horses to drink at the stream; then Skye saw that beneath a rock jutting out, half hidden by a huge fallen boulder, there was a cave.

"Go and see what it is like," she said to Pedro, "and make sure there are no snakes."

She knew from El Diablo of the danger that lurked in such places from rattlesnakes and the *vivora de la cruz*— a viper with a cross on its head.

Pedro swaggered off, not hurrying himself unduly, and she guessed that he was offended because she was now giving orders and he had failed in his promises. But there was no time to concern herself with Pedro's feelings.

He would doubtless blackmail her further before they reached Jácara, but she didn't mind anything so long as they got there. She unsaddled the horses and hobbled them with the reins as she had seen the *gauchos* do.

They were used to being tied in such a manner; and cropping the rough scrubby grass which grew beside the stream, they were quite docile and not likely, Skye thought, to wander away.

She heard Pedro striking matches. She saw the glow of light, then he came back.

"The cave is clean," he announced, "but it smells of fox."

"It is better than sleeping out in the open," Skye answered. "I should have brought a coat."

She shivered as she spoke.

"Poor Señora, but I have something that will make you warm," Pedro said sympathetically.

As he spoke, he drew a bottle from his pocket and held it out to her.

"It is good," he said encouragingly as she looked at it apprehensively.

She pulled out the cork and smelt it. It was a fiery, raw wine, strong in alcohol, which had the potency of Irish poteen. She handed it back to him with a smile.

"No, thank you. The cave will keep me warm."

Pedro threw back his head and took a long drink from the bottle, then corked it up again.

"Be careful, Señora, it is dark inside," he said. "Let me show you the way. I have my matches."

"We could build a fire," Skye cried.

"Yes, of course," he agreed, but without enthusiasm.

"Then, quickly, find wood before it gets too dark to see what we are collecting!"

They were lower down the mountains than they had been for hours and there was an abundance of dried-up shrubs and leaves from the previous autumn scattered around the hillside, besides an occasional branch from a pine tree.

Skye soon gathered a huge armful and then, as the sun sank blood red, the peaks standing out against the still faintly blushing sky after all else had turned black, she collected another and yet another before finally it was too dark to see any more.

She was so tired that it was almost a torture to force herself to move over the rough ground, to bend down, to carry her heavy load, and she was annoyed to see that Pedro had not brought in nearly as much as she had.

But with an effort she fought down her irritation and asked him to light the fire.

"You will be able to collect some more fuel by the light of the flames," she said pointedly.

He laid the fire cleverly, lit it skilfully with one match and the fire flared up yellow against the night.

"That is better," Skye approved with a little sigh. "At least it will keep away the foxes from their home. I do not wish to share my bed, hard though it may be, with a wild animal."

She saw as she spoke that Pedro was drinking again from the bottle he carried in his pocket. Now he wiped the top on his sleeve and pressed the cork back home.

"The Señora is frightened?" he asked. "Pedro will protect her."

"No, I am not in the least frightened," Skye answered. "I wish we had brought some food with us; but as we have not, it is best not to think we are hungry. Let us get some sleep. As soon as the moon is high we can move on again."

She was holding out her hands to the fire as she spoke, feeling the warmth of the flames dispel the sudden chill which made her shiver a few minutes earlier. Pedro came across and stood close beside her.

"I will protect the Señora," he said in a smooth, ingratiating voice.

"Then you had better sleep here at the mouth of the cave," Skye answered sharply. "And keep the fire going. I will go inside. Goodnight, Pedro.

She turned and made her way carefully into the cave. It was not very deep and the fire outside illuminated the sandy floor, the rough walls and the pile of whitened bones which lay at the other end. There was no doubt that Pedro was right in saying that it smelt of foxes.

However, at least it was a protection against the cold; and then the light from the fire was partially blotted out and Skye realized that Pedro had followed her.

She turned round quickly.

"What do you want?' she asked.

"I have come to take care of the Señora," he replied, his voice thick and at the same time caressing.

"I have told you that I don't want you in here," Skye said. "Go out at once."

He was not a tall man, but his head reached nearly to the top of the cave and he seemed to fill it, making her feel suddenly very small.

"Do you hear me?" she repeated. "Go outside. I wish to be alone."

There was no fear, only an autocratic authority in her tone. But in reply Pedro, quite unabashed, put out his hands towards her.

"The Señora will like Pedro," he smiled. "All the girls like Pedro; and if the Señora like Pedro very much, perhaps she will take him with her to America."

"Don't you dare touch me," Skye cried furiously, "and go away! If you want to come to America, we will talk about it tomorrow, but not now—do you hear me?—not now!"

"You are very pretty." She felt his hot, wine-tainted breath upon her face. "I like fair girls with white skins and you, too, will like Pedro—he very fine lover."

He caught hold of her as he spoke. Skye gave a scream of sheer terror and then started to fight him with every ounce of her strength. She felt her nails scratch his face, she beat on his chest; she even, at one moment, fastened her teeth on his hand. But she knew that gradually she was being overpowered.

He was a man, he was strong and he was inflamed by

a passion which showed itself in the quick, excited breath which she could hear hissing between his thick lips.

She felt her feet slip beneath her, and as she fell she screamed, screamed and shouted and screamed again. She felt his hands on her neck, felt him pinion her down, as there came a sudden sound from outside—the sound of footsteps and the report of a shot which echoed deafeningly round and round the tiny cave.

Then Pedro fell forward, slumping heavily against her.

Desperately Skye fought herself free of his body, and as she struggled to her feet she saw the outline of someone standing in the doorway of the cave.

There was no need for the flames to leap higher to reveal the broadness of his shoulders or the proud carriage of his head. She knew who it was, knew who had saved her!

She stumbled towards him, her breath coming sobbingly her heart panting so suffocatingly that she could hardly gasp:

"You've come! Thank God . . . you've come!"

She clung to him, her face hidden for a moment against his shoulder. The nightmare of the last few minutes had completely unnerved her. She was trembling so that she could hardly stand, and yet El Diablo did not put his arm around her.

"See if that man is dead," he said in a voice that was sharp and imperative, to someone behind him, "and saddle those two horses."

Vaguely, as she leaned against him fighting for control, Skye realized that he was angry and that she was re-captured; but she did not care.

She was only thankful beyond any expression of words that El Diablo had come in time.

10

Skye's teeth were chattering from the shock and for some minutes she could not think clearly.

She could only stand clinging to El Diablo, feeling that he was the one sane thing left in a world of horror and danger such as she had never imagined before in the whole of her uneventful life.

Yet, vaguely, despite the violent hammering of her heart and the throbbing of her head, she knew what was going on.

She heard a man's voice say, "He's dead all right," and there was the sound of horses' hoofs on the rocky track.

She felt El Diablo take her arm—it was the first time he had touched her since his arrival—and turn her round so that she faced the fire and beyond it the horses.

By the light of the flames she could see his men, their dark eyes curious as they stared at her. She was conscious that her shirt was ripped from the shoulder to the waist, a sleeve torn away from its socket.

Then, as they reached the first horse, El Diablo took his poncho from where he habitually carried it across the saddle and wrapped it around her shoulders.

It was of soft wool and she clutched the warmth of it round her gratefully as she felt herself swung up into the saddle of her own horse and one of the men came forward to lead it by the bridle. She wondered for one moment how they would be able to find their way back over the tortuous path with its deep gullies and narrow foothholds.

Then, as they moved forward she realized that they were going downhill following the stream.

The moon was rising and the stars were gaining in strength. As Skye grew accustomed to the darkness it was possible to see the bushes and trees silhouetted against the luminous indigo of the night.

But El Diablo riding ahead and the men following moved like cats, sure of their way, finding a foothold as if by instinct.

The shrubs and bushes became thicker and more profuse and after they had travelled for about twenty minutes they reached the plain.

Skye knew then that Pedro had so very nearly succeeded in getting her to safety—Jácara could not be far away—perhaps only an hour's ride!

At that moment, with a feeling of utter exhaustion, she felt she could not go on any farther. Only by a supreme effort of will had she kept herself in the saddle as she had been led down the mountainside.

Now the thought of the long ride ahead was too much to be endured.

She had eaten practically nothing all day; it had been a gruelling test of strength to climb those tortuous paths under the hot sun and then to experience the terror and horror of Pedro's attack upon her. She had gripped the saddle with both hands while her horse was being led.

Now she let go. She started to say, "I can't go any farther . . ." but the words died on her lips.

She toppled forward into a deep, endless darkness which seemed to swallow her up.

A long time later she felt water being forced between her lips and something wet and cool against her forehead. She tried to fight against her return to consciousness, but the hand that held the cup was insistent.

"Drink!" a voice commanded her and she was too weak to disobey. She opened her eyes to find El Diablo looking down at her. His arm supported her shoulders.

"I . . . am . . . sorry," the words came stammering.

"Are you all right now?"

She felt she was hardly alive, that unconsciousness was so near that she could slip back into it if she wished; but there was something imperative about him which forced her to make the effort to recover.

"I am . . . all right," she lied.

She thought piteously that she must get on her horse again. She wondered how she could keep upright; but there was no need for her to worry herself.

El Diablo picked her up in his arms and, as if she weighed no more than a child, swung her on to the front of his saddle and climbed up behind her. He put his left arm round her and held her close against him.

It was the way he had carried her when she tried before to escape from him and by a brilliant feat of horsemanship he had lifted her from her horse in full gallop.

She remembered how she had loathed the close proximity of him and the arm that kept her captive; but now she welcomed it. She turned her face against his shoulder and closed her eyes.

His tweed coat smelt of cigar smoke and the faint fragrance of heather and peat which seems to cling to a Scottish tweed all the world over.

It reminded Skye of her father, when he had carried her to bed as a little child and when as she grew older she had run into his arms on her arrival back from school or from America.

It seemed to her now that she missed that masculine smell since he died, but there it was again.

The horses were moving quickly and yet she was not unduly uncomfortable. All that mattered for the moment was that El Diablo's arm spelt safety, why or how she was not prepared to argue with herself.

She was too tired, too low in body and spirit, to think anything out save that for the moment she was safe from Pedro and his clutching hands.

She must have fallen asleep, for hours later she was conscious of being lifted from the horse's back and feeling the sudden agony of cramp in her right leg which had rested against the saddle.

She gave an involuntary cry and then realized that El Diablo was carrying her up the stone steps which led to the terrace.

She wanted to say, "We're home," but her lips would not speak the words. Her eyelids felt as if great weights hung upon them and it was impossible to force them open.

Dimly, as if she lay at the end of a long, dark tunnel, she was aware of being carried across the cave and laid upon her bed.

Later she was aroused by feeling herself being undressed; her boots were drawn from her feet, gentle hands took off her shirt and riding-breeches.

She murmured against the interruption, then felt herself being covered with the light bedclothes. Like a child she turned her face against the pillow.

She thought that someone kissed her lips, but she could

not be sure. The tunnel was so long and dark and everything else was far away . . .

She woke with a sense of terror and started up in bed to find herself alone and knew it was only the first faint sounds of dawn which had awakened her. The camp below was astir. She got out of bed and went to the window to draw back the curtain.

The sun was rising over the horizon, driving away with a swiftness that was almost incredible the purple darkness of the night.

Gazing through the wrought-iron grille, Skye stared at the familiar scene below, with its huts and tents, dogs and goats and tumbling children, and remembered that she might have seen the dawn under very different circumstances.

She shuddered at the thought and realized that she was naked.

She saw her clothes lying in a tumbled mass on the floor and guessed who had put her to bed last night. She remembered then that El Diablo had spoken but a few words to her since she had fought herself free from Pedro's dead body and had run to him for protection. Was he angry?

She tried to remember the expression on his face when she looked up to find him giving her a drink of water.

It had been dark, but she seemed to remember there was a light somewhere, perhaps from a match or an electric torch held by one of his men.

But the events of the night were hazy; she could not remember what had happened. He carried her back across the saddle of his horse, but after that she could remember nothing.

Suddenly she was conscious of feeling extremely hungry. She was still tired but not exhausted, and she knew that when she had something to eat she would feel better.

The rays of the sun were already coming through the window and in a very short while El Diablo would be having breakfast. He rose when his men did at dawn.

She was determined that she would see him before he went out; it was impossible to lie in bed wondering if he was angry with her, frightened as to what he would say and do about her latest escapade.

If she was to be punished, any punishment, however cruel physically, was better than the mental agonies of anticipation.

Quickly she moved across the room and filled the basin with water from the jug that stood beside it.

The dust and dirt of the day before wanted a lot of washing away, but after it was done she felt clean.

Quickly she dressed, choosing a dress of grey muslin with a white collar which made her look like a demure Puritan.

A very pale face looked back at her from the silver-edged mirror, with eyes which seemed unnaturally large in the small oval of her face.

Skye did her best to improve her appearance, but she knew that some of her pallor was due not only to the events of yesterday, but because she was nervous.

She remembered how she had told Jimmy that she was not afraid of any man, not even El Diablo. How gay and lighthearted and how stupid she had been! Now she was afraid not only of him, but of many things in life.

She had believed herself inviolable and that the world was there for her to conquer it—well, she had been conquered, not by the world, but by one man.

A man who was stronger and more overpowering than all the smatterings of civilization which she had thought so important or the money which she had believed could buy her everything she wanted.

Thinking that she heard a sound in the cave outside, she went to the curtain, torn by her desire to see El Diablo and her own fear of what sort of reception she would have from him.

She was afraid—she admitted it to herself; and then, forcing herself to a courage that was almost heroic, she pulled back the curtain.

The outer cave was empty, the table was already half laid with the breakfast things, but El Diablo was still dressing. She could hear him whistling very softly, a tuneless sound reminding her of the song of one of the birds out on the campus.

She went towards the window and stood there waiting, feeling the warmth of the sunshine on her face and wishing it would drive away the sudden hard constriction in her throat.

When he came into the cave, he seemed to come silently and unexpectedly, for he was there before she heard him.

She turned with a sudden start, her eyes wide and frightened, her lips parted and for a moment trembling.

"So early?" he questioned. "I thought you would sleep late this morning."

His voice was calm and pleasant and there was no hint of anger in his eyes. She felt the fluttering of her heart subside; then she came across the room towards him.

"I wanted to say . . . thank you," she faltered. "If you . . . hadn't come . . ."

Words failed her and she made a little piteous gesture with her hands which was somehow more expressive than words.

"Forget it," El Diablo said briefly.

She looked up at him.

"You are not angry?"

"With you? What do you expect?"

She turned away lest she should see the expression on his face leap into fury.

"You warned me . . . your men were like . . . that," she murmured a little unsteady, "but I didn't . . . believe you."

He did not answer her for a moment, but she knew that his eyes were on her face.

"The man is dead," he said at length. "Forget him."

"And you are not going to punish me?"

"I think you have been punished enough."

The sunshine was suddenly very golden. She felt her tension relax so suddenly that it was almost as if he had taken away some support which had held her up.

"Sit down," El Diablo commanded in a tone of authority that she knew so well. "You need something to eat."

She was thankful to obey him, sinking down in the place where she habitually sat for meals. As if by magic the Indians came running in with coffee, eggs, hot crisp rolls and a big bowl full of fruit.

Skye drank a cup of coffee and instantly felt some of her old strength and spirit returning to her.

"Tell me how you managed to come . . . in time," she said at length.

El Diablo put down his knife and fork.

"There have been several occasions in my life," he replied, "when I have followed my instinct in defiance of common-sense. I have never regretted it. Yesterday, when we had been riding for a little while, Pedro asked me if he could return home. He told me that he was feeling ill —his tummy was upset and it was impossible for him to ride further.

"I did not suspect that his story was anything but the

truth; men in these parts often get a type of dysentery which is very painful.

"I agreed that he should go back. Only as he turned to go did it strike me that he was extremely cheerful about it. We rode on without him. My men began to laugh among themselves. I heard one say, "I'll bet you it isn't Pedro's stomach that is troubling him.'

"They all began to laugh and to make remarks about Pedro and his love affairs, to which I paid very little attention. I knew Pedro's type only too well—a rolling stone that will never settle anywhere, a conceited braggart who, in his own sexual way, undoubtedly had a success with a certain type of woman.

"Then I remembered something I had heard about Pedro's past—how two, if not more, women had been found strangled after he had slept with them."

Skye gave a sudden exclamation; she was remembering Pedro's small hands, dark with hairs, that had clutched her throat.

"It was as if something warned me to go back," El Diablo continued. "I recalled a look I had seen Pedro give you once when we were all riding together. A picture of it seemed to float before my eyes. I wanted to laugh at the very idea and yet it persisted. You were young, you were lovely, you were also rich. I remembered that Pedro's reason for joining me had not been because he had been unjustly treated or because he had offended the government of Mariposa, but simply and solely because he had made the place too hot to hold him.

"He had been living with a woman and her husband had caught him out. Pedro was no hero, and no strangler on this occasion. Perhaps because he had a man to deal with, he ran away.

"The urge to return became too strong to be resisted. I turned back and headed for the camp. I arrived only an hour and a half after you had left!"

"Only an hour and a half?" Skye ejaculated.

"That was all," El Diablo said, "and it didn't take much questioning for me to discover the way you had gone. Pedro knew the path over the mountain, but I knew it even better. I took three of my best men and started at once. The others I sent by the usual route to Jácara to intercept you if you should reach the plain before I had caught up with you."

"Then I really hadn't got a chance?" Skye asked.

"A slender one," El Diablo replied; "you had an hour and a half's start; but the route over the mountains is very much slower than when one goes across the plain."

"So your men would have cut me off!" Skye said with a little sigh; "and I thought I was so certain to escape this time."

He smiled at that.

"You are at least a persistent fighter."

"Go on," Skye pleaded. "What else?"

"There is little more to tell," El Diablo answered. "I think you must have lost your way, the path was far worse than I anticipated. The rains in the spring had washed away the track in a lot of places."

"Yes, we lost our way not once but several times," Skye said.

"I was getting worried when I saw your fire," El Diablo went on. "We were only about a quarter of a mile away when my men drew my attention to it. I knew then what had happened; you had got lost in the darkness and been forced to camp for the night. Pedro was no use as a guide."

Skye put up her hands to her face.

"I am ashamed of having trusted him," she said. "Why did you have such a man in your camp?"

"I have to make use of what material is available," El Diablo replied. "Besides, these men are very often only children. They give what they get. Bad laws, bad rulership and corrupt governments make bad men."

Skye put her hands up to her throat.

"But a strangler!" she murmured.

"Tell me what he said to you," El Diablo suggested.

She told him how Pedro had brought her the flowers and put his suggestion of how she should escape.

"It was a clever idea," El Diablo said. "I will grant you that. It is a pity that he had not the ability or the intelligence to carry it through."

"I cannot bear to think of him," Skye cried. "When he came towards me in the cave, I thought I should go mad at the sheer beastliness of it."

"I heard you scream," El Diablo said. "I heard you, too, call out for someone."

She looked down, her long eyelashes sweeping against her cheeks.

"Did you hear what I said?"

"So you wanted me to save you," he said very softly.

"Who else could have done so?" she asked wonderingly.

"No one, of course," he replied, his voice suddenly abrupt; "and once again I am a murderer."

"This time I am not reproaching you," Skye flashed.

He smiled at that.

"It is very easy to condemn as unnecessary the crimes that don't affect us personally."

Skye pushed back her chair from the table.

"I must have seemed very priggish to you that first day when I made such a fuss about the man I found hanged," she said. "I am beginning to learn many things that I never understood before."

She got up and walked across the room.

"So many people in Mariposa seem to trust you," she went on. "Can you really help them?"

"What do you think?" El Diablo enquired.

"I wish I knew," Skye answered helplessly. "It is all too big for me to understand, just as I can't understand you."

He did not move but sat at the end of the table watching her.

"Would you like to explain what you mean by that?" he enquired at length.

"How can I?" Skye asked. "I have hated you with a hatred beyond words; and yet when I had the chance of shooting you, I could not pull the trigger; and when I was in danger I called for you to come and save me. It is all a contradiction for which I have no possible explanation."

El Diablo got to his feet and walked across to her.

"I should not worry your head unduly," he said. "But it might be an idea to obey me and to believe me another time when I warn you about something."

Skye sighed.

"I imagined that I should have been aboard my yacht this morning," she said. "If I had reached it last night, by this time I would have been far away from Mariposa and you would not have been able to find me."

"Have you not yet learned that I never let go of anything that I want? That I never lose anyone I desire?"

She glanced up quickly, for El Diablo's voice had changed and now he put out his hand towards her. But there came a sudden knocking at the door.

Turning away, El Diablo walked across the floor. Through the open door Skye heard the voice of Juan, El Diablo's most trusted guard, say:

"Six men are approaching, Señor. They wear uniforms and carry a white flag."

"Good. You know what to do?"

"Si, Señor."

"Blindfold them before they reach the pass."

"Si, Señor."

El Diablo shut the door.

"Who is it?" Skye asked, unable to curb her curiosity.

"Alejo's men," El Diablo replied curtly. "I was expecting them some time today. I had word yesterday that a deputation was to be sent. This is what I have been waiting for for a long time."

He clapped his hands and the Indians came in to remove the breakfast.

"Have maté and wine ready," El Diablo commanded. Then as they went out he turned to Skye. "What am I to do with you?" he asked. "These men must come in here. There is nowhere else I can talk with them. Must I tie you up and gag you?"

"No! No!" Skye cried. "I promise you, I give you my word of honour that I will stay in my bedroom and not make a sound."

He went close to her and taking her chin between his fingers in his characteristic way, lifted her face to his.

"Can I believe you?"

"I swear it," Skye answered. "Do you think I would trust myself to Alejo after all you have told me about him?"

He looked down at her, at the clearness of her eyes, at the warm softness of her lips, and slowly he bent his head.

"I believe you," he said as he kissed her.

Skye slipped away into her own room. She had only been there a minute when she heard footsteps crossing the floor.

"You may remove the bandages from your eyes, gentlemen," she heard El Diablo say.

Very, very softly, Skye tip-toed to the curtain which divided her bedroom from the outer cave.

There was a hole in the leather—she had noticed it several days ago when it had caught the button of her dress as she brushed past it. She bent her head and peeped through. She could see quite clearly the three men standing facing El Diablo.

One was an elderly man, the other two were young. They were dressed in the blue and white uniform of the Mariposan Army, ornamented with an enormous amount of gold braid. All three sported a considerable number of medals and they wore over their shoulders black cloaks lined with crimson.

"Won't you sit down, gentlemen?" El Diablo asked.

The Indians brought forward chairs as he spoke and then set wine on the table by the couch and carried in the hot maté.

"Your men will be well looked after," El Diablo said, but I regret that they will not be allowed to remove the bandages from their eyes. I am trusting you gentlemen that if by any chance you see a face while you are here, you will forget it when you leave."

"Yes, yes," the older man said testily, "our business is more important than a few fugitives from justice."

"I was certain of that," El Diablo replied.

The leader of the deputation cleared his throat.

"May I introduce myself?" he asked. "I am Colonel Don Pelayo and I have been entrusted by El Supremo to approach you on a matter of great importance."

"Which is?" El Diablo enquired.

"El Supremo feels that the time has come when it is imperative that we throw away our differences and merge our interests. The country's finances will not permit the present state of affairs to continue. A compromise must be reached. El Supremo has empowered me to present you with this paper in which he sets forth various suggestions."

The Colonel held out the paper and El Diablo took it from him.

"You will understand, Señor, that these are but the preliminary outlines of what must be discussed in detail."

"Yes, I understand that," El Diablo said.

"El Supremo therefore suggests that you should meet him tomorrow at the Palace," the Colonel continued.

El Diablo looked up at that, his eyebrows raised in a manner which Skye knew only too well.

"What guarantee have I of safe conduct for myself and my men?"

"El Supremo has thought of that," the Colonel replied. "He suggests that the conference be held in the courtyard of the Palace. All may attend who wish. You and he will sit together in full sight of your followers, and of the whole town. You may bring as many men as you wish, Señor, to see fair play."

"I accept those conditions," El Diablo said briefly. "I

will consider the suggestions put forward on this paper and have my answers ready by tomorrow."

Skye noticed that, as soon as El Diablo had accepted El Supremo's suggestion of a meeting place, there was a look of satisfaction on the faces of the three soldiers; then, having sipped maté, they each accepted a glass of wine which El Diablo poured out for them.

"You have a very comfortable hide-out here," the Colonel remarked, relaxing now that his mission was complete.

"It has been my home since General Alejo confiscated my *estancia* and the land which I was farming," El Diablo replied.

The Colonel coughed behind his hand.

"El Supremo undoubtedly had a good reason for his action," he murmured.

"The reason given," El Diablo answered, " was that the entertaining I did there was not in the public interest. Actually, my friends and the meetings I held with them were concerned solely with the future of Mariposa."

"El Supremo recognizes your devotion to our country," the Colonel said stiffly.

"I am glad of that," El Diablo replied, "for you, Colonel know as well as I do that there is a vast amount to be done if Mariposa is to survive. We are, I can safely say without contradiction, the most backward of all the South American countries; and yet we have a people with fine traditions behind them, a land full of natural wealth, and a climate which has been rightly spoken of as the best in the world. Can any of you gentlemen say that with these advantages it would not be possible to do a great deal more for our people than is being done at the moment?"

There was an uncomfortable silence and the two younger officers looked sideways at their Colonel, waiting for his reply. The older man stroked his chin.

"I am an officer in the Army, Señor," he answered at length, "but I am also a Mariposan. I am not fool enough to deny there is much in what you say. We have made many mistakes; we cannot afford many more."

"Then you certainly cannot afford the greatest mistake of all," El Diablo insisted, "to accept help and money from outside interests who are essentially at variance with the free spirit and desire for personal liberty which is the rightful heritage of every Mariposan."

The Colonel bent forward in his seat.

"If you mean what I think you mean, Señor, such a step is not contemplated by El Supremo."

"If you tell me that in all good faith," El Diablo said, "then I must reply that you have been hoodwinked. General Alejo does contemplate accepting Communist aid for Mariposa. That, as you know, was why I placed myself at the head of those sections of the community who are prepared to fight such a decision. We hope this may be settled peacefully; but if not, we are not afraid to die for the country to which we belong."

For a moment the two men stared across the room at each other and then the soldiers rose to their feet.

"I will convey your message to El Supremo," the Colonel announced.

"And I will come to the Palace tomorrow afternoon," El Diablo announced, "but not until four o'clock, for we must permit General Alejo to finish his *siesta.*"

There was laughter at this small joke and then El Diablo made a gesture with his hands towards the handkerchiefs which had bandaged the eyes of the three men and which now lay on the table.

"I am sure these would be more comfortable if you adjusted them yourselves, gentlemen," he said politely.

The three soldiers bound their eyes and then El Diablo opened the door and let in the guards. There were two to help each officer down the steps to where their horses were waiting. El Diablo watched them go, not moving until he saw them climb the terraces which led to the pass, moving in single file, followed by a dozen of his men who would escort them for several miles on their homeward way.

Then as he turned from the doorway he found Skye waiting for him.

"I don't trust them," she cried.

The frown that had been between his eyes vanished.

"Are you concerned for my safety?" he enquired with a whimsical smile.

"There is something behind all this," she insisted. "Why should Alejo suddenly be so considerate?"

"He is short of money," El Diablo answered briefly. "They are in arrears with the Army pay and the Minister of Finance resigned a week ago. That was why I was certain he would soon approach me."

"But you are not really going to Jácara tomorrow afternoon?"

"Of course."

"They will capture you. It will be a perfect opportunity of taking you prisoner—can't you see that?"

"With several hundred men as an escort?" El Diablo asked. "You heard him say I could bring as many as I like, and I have many supporters and friends in Jácara itself. Don't worry, my dear, you are not going to get rid of me so easily."

Skye turned away from him petulantly.

"I was not thinking of that," she retorted.

"What is troubling me is what is going to happen to you," El Diablo said. "I suppose I shall have to leave you here."

"No . . . no, you couldn't be so mean! I want to see what happens. Let me come with you—I must!"

"So that you can escape as soon as I am busy discussing matters of national importance?" El Diablo asked ironically.

"No, I won't do that—I promise you. If you let me come, I swear to you that I will not escape, even if the opportunity presents itself—not tomorrow at any rate, not until my parole is finished."

El Diablo smiled at her eagerness.

"I thought you just told me that the whole meeting is a trap and dangerous; do you want to run into danger?"

"I am not afraid of danger," Skye replied, "but I am afraid of being left here alone. I could not bear it—not after what happened yesterday."

She went suddenly pale at the thought and put out her hand and laid it on his arm.

"Please take me with you," she pleaded in a small voice. "Please!"

He hesitated.

"I should feel more satisfied of your safety if I was within earshot," he replied. "At the same time, think of the comment it will cause if I go riding into Jácara with a golden-haired Englishwoman whose yacht has been sitting empty in the harbour for over ten days. My reputation might suffer!"

"I will disguise myself," she said quickly. "No one will think it is odd that you have a woman with you. But it will cause comment if she is fair. I will wear a handkerchief pirate-fashion around my head, and a sombrero. The hat will shade my face and I can also put on some dark glasses.

"We might get away with it," El Diablo said doubtfully.

"We can try," Skye pleaded. "No one knows me in Jācara, and anyway, if you are taking hundreds of men with you, I will be lost amongst the crowd."

"I suppose I must agree," El Diablo conceded. "And now I have a great deal to do and to arrange. You are to stay here. Is that understood?"

"If I may come with you tomorrow, I will do anything you say today," Skye answered.

He laughed at that.

"I am not in the habit of making bargains," he said, "but I will remember your offer."

His eyes flickered over her, resting for a moment on her white throat. Then he picked up his riding-whip and turned towards the door.

"*Adios*," he said as he reached it.

"*Adios*," she replied, and with a strange sense of loneliness she heard the door shut behind him.

11

Skye walked across to the window to watch El Diablo.

The sunshine made the camp a pattern of light and shade and his shadow was like a purple question-mark behind him as he walked down the stone steps to where his horse was waiting for him.

As he reached it, Skye saw him stop and hesitate, then speak to one of the men who were waiting for him. He evidently gave an order, for the man turned and cupped his mouth with his hands and shouted out a name.

"Josné! Josné!"

The roar of his voice echoed and re-echoed throughout the caves and in answer to the summons a little man appeared at the mouth of one of them and came hurrying helter-skelter down the terraces to where El Diablo stood waiting.

He was a hunchback and Skye wondered what business El Diablo could have with him. They stood for a moment side by side, Josné deformed and mis-shapen; and in contrast El Diablo's height, broad shoulders and good looks were all the more noticeable.

Then he mounted his horse and joined by his escort of *gauchos* cantered from the camp leaving behind a cloud of red dust iridescent on the sunlit air.

With a little sigh Skye turned back towards the couch. She was uncertain whether she would not have preferred to be with the riders, knowing the joy of a horse moving beneath her, experiencing that sense of freedom and exhilaration that always came to her when she was out on the flower-strewn pampas.

Even in her most bitter moments of hating El Diablo and loathing the circumstances under which he kept her prisoner, her senses never failed to respond to the wonder of those wide rolling plains.

She stretched her arms above her head. Perhaps today it was best that she should rest and keep quiet—there would be excitement enough tomorrow.

Then, as she went to sit on the couch, there came a knock on the outer door and Neengai came in.

"Will you see the tailor now, Señora?" she asked.

"The tailor?" Skye questioned, thinking she must have misunderstood the Indian girl, or had translated the Spanish word wrongly.

"*Si, si, Señora,* the tailor. He wish to measure you."

"What is this?" Skye asked; then, knowing Neengai's linguistic limitations, she added, "Let him come in, I will speak to him myself."

Neengai opened the door to admit Josné, the hunchback. He bowed politely and Skye saw that he was a middle-aged man, his face etched with sharp lines of suffering, his eyes gentle and humble.

"What is it you want?" Skye asked.

"*Buenos diás, Señora.* El Cabeza has commanded me to make a suit for you, *bombachas* and a short jacket."

Skye smiled and understood. It was like El Diablo to have thought of it. If she were to ride with them tomorrow, it was wise that she should be properly disguised, wearing the same clothes as the *gauchos* wore.

Then she remembered how little time there was before they went to Jācara.

"Is it possible for you to make a suit by tomorrow morning?" she asked.

"Si, si Señora. I will work all night. It will be ready if I can take the Señora's measurements now."

"I think it is very clever of you if you can make it as quickly as that; but what about boots? If I wear *bombachas,* I shall need short calf-skin boots."

"El Cabeza has thought of that, Señora. I have told him that there are several young boys here in the camp who have not worn their best clothes since they arrived. There will surely be one amongst them who will have a new pair. I will make enquiries as soon as I have taken the Señora's measurements."

The hunchback had taken out a tape measure from his pocket as he was talking and now Skye allowed him to measure her. He spoke with a greater refinement than the *gauchos,* and watching him she was certain that he came from a superior class.

He was spotlessly clean for one thing, very unlike a large number of those living in the camp, and his own clothes, worn over his mis-shapen body, were of good quality and skilfully tailored.

"Why are you here? Skye asked impulsively.

"The Señora may well be surprised," he answered in a low voice. "I had my own shop in Jācara. I was the best tailor in the city. Everyone who had the money to spend on good clothes came to me."

"What happened?" Skye enquired.

"I made the mistake, Señora, of pressing a member of the Government for his bill. He had owed me a very large sum for over three years. I grew impatient—I made demands upon him. I threatened to take him to the Courts."

"And then what happened?"

"I was warned by friends that I was to be arrested on a charge of sedition. It would have been difficult to prove, of course, but in Jācara men who offend General Alejo can spend many weary months in prison awaiting their trial. I know what these prisons are like and I knew that, if I went into one, it was unlikely that I should come out alive; so I ran away, Señora."

"What a terrible story!" Skye exclaimed.

There was a faint, sad smile on Josné's lips, and his eyes were sorrowful as he replied:

"I left my home, the shop for which I worked so hard. I told my wife to say I had gone on a journey to purchase new materials for my trade. Then I came here to ask El Cabeza for shelter."

"Do you know what happened after you left?'

"*Si, Señora.* The Police came in search of me and with them members of the Palace guard. They told my wife I was a traitor, that I had to stand my trial. It was just as my friends had warned me."

"It is disgraceful that such things should be allowed to happen," Skye cried.

The hunchback shrugged his shoulders.

"General Alejo is very powerful. Señora. But you will forgive me, please, for boring you with my troubles. The clothes for the Señora will be ready early tomorrow morning."

Josné bowed to her as if he were a queen and went from the cave. Neengai went with him.

"Poor man" Skye said out loud.

Dictators were all the same; suffering and injustice were an indivisible part of their régime wherever they reigned!

It was hot and Skye felt suddenly tired. She decided she would rest on her bed—perhaps she would sleep and she would be more comfortable than on the couch in the outer cave. She went to the dressing-table, and pulled the thin muslin frock she wore over her head.

As she did so, a pin concealed in the hem of one of the sleeves caught her arm, scratching her. It must have been left there by the dressmaker who had made the frock for her in London.

It was not a bad scratch, but it bled a little, and when she had staunched it with a handkerchief Skye thought it would be wise to put some iodine or disinfectant on it.

All the time they had been traveling through the Caribbean, Jimmy, who was very careful about his own health, spent his time warning her to be very particular about scratches, insect bites or anything that might become infected.

"How fussy you are!" she had teased him; but he had only reiterated his warning.

"I had a friend who died in the tropics from neglecting a tiny cut he had made on one of his fingers," he told her. "I have never forgotten the agonies he suffered before he died. You've got to be careful, Skye. It is never safe to take a chance in a hot climate."

She remembered his warning now and thought with a wry smile that, as she had disregarded his advice on other matters, she had better be more punctilious over this. She looked through the things that had been in her dressing-case, but there was nothing there that was the slightest use.

Slipping on her dressing-gown over her silk petticoat, she walked across the cave to El Diablo's room. She was sure she would find some disinfectant there.

She had been in his room often enough when he was out for it to hold no surprise for her. There was the six-foot-wide hammock woven of the fibres of the tucan palm, as soft and as pliant as the finest panama hat and the most comfortable of all beds for use in a hot climate.

There were several pieces of furniture—tables, a chest of drawers and a big cabinet in which he kept his clothes.

They, with the things in the outer cave, were old Spanish pieces, gracious, dignified and, of great antiquity, and Skye knew that they came from the *estancia* from which El Diablo had been driven by General Alejo.

As in her own bedroom, there was no outer door to El Diablo's cave, only a window, also with an iron grille, which overlooked the terrace.

Skye looked on the tables and on the top of the chest of drawers for a bottle of disinfectant or of iodine. There was a various assortment of articles, but not what she wanted, and cautiously she tried the drawers of the chest.

The two top ones were filled with ties and handkerchiefs, the next one contained underclothes, and the bottom one shirts. She was then about to try the big cabinet when she noticed that the small table beside El Diablo's bed had a drawer in it.

It was too narrow to contain a bottle and yet, inquisitively, since she had started to look around, she thought she would also search there.

She pulled at the drawer—it was locked.

She gave it another tug, from impatience rather than the thought that it would open, and to her surprise and momentary consternation a piece of wood holding the lock in position fell away and clattered on to the floor.

Skye realized then that the table was as old as the rest of the furniture. Beautifully inlaid, it had the appearance of exquisite old marquetry and she realized uncomfortably that her roughness had damaged a centuries-old piece of craftsmanship.

She picked up the piece of wood which had fallen to

the floor, wondering if she could stick it back again. Then she saw that the open drawer contained papers.

Her curiosity was aroused. What, she wondered, could be of such importance that El Diablo kept it here beside his bed rather than in the desk in the outer cave where, she knew, the majority of his things were housed?

She pulled the drawer a little further open. They were legal documents, she thought.

Then, as she moved the papers tentatively with one hand, she saw what looked unmistakably like a British passport. She pulled it out.

For a moment the disquieting thought came to her that she was prying into things which did not concern her; and then with a little toss of the head she told herself that anything was permissible when she was dealing with someone like El Diablo.

Something hidden here might prove to be a weapon against him, and why should she scruple to use any methods, however morally reprehensible, to get the better of her opponent?

It was a British passport! There was no mistaking the dark blue cover, the neat inlet for the owner's name and for the number. Skye stood very still, staring at the name that was inscribed on the passport; and then, quickly, she opened it. El Diablo's face looked back at her.

He had obviously been much younger when the photograph was taken, yet there was no mistaking those strong, hawklike features, the deep-set eyes under straight eyebrows, the square chin, determined mouth and the way his dark hair grew back from his forehead.

Yes, the photograph was of El Diablo, but the name was Guy Tremayne!

It was written clearly on the outside of the passport—Mr. Guy Tremayne—and under the photograph the signature, in El Diablo's writing, was the same!

This was something Skye had never expected, and now she scanned the opposite page for particulars of him. He had been born at Bredon in Worcestershire, he was thirty-four this October, and he was of British nationality!

She gave a sudden exclamation which was almost a cry—somehow it did not seem possible that El Diablo could be British. From the very beginning she had thought of him as being Mariposan, and now she realized how stupid she had been not to have guessed before that he was not what he seemed.

In appearance he undoubtedly had some of the more characteristic features of the race and the sun had tanned him until he appeared as dark as, if not darker than, the average Mariposan, with his Spanish ancestors.

But Skye guessed now that where his skin had not been exposed to the sun it was as white as hers.

She might have guessed he was not entirely what he seemed on the surface. For instance there was the way he spoke; not only his command of the English language, but the idioms he used; and she remembered the slip he had made the night he spoke of Rowland Ward. She had been sure at the time that it had been a mistake on his part, and yet . . . British!

She could hardly believe it, especially as she knew too well how much he apparently hated England. He never spoke of the country of his birth without sneering or saying something unpleasant about it.

Hundreds of times he had made disparaging remarks about British people, especially women. There was a mystery here; but for the moment Skye could only grasp that El Diablo was British, and in some subtle way which she could not clarify to herself it made it infinitely worse that her captor and conqueror should be of her own blood.

She remembered now that she had asked him why he was called El Diablo.

"A woman christened me!" he had replied.

"Why and when?"

"Many years ago at one of the first meetings I had of those who suffered from Alejo's tyranny and injustices."

"What happened?"

"The lady in question disagreed with me for personal reasons. "Don't listen to him," she cried. "He speaks like the devil, he looks like the devil, he makes love like the devil—in fact he is the devil!' "

"What happened then?"

"She tried to knife me. When I prevented her from doing so, she threw her arms around my neck and kissed me."

"Was that all?"

"The meeting cheered vociferously."

"Because she kissed you?"

"Because I had the power to make her want to—the devil's power, of course!" he added mockingly.

"Of course!"

"A power which has proved effective with everyone, it seems, but you. Why is that?"

Skye shrugged her shoulders.

"Perhaps I am specially protected by Heaven!"

"I doubt it! Come here!"

She glanced at him anxiously. He was lying back in an armchair, seemingly relaxed and at ease. She wanted to refuse his command, but she knew only too well by now that resistance was useless.

Slowly she rose to her feet and walked across the cave to stand in front of him.

The light from the candles was on her hair, on the white beauty of her shoulders and the proud indifference of her little face which would not betray the sudden tension of her nerves.

His eyes appraised her, taking in every detail of her appearance.

"I am looking for flaws," he said at length.

"Like a slave in the market-place!" Skye stormed at him, forgetting all caution in her anger. "Would you like to see my teeth? The buyers always look at them, I believe."

"If we are to be historically accurate," El Diablo said slowly, "you have forgotten one important fact."

"What is that?"

"The slaves were naked!"

There was a sudden silence. Then, as the blood rose crimson in her face, Skye's face fell before his.

"You are aptly named," she cried furiously, hating him because as usual he was teasing her, torturing her in his own strange, inexplicable fashion.

Now she put her hands for a moment to her eyes, trying to think clearly, trying to formulate to herself why his nationality should make so much difference, should make everything about their relationship seem even more intolerable, more insupportable than it had seemed before.

Then, hurriedly, as if action was an escape from her thoughts, she took all the papers out of the drawer.

The legal document had a heavy seal to it. It was written in Spanish and was difficult to translate. Finally she realized that it referred to El Diablo's change of citizenship. He had become a subject of Mariposa. Skye read the document through several times, but still the full meaning of it eluded her. "Being of Mariposan blood," it said in one place.

She knitted her brows together—that could not be right. She must have read it wrongly. But one thing was sure—

Guy Tremayne had become Guido Tremayna, a subject and citizen of Mariposa.

She folded the document together again. With the document was an envelope. She opened it to find a photograph. It was of a woman.

Taken by a famous Mayfair photographer, it showed a very pretty young woman with fair hair and smiling, provocative eyes.

She was unmistakably English, unquestionably what is called "a lady", and yet at the same time she gave the impression of having an awareness of sex, of her own allure.

Skye stared at the pictured face. Was this the cause of El Diablo's dislike of England, the reason he despised all English women?

She felt a strange repugnance for this unknown woman. Impatiently she looked to see what else was in the drawer. At the back was a small box, thin and narrow. Skye pulled it out and as she did so a little piece of paper fluttered to the floor. She picked it up. It was a cutting from a foreign newspaper.

She read it almost automatically, but with a sense of growing incredulity.

"The London Gazette has announced the award of the Distinguished Flying Cross for conspicuous gallantry in action to Squadron Leader Guido Tremayna, a Mariposan serving with the R.A.F. in the Middle East."

There was no need to open the box to know what she would find there—the black and white striped ribbon and the cross which was coveted by all those who flew.

El Diablo might rail against England, but he had been ready to fight for the country of his birth when she was in danger. Mariposa had remained neutral.

As a Mariposan there had been no reason for him to join the R.A.F. Why had he done so? Skye felt almost stifled at the impossibility of finding an answer to her questions.

Slowly she put the box and the newspaper cutting back behind the passport and laid the photograph and the big document with its red seal on top; then she closed the drawer tightly and replaced the piece of broken wood.

She pressed it into position, hoping that it would hold until El Diablo opened the drawer himself; then she ran from the cave back to her own bedroom. She threw herself on the bed, pressing her fingers to her eyes, striving to think, conscious only of the chaos of her feelings.

British! A man who had fought with gallantry in the war and received the D.F.C., a man who had kidnapped her, married her and ill-treated her with a barbarism which could only have been explained by the fact that he knew no better.

He was of British blood! He must have been brought up in England, have lived there when he was a child, in perhaps the same sort of environment as her own.

It was impossible to think about it sanely. It was incredible, frightening, and at the same time embarrassing beyond words. She thought then that she could never bear to face him again now that she knew his secret.

" 'Guido Tremayna', 'Guy Tremayne'." She repeated the names aloud.

Why had she not guessed before? Why had she been so stupid and blind? And yet how could an Englishman dare to do this?

She thought of his cruelty, of his despotic power over her and over all those who served him. And she remembered his love-making and felt her cheeks burn again with the shame of knowing that he, too, was British.

Once she had stormed at him, "You are a barbarian!"

"Why not?" he enquired.

"In any civilized country you would be put in prison or treated like a madman for behaving like this."

"We do not pretend to be civilized in Mariposa," he replied, but he had only been mocking her and she had known it even at the time.

He had the utmost contempt for what he called "the playgrounds of Europe and America" and for the socialites whom he described as degenerate and half-witted.

One day when he had seen her enjoyment as they were riding over the plain and the sun was sinking in a blaze of glory he had asked:

"Could anything be more beautiful than that?"

"Nothing," she answered softly.

"Why don't you tell the truth," he asked harshly, "and say that you prefer the lights of Broadway or the night-clubs round Piccadilly Circus? That is your life, isn't it? With Mayfair half-wits chattering ceaselessly to each other about each other. How you must be missing those empty conversations with empty-headed young men!"

There was an anger in his voice which surprised her.

"I dislike all young men—empty-headed or otherwise," she answered. "But why do you assume that they are worse in England than anywhere else?"

He shrugged his shoulders.

"You will find the same sort of cocktail-drinking fools in Jácara," he admitted, "but here in the country itself everything and everybody is different. But, of course, you wouldn't understand."

She had longed for one moment to tell him that she did understand; but she would not give him the satisfaction of hearing that she agreed with him.

Instead she had said in what she hoped was a scathing tone:

"I don't want to understand you or your behaviour."

He had laughed then at her attempt to snub him and the moment for talking seriously passed. She had been so intent on her own feelings that she had never thought it strange that he should speak in such a strain. But now that she knew who he was it explained so much.

And yet why, if he was British and hated so many things that belonged to England, had he singled her out to bring her here? Was there some obscure idea of revenge about it?

By punishing her did he feel he was punishing the Englishwoman whom he hated, of whom he spoke so scathingly, of whom he had always had something disparaging to say?

Was the fair-haired woman in the photograph the reason for his bitterness?

Skye gave a little sigh. It was all too difficult to understand. She only knew one thing—she felt a new shyness and a new embarrassment about El Diablo.

She almost wished she had not discovered the truth about him!

Yet late that evening, when he came striding into the outer cave where she was waiting, she thought she must be mistaken—the air of autocratic authority and virile purposefulness about him, the quick grace with which he moved were all utterly un-English.

"Everything is arranged," he said, throwing his *rebenque* and gloves down on the chair.

He bent towards her and taking her chin in his fingers raised her face to his and kissed her lightly on the lips.

"I'm late, but it won't take me more than a few minutes to change, and then we will have dinner."

He did not wait for her to reply and was gone before she could think of what to say to him. There was an easy familiarity in his greeting which made her burn with indignation.

She was only the woman who must wait for him, her feelings unimportant, unconsidered. He treated her as an Eastern potentate might treat his concubine—and he was British!

She longed to accuse him of it, to hurl fresh terms of abuse at him for his treatment of her. Yet she knew she was afraid.

She dared not tell him that she had been spying on him, dared not confess that she had inadvertently forced open a drawer that he kept locked.

She looked at his whip on the chair and shuddered. The weals on her back were fading, but she knew that even when they gone the memory of them would never be erased from her mind. Restlessly she rose to her feet and walked across the cave.

She had done so a hundred times already since she had been waiting for El Diablo's return, and now she felt she could not keep still, any more than she could keep her mind steady or calm enough to consider the whole situation in the light of her new knowledge.

"Are you hungry? I am sorry to keep you waiting."

El Diablo's deep voice made her start as he came back, his hair still wet from the shower, his neck golden brown against the white silk of his evening shirt. She did not speak as he walked across the floor and stood looking at her.

She was wearing a dress of hyacinth blue chiffon with a sash of pink and silver lamé. His eyes travelled over her, taking in every detail of her appearance, before he said:

"Come and enjoy your dinner. It may be the last you will have here!"

"What do you mean by that?" Skye asked, startled.

"Who knows what tomorrow will bring forth?" he answered lightly.

"You mean that Alejo——" Skye began.

"I mean nothing," El Diablo interrupted, "except that our charming Dictator may have a clever trap up his sleeve. If he takes me prisoner, it might solve many of his problems. Men have been known to agree to strange things in the prisons of Jácara."

Skye remembered that Josné had said much the same thing.

"But if you think he is not to be trusted, why go?" she asked.

"My dear, I can't afford to ignore any olive branch however suspicious it may appear. Besides, it may be a genuine change of heart. Alejo wants to come to an agreement over these mountains and I don't suppose he wishes to fight for them any more than we wish to defend them. And I can assure you that I propose to take every possible precaution."

"But what happens if things go wrong and . . . you are captured?" Skye asked in a low voice.

"Then you will be free," El Diablo replied. "I have given instructions to Juan and to the others I can trust that, should anything happen, they are to take you at once to the yacht. Get out to sea as quickly as you can. I don't need to tell you that once you are away from Mariposa you should forget me and everything that has happened here."

"It would not be as easy as it sounds," Skye retorted.

He raised his eyebrows at that.

"No? Then you can think of me being tortured by Alejo with a lighted cigar and any other fascinating gadgets which dictators employ on those who are unable to retaliate, and you can feel with satisfaction that you are getting some of your own back."

"Don't!" Skye cried sharply. "It makes me feel sick to think of anyone, even you, being tortured."

"I will say this to your credit, that you are not as tough as you pretend," El Diablo teased.

"Did I ever pretend to be tough?" Skye enquired.

"But of course," he replied. "The incomparable Miss Standish who could go everywhere and do everything, armoured with dollars and, of course, her most valuable weapon—a British passport."

Skye felt her temper rise at the mockery in his voice, but with an effort she kept it under control and said quietly:

"You are determined to make our last dinner a memorable one."

He pushed back his chair as if to look at her more comfortably.

"I really believe that I shall miss you," he said. "It is not often that I have been able to say that to a woman with any semblance of truth."

"How flattered I should be!" Skye replied sarcastically. She realized as she spoke that he was not really listening to her, but was thinking of tomorrow. There was silence for some minutes before he said:

"I shall ride in with a hundred men—I don't want to appear aggressive. I will leave another hundred outside—Alejo will know about them, of course, but it might make him think twice before trying any tricks."

"Only two hundred in all!"

"That is a point," he replied. "I don't want to take any more in case this is a ruse to draw me away from here so that he can attack the mountains in my absence. I don't think that is his idea, because he would have to have his troops ready by now and there has not even been a whisper of any movement. But I can't afford to take chances. It is a moment when I don't know whom I can trust or whom it is safe to believe."

El Diablo's voice had a worried sincerity about it which moved Skye to an unexpected sympathy. For the first time she realized the strain under which he was labouring. How little he had to support him in his stand against the acknowledged leader of the country!

As he said himself, it was difficult to know whom to trust, how to sift the information that was worth while from the rubbish.

They rose from the table and the Indians came to clear away. Dinner had been much later than usual and already the noise and music of the camp was fading away into the silence of the night.

"We must start early," El Diablo said, "not because it takes so long to get to Jácara, but because it would be a mistake to arrive with tired men and tired horses. We shall do the ride in easy stages, resting and taking both a meal and a *siesta* before we arrive at the Palace."

Skye seated herself on the couch and as the Indians left the room, El Diablo sat down beside her.

"And now I want to forget everything for the moment and think only of you," he said. "That is your job, didn't you know it? It is what women are for, to soothe men, to minister to them, to make them forget the strain and worry and toil of the day so that they are fresh for the morrow."

"A chattel," Skye retorted, moving as far away from him as she could.

"On the contrary," El Diablo contradicted, "a woman has a supreme position if she chooses to be a woman and not a pale imitation of a man."

"A supreme position as what?" Skye asked. "As a plaything?"

He laughed at the anger in her voice, and reaching over put his arm round her and drew her close to him.

"Would you rather be told that you had a brain than that you were beautiful?" he asked. "I suppose you would. It is the contradiction of your sex. And yet no man, if he is honest, has ever fallen in love with a woman's brains."

He tilted her head back against his shoulder.

"I don't know what your brain looks like," he said, "and I don't think I care very much. But your body is very lovely."

As he spoke he ran his fingers down the warm column of her neck; and then, as she struggled against him, his hold on her suddenly tightened, his arm became a band of steel against which there was no escape.

"Still insubordinate?" he asked. "I wonder if I shall ever train you to accept the inevitable?"

"Never! Never!" Skye cried.

"It is strange," he said reflectively, "how much fight there is in such a very little person. Sometimes when I hold you in my arms I think how easy it would be to kill you by mistake—you are so small, so weak, that sometimes I am afraid of crushing you. And yet you go on fighting me, spitting your venom at me, defying me with a spirit that has really something rather valiant about it."

He was speaking slowly and quietly, almost as if he talked to himself rather than to her; and now his fingers tightened on her throat, feeling a little frightened pulse beating beneath his hold.

Skye made a desperate effort to distract his attention.

"Please tell me something," she pleaded.

"What do you want to know?" he enquired.

"What will happen after tomorrow?" she said. "I have given you my word of honour that I will make no effort to escape while we are in Jācara. I shall keep my promise, you know that; but if Alejo agrees to your terms and the mountains can be utilized in the way you wish, for the good of Mariposa, what happens then?"

"To you or to me?" El Diablo asked.

"To me," Skye replied.

Without replying he bent and pressed his lips against hers. His lips were hard, warm and compelling, and they held her mouth captive.

She tried to move away from him, but he pulled her close against him; and when at length he raised his head and set her free, she was breathless.

She dared not look at him for she dreaded the fire she knew was smouldering in his eyes.

"That is my answer to you," El Diablo said in a deep voice, "for I cannot let you go. Not while your kisses have the power to excite me, however tired, however weary I may be. You are a very exciting person, Skye!"

"But how can we go on like this?" she asked desperately.

"What shall prevent us?" El Diablo asked. "Is there anyone waiting for you in England? Have you promised to be anywhere by a certain date?"

He knew the answer to his questions and he laughed as he saw her face.

"You covered your tracks too well," he taunted her. "Your cruise into the unknown has brought you the adventure you were seeking, and now you don't like it. Aren't you a little ungrateful?"

He was teasing her and yet there was still that deep, frightening note of passion in his voice.

"Let me go!" Skye hardly seemed to breathe the words, but he heard them. Instinctively he reached out towards her. Then unexpectedly he swung her legs off the floor so that she lay on the couch, her head on the soft cushions, his arm across her body so that he looked down at her.

"No, don't move," he commanded as she tried to struggle up. "We are comfortable like this. For the first time today I am at peace with the world."

"You think only of yourself," Skye said accusingly.

"Of course," he replied. "What man doesn't? There is a delight in coming home to you, in fighting a battle different from the one I fight all day, a battle in which I know I must win because I am stronger."

Again she tried to rise from the couch, but he put his hands on her shoulders to hold her down and bent his head to kiss her.

"Fight me as you will," he murmured against her lips, "you are not strong enough because what I want I take."

"I hope Alejo will torture you tomorrow," Skye cried, stung beyond endurance.

"He will if he can catch me," El Diablo smiled.

"Then let us hope he is clever enough."

"So bloodthirsty?" he enquired; "don't look at me like that."

He kissed her eyelids. Then she felt his lips travel over her cheeks to the softness of her mouth.

She knew how hopeless it was to struggle further.

His kisses were growing more passionate, more demanding; there was a fierce possessive hunger in them as if they demanded her very soul.

Striving to make herself rigid, Skye felt him bury his face in the softness of her neck.

He was drawing closer and yet closer to her.

She knew his desire was increasing second by second and as, helpless, she let the tempest of his passion rage over her, she wondered if this was how he had felt towards the woman in the photograph.

12

The clothes that Josné, the hunchback, had made fitted Skye extremely well.

She twisted and turned in front of the silver-framed mirror to get a better view of herself and was forced to admit that not even an English tailor could have succeeded better.

The calf-skin boots that he had provided were a little big, but not enough to be uncomfortable. Skye gave Neengai four dollars on top of the price asked for them by their owner. When she handed the Indian girl the green dollar bills, she thought to herself that this was the first time her money had had any purchasing power since she came to the camp, and yet because of it there had been misery, pain, torture and death.

She was often haunted by the thought of Yokseyi with his blood-stained back and it still made her feel sick when she thought of Pedro slumping dead on top of her in the cave, while the sound of the shot from El Diablo's gun echoed and re-echoed deafeningly in her ears.

So much misery, a man's life had been lost, and yet she had not parted with one penny.

She thought then that she hated her money. She had never really wanted it and indeed the news of her inheritance had given her more a sense of apprehension than of pleasure.

Now she was sure in her own heart that money was a curse.

What had it brought her that she actually wanted? Clothes, jewels and parties—they had always been foreign to her nature.

She had wanted liberty and freedom, but her yacht had brought her only to Mariposa and there she had fallen into the clutches of El Diablo. Perhaps the poor were to be envied, not the rich!

She awoke from her reverie to find that Neengai was waiting for her to finish dressing and that time was passing.

"My green scarf, Neengai," Skye said and wound it round her neck. Another scarf of almost the same colour was bound round her head, hiding her fair hair.

Knotted over one ear, it gave her the jaunty, irresponsible air of a very young pirate.

On top of the handkerchief she set the hat which Josné had brought with the black *bombachas* and short jacket. It was of black stiffened leather with a low crown and wide brim and had a strap which fastened under the chin.

Skye remembered seeing the grooms of the Argentine polo team wear exactly the same type of hat at Hurlingham and she smiled as she set it on her own head.

How far away Hurlingham seemed at this moment, with its smartly-dressed spectators sitting in the pale English sunshine, the chatter and gossip over the tea-cups and the line of sleek, expensive cars waiting to carry their owners back to London and to the social events of the evening!

Very different indeed from Mariposa, where she was dressing in a centuries-old cave, not for some masquerade but for a matter which might be one of life or death.

She must have laughed aloud for Neengai said in her soft sing-song voice:

"The Señora is happy."

Skye looked surprised for a moment, then answered honestly:

"Yes, perhaps I am, Neengai. I like excitement and sometimes I like adventure."

"The Señora will come back soon?"

There was anxiety in the Indian girl's voice.

"Would you be sorry if I did not return?" Skye enquired.

"Very, very sorry, Señora. I very happy to serve you and I hope that I have pleased the Señora."

"You have pleased me very much," Skye answered. "Thank you for all you have done for me, and I shall be back soon, you can be sure of that."

She spoke with unexpected surety, for she was suddenly convinced that she would return. She had made no plan of escape—how could she when she had given her word to El Diablo? And yet his own doubts and uncertainty of the outcome of this meeting with the Dictator had left her feeling that there might be a change in plan, if not in their relationship.

Yet now, at this moment, she knew that she would come back to Neengai, to the cave, to the strange, terrifying life she had lived here for nearly three weeks.

Was it as short a time as that? she asked herself. She felt as if a thousand years had passed since she last saw Jācara.

She was different in herself, different in what she thought and felt. She had a sudden vision of her white yacht lying peacefully in the harbour. It only could give her a chance of leaving Mariposa, of going home.

Then she put the temptation to one side. She could not break her word, even though it was given to a man who, as she told him so often, had not the slightest idea of the word "honour" or of civilized behaviour.

She turned towards the mirror. It was not likely that anyone would recognize her, she thought, and to make certain she had in her pocket a pair of sun-glasses that she could put on at the last moment.

Many of the *gauchos* wore them, not because they were troubled by the sun, having been used to it all their lives, but because they thought spectacles gave them a North American look which they considered smart and up to date.

"I am ready," Skye smiled at Neengai and pulling on her riding-gloves she went into the outer cave.

Down below in the camp all was bustle and confusion.

Men who were to be on guard while El Diablo was away had been arriving since the night before.

Machine-guns had been erected on the pass and at various other vantage points of the mountain. The two hundred *gauchos* who were to ride with El Diablo were determined to make themselves conspicuous in Jácara.

All wore their best clothes and what they did not possess they had borrowed from their friends.

Their harness, stirrups and saddles were bright with silver, polished until in the sun they were almost too bright to look at in comfort. Their spurs and *cuchillos,* too, were dazzling. All wore their gayest and most colourful *ponchos* of blue, green, crimson, yellow or striped wool.

They were a colourful band who swung themselves into their saddles amid the cheers and cries of those who were to be left behind.

Only El Diablo wore his ordinary clothes—the well-cut tweed jacket, whipcord breeches and high polished boots. There was silver on his harness and on his stirrups, however. Skye knew that the *gauchos* would have felt that he lost face if he had used anything plainer.

Although in some parts of the country the custom was dying out, they all of them in their hearts still considered silver ornamentation a sign of importance.

Yet there was no need for El Diablo to have anything to proclaim him their leader, Skye thought, as he rode ahead with his horsemen out of the pass that led from the camp.

His expression was serious and grave as he took a last look round the defences and stopped to give his final instructions to the sentries.

He was anxious, she could see that, and she knew that there had been a dozen and one crises to be dealt with at the last moment.

There was a vast amount of organization to be done for such an expedition apart from the worry and concern of planning the defences of the camp and leaving instructions as to what should be done in case of attack. Information had been coming in up to the last moment.

There had been an almost constant stream of horsemen riding from the *hacienda* where the telephone was situated and an equal number had come direct from Jácara.

Everything rested on one man's shoulders, Skye thought; and then, because perhaps for the first time she was thinking of El Diablo rather than of herself, she spurred her horse forward to ride alongside him as they reached the plain.

"Is everything all right?" she asked.

He glanced at her and what he saw seemed to soften the grimness of his expression.

"I can only hope that I have thought of everything," he replied.

There was a flatness about his tone, and deliberately to ease the tension under which he was suffering she drew attention to herself.

"Do you like my *bombachas?*" she asked. "It was clever of you to think of them."

He looked at her more closely then, as if he really took in her appearance.

"You make a charming boy," he said, "but of course you must remember that it is as a woman that you interest me."

Yesterday she would have shrunk from the deliberate provocativeness of his reply, but today, seeing the lines of worry about his eyes, she smiled.

"Do you really believe I shall deceive anyone into thinking I am a boy?" she asked.

"Not when you smile like that," he answered.

She laughed.

"You told me once it was too early for dramatics. Today I think it is too early for compliments."

He grinned.

"Perhaps in time I shall teach you to receive them gracefully," he said.

"Simpering over my fan with flirtatious feminity, I suppose?" Skye asked sarcastically.

His laugher rang out free and untrammelled, and Skye knew that for the moment at any rate she had made him forget his anxiety at what lay ahead of him.

As he laughed, she wondered whether those other women with whom he had taunted her so often had managed to make him laugh.

What had they been like? Were they all fair like herself, like the woman in the photograph—the Englishwoman whose image he kept in the drawer?

She had a stupid face, Skye thought spitefully, and wondered if another woman would say the same about hers.

El Diablo's voice recalled her wandering thoughts.

"It is going to be hot today," he remarked, "unless there is a breeze from the sea."

"Think how nice it would be to take a cruise in my yacht," Skye said.

"So you are thinking of that," he flashed. "Can I really trust you to keep your parole?"

"Strangely enough you can," Skye replied. "I was brought up with what I suppose we in England would call a public school sense of honour."

She glanced at him under her eyelashes as she spoke, wondering if he would show any sign at the reference.

After all, as he was British, and undoubtedly a gentleman, he would have been to a public school, perhaps to Eton, or Harrow where her father had been and Jimmy and most of her Standish relations.

But she could not read the expression in El Diablo's eyes as he answered:

"I think really it would have been best if I had left you at the camp, chained to the wall as the slaves were fastened at the beginning of this century."

"What would have happened to me then if Alejo succeeded in taking you prisoner?" Skye flashed at him.

"That is exactly why I brought you with me," he answered in all seriousness.

"But you must not be taken prisoner—there is no real chance of that, is there?"

"I think not," El Diablo replied. "With my escort and the men outside the city, and as Alejo knows well, a great number of followers in Jácara itself, it would be tempting Providence."

"I am frightened all the same," Skye said.

"For me?" he queried.

"No, no, of course not—for myself," she answered hastily, although she had, in fact, been thinking of him.

He laughed softly as if she did not deceive him, and then their conversation was interrupted by the sight of a horseman coming towards them over the plain. He was the first of several they encountered riding out from Jácara with last-minute information and the latest gossip from the streets and Palace.

They rode on until mid-day when they were only a few miles from Jácara and then El Diablo called a halt.

They dismounted where the ground was speckled with marachines, the daisy-like flowers of a wild plant that produces a species of tiny sweet potato.

There were trees to give them shade and the river only a hundred yards away. Each man had brought his own food and one of them carried a luncheon for El Diablo and Skye which had been prepared by Alphonse.

There were meat and chicken pasties, tiny rolls stuffed with cream cheese and fruit. Skye found that she was hungry as she and El Diablo sat at the foot of a majestic ombu tree away from the *gauchos*.

She was thirsty, too, and the light wine they drank tasted like nectar.

For a while they ate in silence, watching the horses cropping the grass, their tails swishing to and fro to keep away the flies, while the humming-birds and the butterflies were vivid splashes of colour against the green of the trees and the pampas.

"It seems a pity that we have to go into a town on a day like this," Skye said reflectively.

"Do you really like the country so much?" El Diablo asked.

"I always feel stifled in a town, especially in summer," she replied. "I remember last year how I hated being in London, but Aunt Hilda had taken a house for the season and so we had to stay, rushing from party to party, at which she hoped optimistically I would find an eligible husband."

"Why didn't you?" El Diablo asked.

"I hate men!"

"Why?"

"Must there be a reason?"

"Of course. It is not natural for a woman to dislike the opposite sex. Who hurt you?"

"How do you know anybody did?" Skye demanded defensively.

"You've answered my question," he said. "Who was it and what happened?"

She turned her face away from him a little petulantly.

"You are assuming that there was something to upset me."

He poured himself out another glass of wine.

"Did someone try to become your lover?" he enquired, his voice quiet, without the mocking note she knew only too well.

She shook her head.

"No . . . nothing like that."

"What, then? Tell me what it was, I am curious."

"I can't think why," she answered. "And if there was . . . something . . . it is not the only reason I dislike men. There is plenty to dislike about them. But I suppose in every girl's life there has to be a first time when one realizes that they are all untrustworthy and bestial."

Skye's voice was suddenly very bitter and El Diablo, watching, saw her eyes darken, her lips tighten as if at the memory of something very painful.

"How old were you?" he asked gently.

"Just seventeen," she replied; "but I suppose I seemed younger. I had seen very little of the world. I had been kept in the schoolroom and not allowed to be social in any way. Aunt Hilda had old-fashioned ideas about that sort of thing . . . and then he came to stay."

"Who did?"

"David Standish; he was a distant cousin. He had been injured in a car accident and came to us to convalesce. He was much older than I—twenty-eight or twenty-nine. At the same time he was the first young man I had ever known well."

"And you fell in love with him?"

"I suppose you would call it that—he was brilliant, amusing, good-looking and everything a man should be. I sat at his feet worshipping him. I can see now how much it must have amused him. He told me I was pretty, and no one had ever told me that before. He made a fuss of me and Aunt Hilda didn't seem to mind. I suppose she thought I was only a child and that I could not possibly take such nonsense seriously. But I didn't think it was nonsense. My whole world was transformed. I grew up overnight, as it were."

Skye drew a deep breath. She was thinking back over those days—seeing the green lawns, sloping down to the river, the delphiniums in the herbaceous border, and David walking slowly round looking at them, his arm through hers, teasing her, making her laugh.

"Go on!" El Diablo's voice commanded her.

Somehow it might have been David's, ordering her about in the way she had loved.

"That's all," Skye said flatly. "I thought he loved me. I was so stupid, so inexperienced . . . how could I think anything else? He kissed me—and they weren't cousinly kisses—the night before he went away, in the summer house behind the tennis court. I thought by that he meant me to marry him. I nearly told Aunt Hilda the next morning after he had gone. Then I decided I would keep it a secret . . . his secret and mine! It was too wonderful for anyone else to know about for the moment."

"What happened then?"

"His engagement was announced three days later. Aunt Hilda had known about it all the time, but he hadn't wanted it talked about until his fiancée returned from India, where her father was a Judge."

Skye's voice died away. She was looking out over the plain, but she did not see the men and the horses, the flower-strewn grass and the blue river twisting through it.

Instead she saw a pot of marmalade. She was staring at the label—"Robinson's Golden Shred"—reading it over and over again while Aunt Hilda's voice droned beside her.

"We must think up a nice wedding present to give David," she was saying. "He might even suggest that you should be a bridesmaid—after all, there are not many Standishes left."

"Robinson's Golden Shred"—Skye could hear her heart crying out "No! no! no!" while she sat saying nothing.

"Poor little Skye, so that is what happened."

She had almost forgotten El Diablo was beside her, and now she started and turned towards him, her voice hard and brittle as she said:

"Stupid, isn't it? But when one is young one minds things so terribly."

"Yes, when one is young," El Diablo agreed.

They looked at each other for a moment before Skye turned her face away.

"Now you know why I distrust all men," she said with a false brightness, "and of course you have hardly endeared me to your sex."

"What David began I have undoubtedly finished," El Diablo remarked, and his voice was hard; "but there are other men in the world."

"I am not encouraged to believe them any different," Skye retorted.

"Who knows? Perhaps one day somebody inestimable will come along," El Diablo said. "He will be what your Aunt Hilda would undoubtedly call 'Mr. Right'."

Skye gave a sudden gurgle of laughter.

"How did you guess that that was that she called him?" she said; and even as she said the words, she remembered there was no reason why he should not guess what Aunt

Hilda would say—or any other Englishwoman of her generation.

He doubtless had innumerable relations exactly like Aunt Hilda and perhaps the girl in the photograph had been "Miss Right" for him, only something had gone wrong.

She wanted to ask him about himself. After all, she had told him the secret she had never before revealed to anyone; but even as she summoned up courage to begin, their moment of quiet intimacy was over.

Another rider arrived from Jācara and El Diablo rose and went away to consult with the man and he remained away until the time came for them to move on.

Despite a strong breeze, it was very hot as they rode towards the town. They had their first glimpse of the sea, emerald blue and mirror-smooth to the end of space, and then in the glimmering golden sunshine they saw the Palace, standing high above the harbour.

Below the trees, the white, flat-topped houses and the spires and towers of the churches gave Jācara an almost fairy-like beauty.

It was impossible to think that treachery or cruelty or injustice could be rife among so much loveliness, and Skye thought how little she had known about Mariposa and its people when her yacht had nosed its way so gaily and confidently into the harbour.

She remembered standing on deck with Jimmy and how she had said to him a little breathlessly:

"Mariposa at last!"

"I only hope it is the El Dorado you believe it to be," he answered.

"Why not?" she enquired. "Surely one doesn't always have to be disappointed?"

He smiled at her enthusiasm.

"Not always," he agreed.

She knew that his hopefulness had been born only out of his fondness for her.

"If only we had known," she thought now.

If only either of them had had the slightest inkling of what lay ahead. She looked sideways at El Diablo as they rode side by side.

His eyes were fixed on the town. He was frowning a little and, as always when his face was in repose, it accentuated his hawk-like features and gave him a slightly sinister appearance.

It was the way he looked, Skye knew, when he was most determined, and it was, too, how he had looked at her the first time they had met. *"El beso del Diablo"*—how well she remembered hearing those words, whispered by the frightened boy who had crossed himself at the sight of the dead man!

Since then she had known many other kisses of El Diablo's—kisses not of death but of love.

She felt herself quiver a little at the memory of them, of last night when he had kissed her lips, her hair, her eyes, her neck a thousand times, wildly, fiercely, possessively, as if it might be for the last time, making love to her with a passion which seemed almost to be born of fear.

They were drawing nearer to Jácara. It was no longer a distant scene, but a living reality.

They were travelling on the red, hard-baked roads. There were houses and gardens, wayfarers on their donkeys, and small boys trying to sell them melons, bananas and red figs and even little native birds in tiny homemade cages.

On the outskirts of the town El Diablo called yet another halt; and then, while the men flicked the dust from their boots, wiped the sweat from their foreheads and set their hats at an even more jaunty angle, he gave his last instructions.

He would ride ahead, the rest would ride in threes directly behind him, Skye in the foremost rank in the centre, with a man on either side of her.

"We will go in slowly," El Diablo said in his deep resonant voice, "we want our friends to see us. We want them, if possible, to follow us to the meeting at the Palace."

"We've got friends in the town all right," one of the men boasted.

"Never be sure of your friend until he fights beside you," El Diablo retorted, quoting a Mariposan proverb, and making them all laugh.

"It's Alejo who should be saying that, not us," someone cried, and there was more laughter.

The men were now looking to make quite certain their pistols were loaded. It was a rigidly observed tradition that no *gaucho* should ever carry an unloaded gun. Skye felt herself shiver.

There was a law that no one should carry weapons in Mariposa, but it was disregarded like so many others. She remembered now how she had patted the revolver at her side when General Alejo's officer had warned her against going far into the interior.

As if he sensed her thoughts, El Diablo suddenly turned towards her and drew her own pistol from the pocket of his tweed coat.

"You had better take this," he said.

She looked up at him in astonishment, too surprised to reach out her hand towards it.

"Why?"

"You may need it," he said.

She knew he was thinking that they might all be trapped and taken prisoner; and yet still, for some unaccountable reason, she hesitated.

"I trust you, today, at any rate, not to plug me in the back," he said with a faint smile.

She took the pistol then and slipped it into the pocket of her *bombachas*. It was heavy against her leg and now for the first time she felt really afraid. This was no light-hearted joke. This was serious.

She had a vision of Jimmy in Valparaiso, and of his horror if he knew what she was doing; and then she knew that she would not miss this moment for anything in the world.

She considered what her feelings would have been if El Diablo had left her in the cave. She could imagine how long the day would have dragged.

She would have been wondering what was happening and longing with an almost physical ache for his return. It would have been a torture beyond words to have been left behind, and she felt a sudden warm sense of gratitude towards him that he had brought her with him.

She was only a worry and a liability, she was well aware of that. There was always the fear, too, that she might be recognized; and then she remembered the sunglasses in her pocket and put them on.

Only that her skin was fair made her different from the men riding beside her. Her size was not particularly noticeable. Many of the *gauchos* were small-boned, and the long hours in the saddle and the hardness of their lives made them thin and wiry without a spare ounce of flesh upon them.

Skye gave the brim of her hat a little tug to shadow her face.

A week ago she might have desired to be recognized so that there could be some chance of escape; but now in one thing at any rate she supported El Diablo—in his hatred of Alejo and of the injustices of the Government.

She thought of Josné, of the Indians who had been deprived of their land, of the farmers whose *haciendas* were to be taken away and of the people of Mariposa whose national wealth was to be exploited by a foreign power.

No, whatever her personal hatred of El Diablo, she was on his side in this fight against aggression.

He looked at his watch.

"It is time we started," he said quietly.

The men got themselves into line, three abreast as he commanded; then he rode ahead. The poor houses on the outskirts gave way to the shops and wide tarmacked roads of the modern part of Jácara.

Here they encountered the smart, shiny American cars which ran the Dictator and his friends round the town and up to the racecourse.

Every minister was entitled to one of these elegant automobiles; and when they grew too old and too shabby for such distinguished use, they were passed down the scale to the secretaries and the lower Civil Servants, until eventually, when they were worn out and no longer smart enough for official use, they would be sold, if possible at a fictitious figure, to the ordinary townsfolk.

El Diablo, who knew of these machinations only too well, deliberately kept his horse to the centre of the road so that the cars were crowded out as the cavalcade passed by.

"El Diablo! El Diablo!" the name began in a whisper and rose to a shout.

Their appearance at the beginning of the town was the signal for a large company of people to come storming on to the pavements, waving and cheering and following them along the old Spanish buildings.

Now the road was cobbled and flanked by houses with fluted tiles and overhanging balconies. Skye knew there were great flowery patios and corridors paved with coloured marble hidden away behind the columned façades.

Here was the elegance of a bygone century and it seemed as if they stepped backwards in time.

The old town wound to the very foot of the Palace. The pull uphill and the crowds in the street made them move slowly.

Children kept darting out of the gutters, women leaned

from the balconies to throw flowers to the riders, many of the *gauchos* catching a rose and slipping it behind their ears.

"El Diablo! El Diablo!"

The streets rang with his name. It was difficult for Skye to see his face, but she thought he must be smiling. There was no doubt that he was welcome or that he was indeed a popular figure in the town.

Alejo would resent this, she thought, for dictators are not fond of rivals. At the same time, it would strengthen El Diablo's hand when it came to striking a bargain.

A rose came flying through the air to land on Skye's saddle. As she caught it, she saw that it had been thrown by a pretty, dark-haired girl who, with several others, was leaning from a high balcony.

True to the part she must play. Skye waved an acknowledgment for the flower and the girls giggled with delight.

At that moment she heard a cry!

"Danger! Danger!"

It was the shrill voice of a man frantic with fear and it rose high above the laughter and cheering of the crowd.

"Danger! Go back!"

Skye could see now who was shouting—a young man who came running towards them down the hill, hatless, his face dripping with perspiration, his whole body strained forward with his haste.

Instinctively Skye tightened her hold on the reins and checked her horse. She saw El Diablo's back in front of her suddenly tense.

Then came the crack of a rifle and the boy, for he was nothing more, toppled forward on to the cobbles.

It seemed to Skye as if there was one second of poignant silence and then the screaming of a hundred voices was drowned almost immediately by a fusillade of shots.

They were fired from farther up the street.

Bullets whizzed past Skye's head and she heard a man behind her give a sudden hoarse cry.

El Diablo wheeled his horse.

"Turn back," he ordered.

Then, amidst the screaming and confusion of the crowd and the rearing, frightened horses, as Skye tried to turn, she saw it happen.

El Diablo's horse crumpled under him. Even as he fell she threw herself from her own saddle.

She was aware that the *gauchos* were shooting over her

head. They had all drawn their revolvers and were firing in response to the fire directed at them.

Then, as she reached the ground and ran towards El Diablo, impelled by some form beyond thought, she saw that he was hit.

He had fallen from his horse and was lying sprawled in the roadway. Among the babel of sound, screams and cries, the crack and whine of rifle- and pistol-fire, Skye was conscious only of El Diablo lying free of his dead horse, his head in the dust, blood pouring from his forehead.

As she reached him, she realized that Juan was there first.

"Get him down a side street," she heard him say to another *gaucho*, and lifting El Diablo they ran across the pavement and into a dark alleyway nestling beside an ancient house.

Skye pulled off her dark glasses so that she could see better and threw them away.

El Diablo's eyes were closed and the blood from the wound in his head was running in a crimson stream down one side of his face. There was blood, too, spreading over the shoulder of his coat.

The men paused for a moment as they reached the shelter of the alleyway.

"Is he dead?" Skye asked breathlessly.

Juan, who had carried El Diablo's shoulders, shook his head.

"No, no, Señora; but we must get him away from here. Those devils meant to murder him and may try again."

"Take him to my yacht," Skye cried. "He will be safe there. Perhaps it is the only place in Jácara where he can be safe."

"As the Señora says," Juan agreed.

The two men started to move down the alley. The fighting behind them was noisy and continuous. El Diablo's men were not retreating, but retaliating.

Swiftly the *gauchos* carried El Diablo down a long flight of steps to the lower road. A grocer's van, driven by a boy, pulled up beside them.

"Want any help?" he asked.

They all got into the van and directed the boy to drive them to the quay.

It was only a short distance and they drove in silence, Skye trying vainly to staunch the blood from El Diablo's forehead.

"Take El Cabeza aboard," she said to Juan, giving a handful of notes to the boy who had driven the van.

Then, as they stepped out into the sunshine and lifted El Diablo to carry him up the gangplank on to the deck of the *Liberty*, she saw the pallor of his face and felt that Juan was wrong and that he must be dead.

She knew in that moment, with a hopelessness born of a sudden despair, that she loved him.

13

Skye felt that she had never been so glad of anything as she was of the calm Scottish stolidness of Captain Maclean as he came from below when they stepped on deck.

"Good afternoon, Miss Standish," he said in an unsurprised voice. "Is anyone hurt?"

There was the firing of bullets in the distance; panic-stricken crowds of women and children were hurrying down the roadway above the quay, and Skye knew that her own appearance, dressed as a *gaucho* and standing beside an unconscious man dripping with blood, must be dramatic to say the least of it.

And yet Captain Maclean was as cool as if they were meeting uneventfully on the shores of his native Aberdeen.

"Put to sea at once, Captain Maclean," Skye said; "we must get away from here."

"I have two men ashore," he answered gravely.

"Never mind," Skye replied; "they can follow us overland to Montevideo. That is where we must make for and quickly. We must find a doctor."

Captain Maclean looked at El Diablo.

"Let us get him below," he said in slow Spanish to the *gauchos,* "and then we will see what can be done for him."

Slowly and with difficulty, for although they were strong, El Diablo was a heavy man, they carried him down the narrow companion-way.

Skye opened the door to the comfortable cabin opposite her own. It was exquisitely furnished and the pink silk curtains over the portholes were echoed by the covers on the bed and on a small easy chair.

As the *gauchos* lifted El Diablo and laid him down, the blood ran from his forehead, dripping on to the pillow until Captain Maclean picked up a linen face towel and laid it across his head to staunch the wound.

Again Skye felt that agonizing throb of her heart and she forced the same question from lips that were suddenly dry and a throat which seemed too constricted to emit a sound:

"Is he dead?"

Captain Maclean was taking El Diablo's pulse.

"No," he answered; "he has been knocked unconscious by the bullet which cut his forehead, and there is some trouble, too, in his shoulder."

He spoke with an air of authority and thankfully Skye remembered that the master mariner of any ship must be experienced in First Aid. She had seen Captain Maclean treat cuts and injuries before, for accidents can happen even on the best-regulated ships.

Now she turned to him with what was almost a cry of hope.

"He will live?"

"Ay, I see no reason to think otherwise," Captain Maclean answered. "I'll send Evans to attend to him while I get the ship under way, if that is what you wish me to do, Miss Standish."

"Yes, yes, we must get away from here quickly," Skye said. "There is no time to be lost."

She looked then at the two *gauchos* standing awkwardly by the bed. Their eyes were on their unconscious leader and Skye knew without being told that they were wondering what was going to happen to them.

"You must get back to the camp, Juan," she said. "Fight General Alejo if you have to, but don't let him capture the mountains. El Cabeza will come back to you as soon as he is well enough—I promise you that."

She saw the sudden light of hope in Juan's eyes.

"El Cabeza will return?" he asked.

She nodded her head confidently.

"It will not be long before he is with you again," she said more reassuringly than she actually felt. "Don't worry about him. Take charge yourself and collect men from the town."

"I understand, Señora."

Juan touched his hat to her, and as he and the other *gaucho* left the cabin Skye felt the purr of the engines beneath her feet. She drew a quick breath of relief.

They would soon be moving away from Jácara, from Alejo and his treachery. But for the moment she could only think of El Diablo, silent and still, so different from how she had ever known him.

She went to his side and touched his hand; and as she stood there indecisive, hardly aware of what she felt beneath the frightened beating of her heart, Evans came hurrying to the cabin.

Afterwards she remembered very little of how they managed to cut El Diablo's blood-soaked coat and shirt away from his wounded shoulder. Evans wanted to send her from the room, but she insisted on helping.

It was only when Captain Maclean came back with a box of surgical instruments that she felt she could no longer bear to watch.

White-faced, Skye slipped away to her own cabin.

The sight of El Diablo's shoulder, with its gaping wound where the bullet had entered, had made her feel near to fainting.

The gash, too, in his head would need stitches, although, as the bleeding gradually diminished, she had seen that it was not a dangerous wound.

The bullet had struck him a glancing blow, and while it had knocked him unconscious and cut open the flesh, no vital damage had been done.

In her own cabin Skye went to the porthole. The yacht was moving out to sea. As they drew away from the harbour, Jácara had an almost unreal beauty. The heat made it shimmer hazily, and high above the town the Palace windows glittered iridescent in the sun. It was hard to believe that just a little while ago they had been fighting for their lives in the sunlit streets.

Skye shut her eyes for the moment. She could see El Diablo all too clearly as he had lain in the roadway, his face turned up towards the sky, one hand still entangled with the reins of his dead horse.

That must have been the moment, she told herself, when

she knew that she loved him, that moment when she felt as if a bullet had pierced her own heart.

Then she knew that subconsciously she must have loved him for a long time—that night she had seized his revolver but had not the courage to shoot him, that moment of horror when she fought with Pedro in the cave and called El Diablo's name and felt an inexpressible relief when he had come in time to save her.

How blind she had been, how stupid! She might have guessed it, too, when she found a woman's photograph among the papers by his bed and felt the first bitter pangs of jealousy.

She loved him! She loved him!

Slowly she began to take off the suit which Josné had made so cleverly and so quickly. She threw it down on the floor of the cabin and then, taking the first dress she found in the cupboard, slipped it on.

She loved El Diablo and she could think of nothing else and was scarcely conscious of what she did or even of seeing her own reflection in the mirror of her skilfully-fitted dressing table.

When she had changed, she went from her cabin to stand for a moment outside the one opposite, half afraid to go in. She was still there when Captain Maclean opened the door.

"Is . . . is everything all right?" she stammered.

He came out into the passageway, closing the door behind him.

"Ay, he'll be all right. It is better than I hoped, but the puir mon's in pain just now. I have given him something to make him sleep. Don't go in, for he won't recognize you and there's no call for you to be upsetting yourself."

"It won't upset me," Skye said, but without conviction.

She knew that Captain Maclean was well aware why she had gone from the room while he dressed the wounds.

"There'll be doctors in Montevideo who will set him on his feet again," he said cheerily. "We should be there by noon tomorrow at the very latest."

He turned towards the companion-way and then, as he reached it, he turned back again.

"Can you tell me the gentleman's name?" he asked.

Skye hesitated.

"He is sometimes referred to as 'El Cabeza'," she said at length.

"And by another name as well," Captain Maclean added

with a twinkle in his eye, and she knew that he was well aware of the identity of her guest.

She waited until he had gone above and then went quietly into the cabin where El Diablo lay. The curtains had been drawn, but the light percolated through them. Evans was sitting by the bedside and he rose as she entered.

She motioned to him to sit down again. He was a small, wiry little man, older than he looked, and had been at sea all his life.

He had, as Skye well knew, hands that could be as gentle as any woman's and she personally would rather have been nursed by Evans when she was ill than by anyone else she had ever met.

She saw that Captain Maclean and Evans had got El Diablo into bed. There was a bandage round his forehead and bandages covered his wounded shoulder, but the other showed naked above the soft linen of the sheet.

His skin was very white and Skye remembered as she looked at it that he was British.

She walked across and stood close beside the bed, looking down at El Diablo. There was a little more colour in his face than there had been earlier on.

"Will you sit with him for a moment, Miss, while I get a cup of tea?" Evans asked in a low voice. "He won't wake now, but in case he gets restless it's best that someone should be close at hand."

"Yes, I'll sit with him," Skye replied.

"I won't be more than a few minutes, Miss," Evans promised.

He slipped away from the cabin and Skye sat down on the chair that he had left vacant. El Diablo was breathing deeply and evenly.

He looked younger and more vulnerable when he was asleep, she thought; and she could see now that he had not altered so very much from his photograph in the passport, taken when he was only a young boy.

The lines from nose to mouth had deepened, his lips were set in a harder line, his chin was squarer. It was his expression which had changed most, she thought.

How hard she had fought him! And now, at the end of it all, what she wanted more than she had ever wanted anything in her life before was to feel his lips against hers.

She felt a sudden impatience with herself that so much time had been wasted. Why could she not have realized before that her fruitless struggling would end in love?

Then suddenly a cold hand clutched at her heart. She could hear El Diablo's voice saying.

"It is the mawkish sentimentality which most women call love which I find intolerable."

Skye put her hands up to her face. Was this what he meant? Was it this throbbing of her heart, the sudden dancing within her veins that he hated and despised?

Would she now become as undesirable and as unwanted as those other women, the women with whom he had taunted her so often, shaming and humiliating her because she must be continually reminded that they had been in the camp before her?

In a sudden terror she rose to her feet. He could not mean that, he could not—and yet, as she looked down at him, impersonal in his unconsciousness, she knew that he had spoken the truth and that he had no use for love.

A pretty woman was a solace and a respite, an entertainment to which he could return in the evening, one who would for the moment take his mind off the innumerable problems and difficulties which beset him on every side.

He wanted no more from her than that she should be lovely and excite his desires. He had no time for dramatics, as he called them, for the heart-searchings and the heart-breakings of tremendous emotions.

"Oh, God! What am I to do?"

Skye saw for the first time the pit into which she had fallen. She interested El Diablo because she was different, because, although through expediency he had made her his wife, she had refused to accept him as her husband and had continued day after day to fight him with every weapon left in her power.

Now, she would be no different from the others—the women who hungered for him, who wanted to possess him, to share their love, to command his affections.

"I love you!" She said the words in a whisper of despair, and then she bent down and let her lips touch for one moment his hand resting outside the sheets.

It was with a sense of growing depression that, when Evans returned, she went up on deck. Jácara was out of sight. They were running down the coast, the evening light revealing the vivid colours of cliff, sea and sky.

But Skye could think of nothing but her own aching heart, her new-found fear.

"Why," she asked herself, "did I think I was different

from anyone else? Why did I think I was immune from love?"

She knew the answer to that. Although she had sworn that she hated men, in reality and perhaps unconsciously she had been looking for someone exceptional, someone different.

The men who had seemed pale and unattractive in London and New York had indeed been but pale imitations of manhood when one compared them with El Diablo.

She wondered now that · she had not recognized his power to attract her from that first moment when he had come galloping over the plain, so forceful, vivid and virile in his autocracy.

She had hated him then and she had hated him with every nerve in her body when he had married her by force, kept her prisoner and made love to her just for his own amusement.

But now, watching the coast of Mariposa fade away into the distance, Skye admitted to herself how much she had learned from him. How incredibly ignorant, stupid and foolhardy she had been when she came to Jácara such a little while ago! A silly girl with too much money . . . and, now she was a woman, experienced in many things, and, most important of all, in love.

Not only had she learned to love from the point of view that every breath she drew seemed to bring her an uncontrollable longing for El Diablo, but she had learned to love other things too—the men and women in the camp, in the *haciendas* and the mines, the people of Mariposa for whom El Diablo fought and in whose service he had at this very moment so nearly lost his life.

And the life she had lived in the camp—she loved that too. She was beginning to understand what it meant to be part of a community, to want to help rather than to receive and give rather than take.

"I love him!" she told the sea and the sky.

And at that moment she asked herself what she had to offer with that love. It was a moment of self-revelation, of humiliation far lower than anything she had experienced physically.

It was a humiliation of the soul, of feeling that she was useless and empty, with nothing to give to any man except a pretty face and a well-made body.

"No wonder he finds only one use for women, she whispered and went down into the purgatory of her own conscience.

All that evening, as she sat on deck or relieved Evans at El Diablo's side, she condemned herself and the emptiness and fruitlessness of her life until now.

Her money had brought her new possessions but no new interests. She had done nothing with her millions, neither good nor evil, and that was perhaps more reprehensible than anything else.

When it grew late, Evans insisted that she go to her own cabin for four hour's sleep, promising that he would call her to take his place so that he could rest in his turn. Skye found it hard to relax, but eventually she drifted away into a restless slumber.

There were dreams occurring and recurring, in which always she was lost, lonely and afraid. She woke to the sound of her alarm clock, for she had not trusted Evans not to take the whole burden of nursing upon himself.

She jumped out of her bunk, thankful to escape from her dreams and, putting on her dressing-gown, she went into the cabin to find Evans watching his patient.

"He's a bit restless, Miss," he told her. "Perhaps I'd better stay."

"You go and lie down, Evans. I will manage. If I am at all worried, I will ring the bell for you."

"You promise that, Miss?"

"Yes, of course I promise," Skye smiled.

He went away reluctantly and Skye sat down at El Diablo's side. The drug was wearing off, he was moving about in bed, as if he were uncomfortable, his head turning from side to side.

One of the bedside lamps was lit, but shaded so that she could see his face while there was no chance of the light disturbing him.

She got up to prop his pillow in a more comfortable position. As she did so, he opened his eyes. For a moment he stared with the dazed look of a man who comes back slowly to consciousness, and then in a voice low and husky he asked:

"Where am I?"

"Aboard my yacht," Skye answered. "You've been wounded and we are going to Montevideo to get a doctor for you."

"Wounded?" He said the word reflectively and added, "I

remember now. They shot Marcos who came to warn us of a trap."

"That's right," Skye said; "there must have been men hidden a little further up the street."

"Did the others get away safely?"

"I don't know," she admitted; "there was a lot of shooting, for our men returned their fire. I was concerned only with getting you away. Juan and another man—I don't know his name—carried you down a side alley and we brought you to the yacht in a grocer's van."

"I must get back!"

El Diablo tried to sit up, but the pain in his shoulder was too much for him.

"Don't be so ridiculous," Skye said. "How can you go back like this? Besides, we are going to Montevideo for you to see a doctor."

"But the men—I must be with them!"

"Juan knows what to do," Skye said firmly. "They are going back to the camp to wait until you can be with them. They will hold it against Alejo, whatever happens."

"How can you be sure of that?"

"Juan told me that was what they would do, and you can trust him."

"Yes, I can trust Juan; but will the others follow him? That's what matters."

"If he tells them it is what you want, they will do it," Skye said positively.

"I ought to be with them . . . blast this shoulder!"

He got his right hand, which was uninjured, up from under the bedclothes, but as he went to touch his bandaged shoulder he put it to his forehead.

"My head, too?" he asked. "What happened there?"

"A glancing bullet knocked you unconscious," Skye told him—"you had to have six stitches in the wound."

"I suppose that is why my head aches," he said. "Well, it is no thanks to Alejo that I am not dead. That is what he intended."

"If that boy had not warned us," Skye said, "I suppose there would have been little chance of any of us escaping alive."

"None, I imagine," El Diablo said grimly. "We should have been caught between two crossfires. It would have been impossible to miss us in that narrow street. It was a clever idea; I ought to have anticipated it."

"But how could you?"

"I was expecting something to happen at the Palace—that is where I made my mistake. Alejo's plan was shrewd; we were to have been killed in the town and he would have disclaimed all responsibility. He was waiting for us at the Palace, he would have explained, how could he help our having unknown enemies in the streets? We can be thankful that Marcos found out in time."

"Marcos was your spy in the Palace, I suppose?"

"One of them," El Diablo said briefly.

He tried to move again, but the pain made him close his eyes for a moment and press his lips together.

"How soon shall we arrive in Montevideo?" he asked.

"Noon today."

He opened his eyes and looked at her.

"I suppose you are not kidnapping me as I kidnapped you?" he said.

"Is that likely?"

"No, and I assume you are being magnanimous or you would have heaved me into the sea and that would have been that."

He tried to smile at her and she could see that he was striving at the same time to hide the pain. She reached out and touched the bell.

"What are you doing?" he asked suspiciously.

"Ringing for Evans. He is the steward who has been looking after you; but is was Captain Maclean who cleaned the wound in your shoulder and stitched up your forehead."

"Captain Maclean?" El Diablo repeated. "I seem to know the name."

"You ought to—you had a letter forged to him purporting to come from me!"

"Yes, I remember now."

He was making an almost superhuman effort, Skye could see, to talk against the throbbing ache of his wounds. When Evans came hurrying into the room, she said:

"El Cabeza is awake and in pain. Will you ask Captain Maclean to give him some morphia or whatever he gave him before?"

"I have some tablets here," Evans answered.

He took a little box from the drawer at the side of the bed.

"I'm all right," El Diablo protested, but he swallowed the tablets nevertheless and drank the water which Evans held to his lips. Then drowsily his eyelids began to fall.

"That's better," he said, "much better. Good night . . . Ice Maiden."

His voice died away on the last word, but Skye heard what he said. If he only knew, she thought, the spring thaws had come and her veins were no longer filled with ice.

"Go back to bed, Miss," Evans insisted, "I feel happier if I stay here, and if he's quiet I'll doze beside him."

He was so insistent that Skye obeyed him and going back to her cabin fell into a dreamless slumber.

She woke early and went on deck.

"I have wirelessed to the Harbour Master to have a surgeon waiting when we arrive," Captain Maclean told her.

"That's splendid," Skye said.

"Do you want the gentleman taken into hospital?"

"No, of course not." Skye's reply was instantaneous.

She had not, for one moment, anticipated that El Diablo might be taken away from her.

"I thought perhaps the doctor might consider he would get treatment more easily that way."

"I can't help that. He must stay aboard. There is room for a nurse if the doctor wants him to have one; but the moment he is well enough, we have to take him back to Jācara."

"Very good, Miss Standish."

Captain Maclean never asked questions, neither did he talk more than necessary. Skye was grateful for his reticence. Somehow she could not bear to have to explain anything at the moment.

She walked restlessly up and down the deck. El Diablo was still asleep for she had looked in when she got up and again after she had finished breakfast.

"Is he really all right?" she asked Evans when she saw he was not awake.

"Sleep's the best thing, Miss. It's shock that most people find it hard to get over. I was on a battleship during the war and, when we was hit, the fellows as suffered from shock were far worse than those as got injured. And if you ask me, Miss, the Captain's done a good job on his shoulder."

"I'm glad," Skye said.

But however reassuring Evans might be and however much she might trust Captain Maclean's ministrations, she could not feel anything but anxious.

She was thankful to see the deep brown waters of the

River Plate meeting the Atlantic and ahead, surmounting a little rocky hill, the old Spanish fort built against the Charria Indians which is the first and last landmark of the travelling Uruguayan.

A surgeon was waiting on the quay-side of the beautiful harbour and without any explanations Skye took him down to the cabin.

"A nasty wound, Señorita," he said later when he came up on deck, rubbing his newly washed hands together and, with his bald head and big horn-rimmed spectacles, looking rather like a benign sea-gull.

"But it will be all right?" Skye asked quickly.

"Perfectly. Some years ago it might have caused us a great deal of anxiety, but nowadays with penicillin and the new sulpha drugs to help us there is practically nothing that cannot be cured by care and time."

"Time is important," Skye said, "my . . . my friend has to get back to Mariposa."

"Mariposa?" the surgeon questioned and looked knowing. "Strange things always seem to be happening in that country. But your friend will have to take things easy for some days, at any rate. I will come and see him again tomorrow."

"Does he need a nurse?" Skye asked.

"Not necessarily," the surgeon replied; "your steward seems to understand exactly what to do."

"You don't think there is anything else——?" Skye began.

"My dear lady," the surgeon interrupted her, "I promise you I have done all that is necessary. When it is possible for the patient to be moved without pain, I would like an X-ray. But as far as I can ascertain the bullet has not touched any bones and so we need not worry ourselves unduly."

"Thank you," Skye said, "and thank you for coming."

"It is a pleasure, Señorita," he said courteously, and bowed over her hand before he went down the gangway.

The surgeon's complacency as to his patient's treatment was not shared by El Diablo.

"The damn fool seems to think I can stay here indefinitely," he said. "I believe I could get up by now, despite what he says."

"If you attempt to do anything stupid, Evans and I will have to hold you down or, better still, have you strapped to the bed," Skye cried.

He looked up at her with a twist to his lips.

"So you are giving the orders now," he said, "and getting your own back a little! Wait till I am well!"

She felt her heart leap at the teasing note in his voice, but she answered him in all seriousness:

"Only by being patient will you get well quickly, and you know how important it is, not only to you but to the people waiting for you in the camp."

"Do you suppose I am not worrying about them?" he asked.

"Go to sleep and forget them for the moment," Skye commanded. "Evans says it is sleep that you want, and as he has very likely told you, there is nothing he doesn't know about wounds and shock."

"To hell with Evans!" El Diablo exclaimed. "Kiss me and then perhaps I won't have a nightmare about Alejo."

Trembling so much that she was afraid he might see and guess the reason for it, Skye bent forward and pressed her lips gently against his. It was a light kiss, the touch of a butterfly, and he laughed up at her.

"It that still the best you can do?" he asked. "You are the worst pupil I ever had."

She felt herself flush at the implication of the words, and then his eyes were closed and she knew he was drifting away into sleep.

"The worst pupil!" Always he must compare her with other women, women who had held his interest until they loved him, until he no longer had to fight for their favours.

She went up on deck. A cushioned chair and foot-rest were arranged for her under the awning. She sat looking out to sea. Never in her wildest dreams had she imagined being aboard the *Liberty* with El Diablo.

Yet now she wished only that she had the courage to give the order for the yacht to sail away to the most distant horizon. Perhaps she would kidnap him, perhaps she would take him away with her to some new country where there was no other call on his time, here they could be alone—an ordinary prosaic married couple.

Then she laughed at the very idea. How bored he would be, how quickly he would leave her at the first opportunity! And yet he desired her. But why, why, Skye asked herself for the thousandth time, had he asked no more of her than a few kisses?

Why had he spared her the final humiliation of being captured and married by force, when she knew his body burned for her? It was impossible not to remember his passionate love-making the night before they left for Jācara.

She had not fought against him, telling herself it was useless; but now Skye admitted the truth—it was because she had wanted to be kissed, caressed and—yes, why not admit it?—possessed.

She felt herself thrill and tingle again at the thought of his excitement, and at his goodnight when he had finally risen from the couch to go to bed. The candles had gutted low and it was nearly dawn.

"Are you very tired?" he asked gently, his consideration unexpected.

"Very."

"It's your own fault for being so lovely—you go to a man's head, Skye."

He sat down again.

"What is it about you that drives me mad?" he asked. "I even find myself thinking of you when I am busy."

Skye moved her head wearily.

"I must leave you," he said, but he had not gone.

Instead he bent forward to trace with his finger the dark circles beneath her eyes.

"One day you will become a woman, little Skye," he said, "and you will be infinitely more beautiful and infinitely more desirable—although I cannot imagine how. As you are now, you drive me mad."

He bent his head as if to kiss her cheek, but instead he found her mouth. It was soft with tiredness, and his lips had suddenly grown hard and possessive, holding her captive.

Then with an effort, he had broken free and risen to his feet.

"I think you bewitch me!" he said roughly and had gone from the caves as the candles flickered and went ont.

Why hadn't she reached out to him then? Skye asked herself now.

She was so deep in her own thoughts that she did not hear someone come aboard or hear a step behind her on deck, until a well-known voice said:

"There you are!"

She stared up at that and threw out her hands with a little cry of delight. Jimmy Donaldson stood there, dapper and neat in a suit of light tweeds, his hat in his hand, the sunshine on his greying hair.

"Jimmy! You are the last person I expected to see."

"I wonder why? I got an aeroplane at dawn this morning as soon as I heard the news."

"What news?"

"About the revolution, of course. I expected you would be involved in it."

"But what revolution? What are you talking about?"

Jimmy looked at her as if she were half-witted, and then sat down in a deck-chair.

"Listen, Skye—are you being dense or am I? It was announced on the wireless last night that there was a revolution taking place in Jācara. I thought you might be in trouble and I jumped an aeroplane at dawn and got to Jācara about eleven o'clock. I found the revolution had petered out because the rebels had won and General Alejo had been bumped off."

"Alejo dead?!!" Skye exclaimed.

"So I was told," Jimmy said, "and that the bandit's men—you know, the ones we met when we were riding—have taken over the Palace."

"Jimmy! But what is going to happen?"

"I haven't the slightest idea," Jimmy said, "but does it matter? I found out from the Harbour Master that you had left for Montevideo yesterday; so, having come so far, I thought I might as well see you before I went back. To tell the truth, I didn't think you would have the sense to clear out when the shooting started."

"Jimmy—I can't think for the moment. Say it all again! El Diablo's men have taken the Palace and the town?"

"And everything else as far as I can make out. They told me at the airfield that the townsfolk had risen in support of the bandit's gang. I always told you Alejo had a precarious hold on public opinion."

"But if this is true, he must go back at once. Anything might happen if he is not there."

"If who is not there?" Jimmy asked. "In Heaven's name, what are you talking about?"

"Don't you understand—El Diablo is here on this yacht!"

"Good God!" Jimmy stared at her.

"He was wounded," Skye explained, "so I brought him to Montevideo to see a surgeon. He's all right—or at least he will be in a few days, but we can't wait for that. He must go back at once. He will have to direct things from the yacht if he can't be moved.

"Look here, Skye, have you gone mad?"

"Yes, if you like," Skye smiled.

"But this man El Diablo is a bandit, a revolutionary. What the hell do you know about him?"

"Much more than you think," Skye answered. "Jimmy, don't let's argue. You've got to help me—you must. El Diablo is the only man who can save Mariposa. I will tell you all about it when there is time, but now the great thing is to get him back there. They can't manage without him. They are only children and they will be lost without a leader."

"If you think I am going to help a revolutionary Mariposan bandit you are much mistaken. Nor are you, for that matter. You can put this man ashore and let him fend for himself. You are not going to be mixed up in it, and I most certainly am not."

"Oh yes, you are!" Skye's voice was quiet. "Listen, Jimmy, I know what I am talking about. El Diablo will make Mariposa a decent country if he gets the chance, and you needn't sneer at him for being a bandit—or a Mariposan for that matter. He is British—as British as you and I are—but he doesn't know that I know it."

"British!"

"Yes. His real name is Guy Tremayne."

"Guy Tremayne!" Jimmy ejaculated. "I don't believe you—you are making this up."

"It's true."

"Good Lord! Guy Tremayne! I know all about him."

"Do you?"

"But are you certain? Did he tell you that was his name?"

"No. I told you he doesn't know I know it. I found his passport. He has taken Mariposan nationality."

"So that's where he went to! I made enquiries, but I never dreamed of his doing that."

"You made enquiries?" Skye ejaculated. "How? When? Why? No, don't answer me now. I have to tell Captain Maclean to take us back to Mariposa. Don't you see, he's got to be there now Alejo's dead?"

As she turned to go, something in Jimmy's bewildered expression struck her as pathetic. With a little laugh she put her hand up and touched his cheek.

"It's all right," she said. "I'm not mad or drunk or any of the things you are imagining. I think, though I'm not sure, that I'm happy—perhaps for the first time in my whole life!"

14

Jimmy was still sitting under the awning on deck when Skye came hurrying back to him.

"We are returning to Mariposa immediately," she said. "I have not been able to tell El Diablo yet, because he is asleep, but Evans will let me know as soon as he wakes up."

"What is this all about?" Jimmy asked. "How did you meet this man and why is he here?"

"I will answer your questions later," Skye said evasively; but tell me first what you know about Guy Tremayne."

"I can't really credit that we are talking about the same person," Jimmy replied, "but so far as my story is concerned it is simple enough. A distant cousin of mine, Pauline Donaldson, married Sir Rupert Tremayne a few years before the war. She was his second wife, and while she was nearly thirty when she married, he was in his late fifties."

"Was she fair?" Skye asked.

"Yes," Jimmy replied. "Why?"

"Never mind," Skye answered.

She had discovered the identity of the woman in the photograph.

"She was both fair and pretty," Jimmy went on. "She was what was called a Society beauty and had a great success in London. A great number of people fell in love with her, including myself."

"Oh, Jimmy, I had no idea. Is that why you never married?" Skye asked.

"Perhaps," he answered. "But my feelings are not of importance except that they enabled me to understand a little of what Guy Tremayne suffered when she married his uncle."

"He was in love with her?" Skye asked.

"Tremendously in love I believe. He met her when he was eighteen. Pauline was much older and led him up the garden path, as she had led so many young men one way or another. She was one of those strange, complex characters who like to have men madly, crazily in love with them but who are prepared to give nothing in return. From my own experience of Pauline I would swear on the Bible, if need be, that she had always been strictly moral."

"And yet she made men love her," Skye said.

"It was almost what you might call a hobby," Jimmy replied, with a note of bitterness in his voice. "And Guy Tremayne, I gather, was no exception to the rule. He was as besotted as all the other young fools who hung about Pauline, and then, when he took her down to his home at Bredon to meet his uncle who had looked after him since he had been a child, she decided to marry Sir Rupert."

"It must have been a shock for . . . for Guy," Skye said.

"Of course it was. And it would have been better if he could have gone abroad there and then and tried to forget her, but Pauline had no intention of letting him go."

"She sounds odious!" Skye exclaimed.

Jimmy shrugged his shoulders.

"Women never cared for her, but to men she was irresistible. I did not go to the wedding. I did not see her again until the end of 1938 when my appointment at the Embassy in Buenos Aires was announced. I had a letter from her begging me to see her and her husband before I left."

"That was your first post in South America, wasn't it?" Skye asked.

Jimmy nodded.

"I was very busy, as you can imagine, but I could not refuse the appeal in Pauline's letter so I went down to Bredon and when I heard why they wanted to see me I understood how I could be of use."

"How?"

"Sir Rupert had lost his nephew and heir."

"Lost him?"

"Yes. Guy had disappeared—vanished into thin air. They had no idea where to begin to look for him. They had a vague idea that he might turn up in South America because his grandmother—his mother's mother—had been a Mariposan."

Skye gave an exclamation.

"That was that they meant when they said he was of Mariposan blood."

"Who said?" Jimmy asked.

"Never mind now," Skye said impatiently. "I want to hear your story."

"Sir Rupert was rather guarded as to why the boy had left home. But when I got Pauline alone I forced her to tell me what had happened. She told me then how Guy had been madly in love with her but that after a visit to Bredon she decided to marry his uncle. She was quite frank. She had felt it was time she settled down and the fact that Sir Rupert had both a title and a great deal of money undoubtedly tipped the scale in his favour.

"Guy had taken it hard. I gather Pauline had used all her wiles to keep him at her side. She enjoyed having both a husband and what was, to all intents and purposes, his adopted son at her feet."

"What happened?" Skye asked sharply.

"Pauline had one very unfortunate vice," Jimmy went on; "She was an inveterate gambler. There's Irish blood in the Donaldsons, and Pauline, like many of our forbears, would gamble on anything. She could never resist poker and soon after she married Sir Rupert had to settle her debts for a fairly considerable sum. But he made her promise that she would never play again.

"He went fishing in Scotland that April, and because she was always looking for amusement Pauline went with some friends to one of these smart gambling places in Mayfair which are responsible for so much misery and financial unhappiness. She lost over a thousand pounds.

Like all gamblers she could think of nothing when she held the cards in her hand but the excitement and thrill of the game. It was only when the reckoning came that she realized what she had done—she had broken her word of honour to her husband; what was more, it was impossible for her to meet her debts."

"She sounds an extremely stupid person," Skye exclaimed.

"She had no money of her own and you've never known what it is to be penniless," Jimmy said gently, and she flushed at the rebuke in his voice.

"I'm sorry," she capitulated, "one should never judge other people's temptations by one's own. What did she do?"

"She played for time, knowing that eventually she would have to tell her husband and ask his forgiveness, but putting off the evil hour day by day. The owner of the gambling club became unpleasant, and finally, when Pauline did not answer his letters, he arrived one evening at Bredon and threatened that, if she did not pay him there and then, he would ask her husband for the money.

"I think perhaps the Tremaynes' marriage at that moment was undergoing one of those strained, difficult periods which comes to so many couples when there is a big difference in the age. Sir Rupert was not easy to live with. He had the fiery, tempestuous temper which is characteristic of all the Tremaynes.

He was also a bit of a tyrant and Pauline knew that, if he heard from a stranger of the way she had broken her promises to him, he would never forgive her.

"She was almost frantic at the thought of his anger. Leaving the man who had called to see her shut away in a sitting-room, she ran to find Guy. She poured out her tale of woe, begging him to help her.

"Guy naturally wanted to save Pauline from the consequences of her foolishness. He had a little money of his own, left to him by his parents, but it was all in stocks and shares and this was a Friday. The Stock Exchange did not open till Monday. Pauline asked the owner of the gambling club if he would take Guy's post-dated cheque, but he was in an unpleasant mood.

"'You've staved me off with promises of repayment for over two months, Lady Tremayne,' he replied. 'I will take cash or your husband's cheque, nobody else's. And I'm not leaving here without one or the other.'

Pauline went back to Guy in tears and then she suddenly remembered that the agent had brought in the half-yearly rents of the estate for her husband that very afternoon. She had seen Sir Rupert put the money away in his safe. It was his practice to keep the money there until he could bank it.

"Pauline and Guy decided to borrow the money. 'I will sell my shares on Monday and replace the cash so that the old man will know nothing about it,' Guy said.

"'He won't be going to the Bank until Wednesday at the very earliest,' Pauline reassured him.

"Guy knew the combination of the safe and Pauline's

debts were paid and the owner of the gambling club left the house."

"She would have been wiser to tell her husband," Skye ejaculated.

That is what she thought later, but not at the time. She and Guy were congratulating themselves on being clever when a bombshell burst on them. Sir Rupert went to the safe to get some papers and discovered that the money was missing. He called them into his study, told them that he had been robbed and that he intended to notify the police.

"There was nothing for Guy to do but admit that he had borrowed the money for a special purpose of his own. His uncle was dumbfounded.

"What do you want with a thousand pounds?" he enquired.

One glance at Pauline's frightened face might have given him the answer, but he was too intent on cross-examining his nephew.

"It will be paid back on Monday," Guy replied defensively.

" 'That is not what I asked you,' Sir Rupert barked at him. I suppose, knowing the Tremaynes, the end was inevitable. Both men had fiery and uncontrollable tempers; both men resented the attitude of the other. Guy thought it was unreasonable that his uncle would not trust him, and Sir Rupert was infuriated by his nephew's evasive answers.

Finally, as their tempers mounted, unforgiveable things were said. Sir Rupert accused his nephew of being a thief and Guy finally slammed out of the house, vowing that he would never come back.

"Pauline was upset, but she still had not the courage to tell the truth.

" 'Don't worry, my dear,' Sir Rupert comforted her; 'the young fool knows which side his bread is buttered. He'll come back with his tail between his legs.'

"But Guy didn't come home. The thousand pounds arrived on Monday. A few weeks later they found that he had sold out all his shares, had closed his bank account, disposed of his car, given up the rooms he had in London and disappeared.

"It was when Sir Rupert began to worry that Pauline broke down and told the truth. He was too upset by this time even to be angry with her. Instead, he began to make enquiries as to where Guy had gone.

They thought at first he might be staying with friends abroad. They wrote in various directions and then, when they heard that I was going to the Argentine, they asked me to make enquiries out here."

"And did you?" Skye asked.

"I did what I could," Jimmy replied, "but it was not very much. A continent is a big place to look for one young man. I sent a routine message through to the Embassies. I enquired of friends in Patagonia and Peru if they had heard of Guy Tremayne. I asked a business man who occasionally visited Mariposa to keep his eyes open for the boy. There was not much else I could do."

"Anyway, they could not know he had changed his name," Skye said.

"I never thought of his doing such a thing," Jimmy admitted, "and actually he has only translated his own into Spanish. I think Sir Rupert would have been glad of that."

He was silent as Evans came on deck and stopped beside Skye's chair.

"The gentleman is awake, Miss. He has asked for food. I have given him all the doctor said he was to have, but he still wants more."

Skye smiled, her eyes suddenly alight.

"Give him all he wants, Evans. He always gets his own way."

"Very good, Miss," Evans replied with a slightly reproving air.

Skye walked across the deck. As she waited for El Diablo to finish his meal, she was thinking of Pauline—Jimmy's story told her more than he knew; she understood now many things about El Diablo that had puzzled her before.

His hatred of Society—Pauline was responsible for that. The way he despised women and scorned the idea they could have any sense of honour or integrity. Pauline was responsible for that, too. But he had loved her!

Perhaps he would never love another woman. Skye remembered the times El Diablo had made it very clear that the passion he felt for her had no connection with love.

"Can't you leave me alone?" she had flared at him once when he had pulled her into his arms when dinner was over.

He had laughed at her struggles to get free.

"What else do you expect me to do?" he asked mockingly. "Talk? A woman's lips were made for kisses."

"The sort of women you know!" she retorted angrily.

"There are only two sorts of women, those who are desirable and those who are not."

"Your opinion would be farcial if it was not insulting."

"Not to you, for you are very desirable."

"For you to think so is the greatest insult I can imagine."

He laughed at her anger.

"Think how much more humiliating it would be if you were without sex appeal—an unwanted woman."

"I would thank Heaven on my knees if I was unwanted by you."

"The day will come," he reassured her; "passion doesn't last."

"Only love! Skye was not certain why she spoke the words. He had looked at her strangely.

"Love," he repeated slowly, "is something about which you and I need not worry ourselves! Let us think instead of passion."

His arms had tightened round her body and there had been a cruel twist on his lips as he sought her mouth.

The memory of those words stabbed at Skye now with an almost intolerable pain. With an effort she remembered that Jimmy was waiting.

"I want you to come down and see El Diablo," she said. "But what are you going to say? Are you going to tell him that you know who he is?"

"Why not? Although I have only got your word for it," Jimmy replied.

"I know, and he has always refused to tell me his full name."

"I see no reason for subterfuge and intrigue," Jimmy said stiffly, suddenly becoming very English.

"All right, have it your own way. It can't matter now," Skye retorted.

She led the way down to the cabin. As they entered Evans was just carrying out a tray. El Diablo was propped high on his pillows. He was wearing blue pyjamas which accentuated his suntan, making it hard to believe he was of British nationality.

"Hello, Ice Maiden. Have I been neglecting you?" El Diablo asked lightly, as Skye went into the room, and then he saw that she was not alone.

His eyes rested on Jimmy with an expression of interrogation in them.

"My cousin, Jimmy Donaldson, has brought news that will interest you," Skye said, going up to the bed.

"Indeed?"

She fancied there was an atmosphere of tenseness between the two men.

"General Alejo is dead," Skye announced; "your men have taken control of Jácara, and we are returning there at this moment."

"So they've killed Alejo!" El Diablo said quietly.

Skye felt almost disappointed at the way he had taken her announcement. She had expected some startled exclamation from him.

"He is no loss, I imagine," Jimmy remarked.

"None," El Diablo agreed, "but someone will have to take over the country."

"I imagine you are expected to do that," Jimmy said drily.

"Tell me exactly what has happened," El Diablo commanded.

Skye thought for a moment that Jimmy might resent the note of authority in his voice. To her relief her cousin sat down on the chair by the bed and told how, having heard the announcement that a revolution had broken out in Mariposa, he had flown to Jácara and later on to Montevideo to find Skye and the yacht.

"What has happened to the Army?" El Diablo asked.

"There was no fighting by the time I got there," Jimmy replied. "People were rushing about the streets, waving flags and behaving as if they had suddenly been granted a holiday. The shops were closed and some of them were boarded up. Everybody was in such a festive mood that it was hard to get any sense out of them."

"There couldn't have been much bloodshed at that rate," El Diablo said.

"As far as I could see it was no more dangerous than a Bank Holiday on Hampstead Heath might have been," Jimmy replied.

"I'm sure you were glad about that," Skye said teasingly.

"I was," he agreed. "If there's one thing I really dislike it is a trigger-happy *gaucho*."

"How soon can we get back?" El Diablo enquired.

"By tomorrow morning," Skye replied.

"Can we wire Juan that I am coming?"

"Of course. Where shall I send it?"

"If you will give me some paper and a pencil I will write out a message."

She brought him a pad and held it steady while he wrote several messages. She saw him wince as he tried to raise himself a little higher on his pillows and she knew that he was in pain, however much he might try to disguise it. He looked pale, too, and she remembered that he had lost a great deal of blood.

"You won't be able to go ashore," she said quietly; "you can give your orders from the yacht and those you want to see can come aboard."

"Nonsense," he replied. "I shall be all right by to-morrow."

"If you are going to kill yourself, I shall refuse to take you back to Jácara," she answered. "For once you will have to listen to me. There is no escape from the yacht unless you swim."

He looked up angrily and then unexpectedly he smiled.

"So the tables are turned," he said softly.

"You are more use to Mariposa alive than dead."

Her eyes met his and she felt herself quiver and something warm and wonderful seemed to open its petals within her heart.

She wanted to reach out to him then, to tell him that he must take care of himself because of what he meant to her as well as to Mariposa.

"Very well, I capitulate—for the moment," El Diablo said.

"I don't know what all this is about," Jimmy interposed, his voice making Skye start, for she had forgottten his existence, "but I am certain of one thing—that you are the nephew of Sir Rupert Tremayne. You have a decided look of him. If I shut my eyes it might be him speaking."

There was a sudden tense silence.

"Whom are you talking about?" El Diablo asked at length.

"You!" Jimmy replied; "and I'm glad to meet you—Guy Tremayne. I have been looking for you for a great many years—since the end of 1938 to be exact."

"Guy Tremayne doesn't exist," El Diablo said fiercely.

"I think he does, even though he has changed his name," Jimmy replied. "Did you know that your uncle was dead?"

"No. When did he die?"

"In 1943. A heart attack brought on by doing too much

in the local Home Guard. He always hoped, until the very last, that you would come back."

"I have finished with England." There was a pause before he asked in a low voice, "What has happened to Pauline?"

Skye felt her heart turn over at the question. She hated this woman whom El Diablo had loved and whose cupidity and cowardice had driven him away from his home.

"Pauline is dead, too."

The words, spoken in Jimmy's even tones, were somehow sensational.

"Dead?"

"Yes. She was killed in an air raid early in 1945. She went to London after your uncle's death. Her excuse was war work, but I think actually she enjoyed the excitement of seeing people, of being in the thick of things despite the danger from bombs."

"Poor Pauline!" There was a gentleness in his tone that made Skye hate her the more; and then El Diablo said with a sigh:

"That lays the last of my ghosts. Now I am free of England for ever."

"Can't you forgive him after all these years?"

It was Skye who spoke, unable to keep back the words which came impulsively to her lips.

"Forgive my uncle?" El Diablo repeated, and then added reflectively, "I suppose it doesn't mattter now whether I forgive him or not. I can't imagine him dead. I have always thought of him as being at Bredon, cursing me, believing me to be a thief. I have hated him all these years and half of the time he was not there to hate. What a fool one can make of oneself!"

It was the most self-revealing speech Skye had heard from him. Impulsively she put out her hand and laid it on his.

"You must have suffered," she said. "You were too young to go out into the world entirely on your own."

"I took some hard knocks," El Diablo agreed, "but it made a man of me. It taught me to . . . trust no-one."

There was a little pause before he said the word "trust" and Skye knew he could easily translate it into the word "love". It was Pauline who had done this to him, she thought. He had loved her, rotten though she must have been at heart. She also had been a coward.

He would not be able to forgive her for that, because he

respected courage; and yet perhaps fruitlessly he had gone on loving her.

Skye dared not look at him lest he should see how much she understood. It was her newly-awakened love for him which had given her an understanding that she had never had before; and then, while she stood there wondering what to say, El Diablo turned to Jimmy.

"Thank you for what you have told me," he said, "but I want my past to be forgotten. My name is now Guido Tremayna. I am a Mariposan and proud of it. As you doubtless know, my grandmother was of the Veremundo family. They were for centuries one of the finest families in the country, but the line came to an end and their estates were scattered. One day I may try to restore the family fortunes, who knows? But in the meantime everyone in Mariposa knows I am of Veremundo blood and they respect it."

"I, too, will respect your wishes," Jimmy said; "but remember, if you take over the government of Mariposa, Britain can prove a good friend to a young democracy."

"I am well aware of that," El Diablo said, "and I need your help."

"I shall be glad to give it to you," Jimmy said formally.

Evans came into the cabin and whispered in Skye's ear.

"We are to let the patient sleep," she said to Jimmy. "Evans says we have been here far too long already."

"I am not tired." El Diablo said, but she knew that he lied.

"Sleep as long and as much as you can today," she said, "there will be a great deal to do tomorrow."

He was asleep almost before they left the cabin. Evans would not allow Skye to act as nurse when night came. She pleaded with him, but the steward insisted that he preferred to sit up with El Diablo rather than toss restlessly on his own bunk, wondering what was happening.

"I am used to nursing, Miss. I can sleep with one eye open like a cat. I got a bit of a lie down this afternoon, so there's no need to worry about me. You go to bed. There'll be plenty to keep awake for tomorrow, I'm thinking."

Skye smiled at that and she knew that the whole crew was agog with excitement at the thought of going back to Mariposa.

There was no sign in Montevideo of the two they had left behind. Captain Maclean had wirelessed the Harbour

Master at Jácara to tell him if possible to get in touch with the men and inform them of the yacht's return.

There would be a lot of people, Skye guessed, waiting to greet them when they arrived back. That was her last thought before she went to sleep, and she awoke to find it very much of an understatement.

There were not lots of people on the quay as Captain Maclean brought the yacht into the harbour, but thousands. The whole population of Jácara seemed to be there, and standing to the forefront was Juan and hundreds of other *gauchos*, all cheering and waving in a way that gave Skye a lump in her throat.

She had risen early so as to be on deck as they came into port and now she ran down below to El Diablo's cabin. He was awake and Evans had just finished shaving him as she burst in.

"There are crowds, enormous crowds, on the quay," she said excitedly, "and Juan is there with your men."

"I shall have to try to get up," El Diablo exclaimed.

"No, no, sir! It is impossible," Evans insisted. "If your shoulder starts bleeding again, you will undo all the good we've done. Let them come down to you."

"Why does this have to happen to me now?" El Diablo said angrily.

"It is perhaps because they realize they might have lost you that the people have awakened to the fact that they can't do without you," Skye replied.

She spoke more truly than she knew; and when Juan and El Diablo's other head men came aboard, they confirmed exactly what she had said.

It was the thought that El Diablo might have been killed which made the people of Jácara decide that they had had enough of Alejo and his injustices.

They had rallied behind El Diablo's men, marched on the Palace and overpowered the guards.

The Dictator was taken entirely by surprise. He had planned his treachery very carefully, and he was sitting complacently in the courtyard of the Palace. He had thought that El Diablo's death would scatter the whole opposition to his plans and that he would then have everything his own way.

He had not reckoned on the sound common-sense of the Mariposans themselves. Those who had sat on the fence, undecided whether to throw in their lot with the lawful government or with El Diablo, had made up their minds in the flash of a second.

No-one knew who had killed Alejo. When the fighting was over, he was found dead in the courtyard. The Army had surrendered unconditionally.

In fact, a large number of officers had been secretly against the Dictator's policy for a long time.

Everything was quiet; the people were only waiting to welcome their new President, who had been chosen unanimously. All day long men came and went on the yacht, talking with El Diablo, drinking the wine which Skye offered them on deck, then hurrying away to carry out the instructions of their new leader.

"His body may be a bit the worse for wear, but his head's all right!" a civic dignitary said to Skye and she laughed to hide her anxiety.

El Diablo must be very tired. She was wondering frantically how she could interfere and what she could say to stop the stream of callers which seemed never-ending, when Evans took the initiative.

To Evans a patient was a patient whether he was a President or a deck hand.

It was Evans who shut the cabin door decisively and came up on deck to say, "No more visitors."

"You'll kill him—and then what will you do?" he asked aggressively when someone argued that they had to see El Diablo, that what they had to communicate to him could not wait.

"He'll be here tomorrow if you haven't harried him into the grave," Evans continued. "Nine o'clock's the time for visiting and not a moment before. Sorry, gentlemen, but them's the doctor's orders."

Skye heard what Evans had said being translated by those who understood English for the benefit of those who only spoke Spanish; and then, as Evans came walking across the deck like a cocky sparrow, she said to him quietly:

"How is he?"

"Tired, Miss, dead tired. I'm going to give him something to eat and he'll be asleep the moment he's swallowed it, you see if he ain't."

But El Diablo was actually asleep before he swallowed anything, and Evans, muttering to himself, had to carry the uneaten supper back to the galley.

The Mariposan doctor who came on board at eight

o'clock next morning was delighted with the condition of the wounds.

"His Excellency is much better than I had dared to hope for Señorita," he said. "I heard what had happened and I felt that, if the bullets had not killed him, they must have done inestimable damage. This is a miracle!"

"Yes, it is a miracle," Skye agreed, "sent because he is so vitally needed in Mariposa."

"That's true enough," the doctor cried. "And if you get a chance, Señorita, will you speak to His Excellency about the hospital? It is in a terrible state of disrepair. We need funds for new laboratories as well as for the repair of old buildings and the furnishings of new wards."

"I will do what I can," Skye promised.

It was the first of many similar requests she was to have before the day passed. She found herself promising to speak for Institutions and Ministries, for Orphanages and Schools, for Welfare Services and even for new sanitation and drainage schemes.

The day proved exhausting. There was never a moment when the yacht was not filled with people and when she was not offering hospitality of some sort or another and trying at the same time not to worry too obviously about El Diablo.

He insisted on getting up to sit under the awning on deck, holding meetings, giving interviews, issuing instructions until his face was grey with fatigue and they had almost to carry him back to his bed.

Skye saw him alone for a few minutes just before Evans shut him up for the night. He was looking very tired. She knew, at the same time, that he was content.

"Things are shaping well," he told her; "there are plenty of good men to do the jobs. It was only that they were afraid to come to the front so long as Alejo was there."

"You are not in pain?" she asked.

He put out his hand to take hers.

"Worrying about me?" he asked. "You ought to be pleased that I am too busy to make love to you."

She felt herself flush; then his fingers tightened on hers.

"You are looking very lovely," he said, "and a great many of my callers told me how kind you had been to them."

"I listened to their pet schemes," Skye said. "They all imagine I have a lot of influence with you."

"And haven't you?"

She smiled at that.

"I don't think even a bulldozer would move you once you had made up your mind on a course of action," she replied, "and I am certainly not going to try."

"I've told Juan to bring your clothes back from the cave."

"Fancy you remembering to do that," Skye exclaimed and added, "I suppose we won't be going there for some time?"

He raised his eyebrows.

"We?" he questioned.

She looked away from him, her eyes on the brown hand that held hers, on the long fingers and well-kept nails. They could, she knew, be both brutally strong or surprisingly gentle.

"I am being sworn in as President on Thursday," El Diablo said after a moment. "There will be a reception that evening at the Palace. I want you to come to it."

"Of course," Skye smiled. "But Thursday is only three days ahead; will you be strong enough?"

"I shall be well by then," he answered; "but I admit to feeling tired at the moment."

She waited for him to command that she kiss him goodnight, but Evans came into the cabin. He let go of her hand.

"Sleep well, Skye."

She was dismissed; and though she longed to stay, she could think of no excuse why she should do so.

The next three days were even more hectic. El Diablo presided at meetings and committees which would have gone on endlessly had not Evans intervened to insist that his patient take food at regular intervals.

"I have never known a wound heal so quickly," the doctor told Skye.

He came night and morning to do the dressing, much to Evans' disgust; but Skye gathered that it was not El Diablo's wish but the wish of those in Jácara who for the first time in years valued the life of their President.

"He is extremely fit, that is the answer," she said.

"He is indeed. I do not think I have ever seen such a strong man."

There was no doubt that El Diablo was picking up in health and that his spirits were high.

One evening, when they were at last alone after a

gruelling day, he outlined his plan of government to Jimmy, who was from that moment whole-heartedly optimistic about the possibilities of transforming an old-fashioned, out-of-date and practically bankrupt state into a prosperous modern one.

"He's got the right ideas," Jimmy said. "It may take time—of course it will—but he will do it. You mark my words."

"I will," Skye answered faintly.

She was begining to wonder where she came in on all this. El Diablo was planning the future of Mariposa, but there seemed to be no place for her. He was charming, he was courteous, he teased her a little when they were alone together; but their old relationship had undergone such a tremendous change that it was difficult for her to know where she was and where she stood.

It seemed almost impossible that he could have stayed six days aboard the *Liberty* and yet she should not have had more than a few minutes alone with him.

She found herself longing for the times they had spent together in the camp. Her clothes had come back to her. She had almost cried when she thought of Neengai packing them and thought of her bedroom with its soft blue hangings standing empty.

It was difficult these days to be natural in El Diablo's presence.

Every day it seemed that her love for him grew and deepened and even the sound of his voice made her quiver with a new awareness of her feelings. She had not believed it possible that she could be herself and yet be so different.

She was almost ashamed of her yearning she had for him as she lay alone in her own cabin, separated from his only by the narrow width of the gangway.

It required all her will-power at times not to go to him, to tell him that she loved him, that she no longer wanted to fight him or to run away.

It was not something one could put into words, she thought. Perhaps when next he took her into his arms he would know instinctively.

It would be impossible for her not to turn towards him then, not to surrender herself. If only she had known of her love sooner!

Fool that she had been to go on fighting a battle she had already lost.

Then inevitably her mind came back to those other

women—not only Pauline whom he had loved and who had failed him and made him hate England and English-women, but those others, the women with whom he so often compared her.

They had loved him and bored him by their love. She could hear his voice saying:

"It is the mawkish sentimentality which most women call love which I find intolerable!"

"Passion doesn't last."

"Love is something about which you and I need not worry ourselves!"

She was haunted and tortured by his words.

"What am I to do?"

Skye asked the question aloud and then buried her face into the pillow, holding on to it with both hands as if it were only in that way she could prevent herself from running into El Diablo's cabin.

She wanted him! She knew now for the first time in her life what it meant to desire a man, to quiver and tremble with passion at the thought of him!

15

Skye took from the wardrobe in her cabin a dress which she had never worn.

It was of white lace so fine and so fragile that, when she slipped it over her head and fastened it round her slim waist, she might have been dressed in the proverbial fairy cobweb.

It made her seem very young, and above the strapless bodice her skin glowed with the soft radiance of a pearl.

She had brushed her hair until the curls were like tiny

golden flames over her small head, and the only jewellery she wore were the ear-rings of aquamarines and diamonds that El Diablo had given her on the night of the *fiesta*.

She thought, as she put them on, how she had sworn then to return them; but she knew now that she would never willingly give them back.

When she was dressed, she looked at herself from every angle in the mirror of the cabin, wanting to criticize, wanting to find any fault that might be rectified, for tonight she wished, above all things, to look lovelier than she had ever looked before.

She would have been blind if she had not realized that her eyes were wide and radiant, at the same time with an almost mystical depth in them. Her lips were tender, warm and red, and the quick breath which parted them betrayed the quickened beating of her heart.

It seemed a century of time must have passed since she had seen El Diablo yesterday.

He had left the yacht early in the morning, much to Evans' disgust, who swore he was still not well enough to take up the burden of everyday life. El Diablo had laughed at him.

"I am well," he said, "thanks to you."

And even if his wounds were not completely healed, there was no doubt that they were no longer troubling him unduly.

He had said goodbye to Skye in front of the others, and though she had sought for some personal message in his expression, she had to be content with the brief remark:

"I will see you tomorrow."

She could hardly believe that he had gone, as she watched him leave the quay, scorning the car which Juan had brought in case he should not feel equal to riding a horse.

He had gone, and she must content herself with five barren words—"I will see you tomorrow."

This morning El Diablo had been sworn in as President, and he had arranged for the ceremony to take place in the courtyard of the Palace so that everyone who wished could be present.

Skye had heard the cheeers echoing and re-echoing in the distance; but when she had wanted to go and watch the ceremony, Jimmy had prevented her.

"It would be better not," he said.

"Why?" she asked.

"We are foreigners. This is something which concerns

Mariposa and Mariposans. Let his people have him to themselves."

"But I want to go," Skye retorted obstinately.

Jimmy watched her face as she stood on deck looking up at the town with its mixed architecture of old and new. She had altered tremendously, he thought, but was wise enough not to say so. He had no idea of those words that were trembling on her lips, that she was considering, as already she had considered a thousand times before, telling him that she was El Diablo's wife.

She was no stranger, she wanted to assure Jimmy, and it was her right to be at the side of the new President.

Yet even as she formulated the words her lips refused to say them because El Diablo himself had said nothing. He had never referred to their marriage since he had been aboard the yacht.

Suppose, Skye tortured herself, he never did mention it again? Suppose he denied that the marriage had ever taken place?

Because of her doubts and inward questioning she had done as Jimmy wished and stayed on the yacht; but her thoughts had been with El Diablo, vowing service to his people in the great open courtyard.

"He will make a good President," she said reflectively.

"I am sure of it, Jimmy replied; "he is just what these people want—a buccaneer with ideals."

"Why do you call him that?" Skye enquired.

"All the great pioneers have been the same," Jimmy answered. "Raleigh, Clive, Rhodes—they all had their heads in the clouds, but their feet firmly planted on the earth. If anyone can make a success of Mariposa it will be our friend Guido Tremayna."

Yes, El Diablo would make a success of it, Skye told herself, as when dinner was over they drove towards the Palace. She had a sudden wild desire to tell Jimmy all she wished to do to help him.

How she, too, wanted to work for the people of Mariposa, to spend her money on something worth while, to set up welfare organisations, to sweep away those unsanitary slums, to build new houses, new hospitals, new schools, and many other things which Mariposa needed so badly.

The car wound its way up the narrow street with its overhanging balconies, where Alejo had tried to murder his enemy and had failed.

The sun had set, but there was still a luminous glow in

the sky, and against it, shining like some brilliant, glittering jewel, was the Palace, with the courtyard floodlit, lights shining in all its windows.

Great crowds of people hung round the open gates; and then, as they stepped from the car, Skye saw that the courtyard, too, was filled with them—people of every type, well-to-do shop-keepers, beggars, negroes, *gauchos*, peasants and barefooted children.

There was a very narrow passageway through which the arriving guests could pass, and they moved slowly, climbing the wide marble steps.

Skye saw with astonishment that no one was passing through the great open doors at the top. All were waiting —diplomats with their shining decorations, women in evening dress, officers in uniform and innumerable civic dignitaries wearing their chains of office.

"What is happening?" Skye asked Jimmy, but before he could reply, El Diablo came out of the Palace.

A great shout went up from the crowd at the sight of him, and Skye, who had wondered vaguely what he would wear at this, his first reception as President of Mariposa, saw that he was dressed as a *gaucho*.

It was a gesture that was appreciated by the crowd, for they cheered full-throatedly, their voices ringing out wildly into the darkness of the sky.

Only El Diablo would have thought of anything so clever, Skye thought proudly; and the raven black suit, with its short, tight-fitting coat, and wide *bombachas* became him as nothing else could have done.

He wore shining black boots with huge silver spurs and the traditional six-inch-wide leather belt holding a *cuchillo* and a revolver.

In the flood-lighting it was easy to see the great jagged gash, blood-red against the whiteness of his forehead, from Alejo's bullet. And he stood there waiting—tall, commanding and absolutely sure of himself.

Skye knew indeed that he was the man whom Mariposa had wanted for so long, the one man who could lead the country to greatness.

At last the cheering subsided a little and then, as El Diablo started to speak through a microphone, there was a sudden hush over the great throng.

"My friends and countrymen," he said, "I am glad you are here tonight because those who have been invited to the Palace come as your guests, and it is in your name that I entertain them. This is the first party I have ever given here in Jācara and it will be the last for a long time.

"There is work to do, for, as I told you this morning, you and I are going to work so that Mariposa can take her place among the other great states of the Americas. Tonight, then, I wish to get to know the people who have long and honourable connections with our country and whom we can trust to help us in the future. In your name I bid them welcome and I would like you to show that you welcome them, too."

Cheers and shouts went up at that. The cheering continued as El Diablo received his guests in full view of the people outside. They shook hands and then went past him into the Palace.

Skye slipped her hand into El Diablo's. She felt herself tremble as his fingers touched hers, and something in his eyes as he looked down at her upturned face made her heart leap with a sudden gladness.

He wanted her still—she was sure of it. There was the same magnetism about him, the same strange air of compelling possessiveness which she had felt so often and fought against so fruitlessly.

Another guest claimed his attention and she walked with Jimmy at her side into the Palace. It was even lovelier than she had imagined.

Time and a succession of dictators had not spoiled the old Spanish atmosphere or its original architecture. The great cool rooms, carved ceilings, the walls patterned with beautiful woodwork, painted and gilded, had remained unchanged through the centuries.

There were courtyards and flowery patios, marble halls and mosaics, eighteenth-century crystal chandeliers glittering with light, and balconies on which one could stand and look out over the sea which reflected the shimmering stars and the silver pathway of the moon.

Skye and Jimmy wandered down the long corridors and in and out of the rooms. There was so much to see, so much to admire.

Eventually they went back to the reception-rooms where the new President moved among his guests.

There was no exaggerated or extravagant entertainment. El Diablo was showing the people of Mariposa from the very start that his régime was going to be one of stern austerity.

Skye thought as she looked around her that many of the

Mariposans seemed to appreciate this, even those who might have expected to be fêted royally so that he could gain their support.

The women had other reasons for appreciating him.

"He's magnificent," Skye heard one say.

"Why not?" a Dowager replied stiffly. "He's a Veremundo."

"More than that," the younger one smiled, "he's a man!"

She was right, Skye thought with a sudden leap of her heart, and she longed to go to his side. But it was no use trying to talk to El Diablo—so many people had a prior claim on his attention, and after a while she walked back with Jimmy to the suite of rooms on the ground floor which one of the servants had told them constituted the President's private apartments.

Here the rooms were big and airy, all with balconies overlooking the sea. In the sitting-room there were innumerable bowls of flowers, some of which were gifts sent to welcome the President to the Palace.

Skye felt a pang of jealousy. So many people would want to make a fuss of El Diablo now that he was in a position of authority and importance.

"He is a man!" She could hear again the throb in the young woman's voice and it made her move restlessly around the room, touching the books that lay strewn about, picking up a newspaper only to put it down again, her white dress in the soft light giving her the appearance of a restless ghost unable to find peace.

Jimmy had been unusually silent all the evening, but now, as she looked up to meet the anxiety in his eyes, she saw that he was about to say what was on his mind.

"Listen to me, Skye . . ." he began.

"Don't talk to me," she cried impulsively; "don't ask me anything—there's nothing I can tell you, yet!"

He was wise enough to understand and to leave her alone, and Skye walked to the balcony to stand looking out at the magnificent panorama of sky, sea and land.

The lights of the town twinkled below her and the stars shone above. She felt suddenly very insignificant and very lost; and then she repeated to herself some words of El Diablo's which had been her only comfort these past days.

"Have you not yet learned that I never leave go of anything I want—that I never lose what I desire?"

He desired her still—she was sure of it.

There was still the fire behind his eyes as he looked at

her, there was still that feeling of magnetism between them, she could not be mistaken about that.

She stood there for a long, long time, the night wind stirring her hair, until she heard a door open and shut again and, turning round, saw that El Diablo had come into the room.

He undid the heavy leather belt which he wore round his waist and threw it over the back of the chair; then he stood looking at her.

They were alone as she had prayed they might be; and yet, because of a sudden, almost overwhelming shyness, she had to speak of unimportant things.

"I have been admiring your view," she said. "Is the party over?"

"Yes, everyone has gone," he answered.

She came from the balcony into the room. The light from the lamps shone on her hair, and the delicate fragility of her gown was silhouetted against the darkness behind her. His eyes were on her—a strange expression on his face.

"I am glad you waited," he said at length. "There is something I want to tell you."

"Yes?"

It was hard to contain the joy rising in her breast.

"I have arranged with your cousin that he shall take you away tomorrow."

For a moment she stared at him as if she could not have heard aright, and then, numbly, she repeated.

"Take me away?"

"Yes I have told him the truth—told him that I forced you to become my wife against your will. It will not be difficult for you to get a divorce or an annulment. Your cousin will see to all the international difficulties and I will provide you with the necessary evidence. Discreetly handled, no one need ever know."

As he spoke Skye felt the blood drain from her cheeks, felt as if any movement was an impossibility; and because she was afraid of what she might do or say, she managed with a desperate effort to turn round and stand with her back to him, looking out over the sea.

"Do you want me to leave?"

Her voice was almost stifled in her throat.

"You are free to do so. Wasn't that what you wished?"

She wanted to scream then, at the very word—how she

had longed and prayed to be free of him; and now that it had come, it was too late!

So he was bored with her! She had joined the ranks of the other women who had loved him and of whom he had wearied.

He had warned her; he had made it clear from the very beginning that when she no longer interested him he would set her free.

Skye gripped her fingers together until the nails bit into her flesh; and then, as the sea, sky and stars suddenly swam before her eyes, she heard his voice.

"Shall we say goodbye now? Your cousin said he would send the car back from the yacht for you."

Skye tried to answer with dignity, but her voice was lost, choked in her throat. She could only stand there, fighting against the tears which threatened to overwhelm her.

"Why don't you say something?" His voice was sharp. "I thought you would be glad to know that you are no longer a prisoner."

"Glad!" her voice broke on the word, and now for the first time she heard him come a step nearer.

"Why do you say it like that? Skye, you are not—crying?"

It was impossible for her to answer him, and after a moment he went on.

"But I have never known you cry. Turn round, let me look at you."

She shook her head.

"I command you to turn round. Have I got to make you obey me?"

She turned then with a sudden jerk, as if she were a marionette controlled by strings, and in the light of the lamps he saw her face with tears glittering on her long lashes and running unchecked down her cheeks.

"Very well, then," Skye said in a low voice raw with suffering; "look at me! Look at me and laugh! This is what you wanted, isn't it?—to make me love you and then throw me away, as you have thrown away all those other women who were foolish enough to lay their hearts at your feet. I thought I had no heart; I thought I hated you! But you've won—I love you! and now . . . now . . . laugh!"

Her voice died away on a heartbreaking sob, but still she faced him.

"You don't know what you are saying." El Diablo exclaimed.

"I do," Skye contradicted. "I love you, I am not ashamed to say it. I love you."

"You are mistaken!"

"Not about this . . . I love you—let me stay!"

"No!"

His eyes were dark and hard as agates.

"Please . . . please . . . it is not much to ask. . . ."

"No!"

She put out her hands beseechingly, all pride forgotten.

"I won't be a nuisance . . . I won't ask anything if you only let me stay."

"It is impossible!"

"But why? I will make no claims upon you, no one need even know I am your wife unless you wish it."

"That is not the point."

"Then let me remain . . . in Jácara . . ."

"No!"

With a sudden defiance which was somehow heartbreakingly pathetic she said:

"So you have found . . . the flaws in your . . . slave."

He did not answer and she went on:

"Or perhaps you have chosen . . . another? One who will . . . amuse you until she, too, is fool enough to offer you . . . 'mawkish sentimentality'."

"There is nothing like that!"

"Then why . . . why?"

"Explanations will get us nowhere. You leave tomorrow."

"I beg you to——"

"It is useless to say any more."

She saw the inflexibility of his expression and she knew only too well his determination when he had made up his mind about something. With a little helpless gesture of utter despair she shut her eyes.

She knew then that she could not live without him, could not go on alone—the emptiness of the years ahead with only her memories to support her was too bitter to be contemplated.

She opened her eyes. He had walked away from her to the fireplace on the other side of the room. She thought that he could not even bear to look at her.

Like a sleepwalker she moved towards the leather belt he had thrown over the chair on entering and, still as if she were in a dream, she drew from it his revolver.

He turned as she took it in her hand.

"Still intent on killing me?" he asked grimly.

"Not you," she answered, ". . . myself."

His instinct must have warned him what she was about to say before she spoke.

He sprang forward before the last word had passed her lips and with a swiftness which was almost superhuman he reached her side and struck her hand upwards as she pulled the trigger.

The bullet passed through her hair, singeing the curls and burying itself in the wall.

For a moment they stood looking at each other. El Diablo's face was as pale as hers. Then, as he took the revolver from her nerveless fingers, she sank down on the floor at his feet, shaken by a tempest of uncontrollable weeping.

She was like a broken flower, her white dress billowing out around her, her face hidden in her hands, her whole body bowed in utter abandonment.

El Diablo stood staring at her bent head, an expression on his face that no one had ever seen before.

There came a loud knocking at the door.

"Señor! Señor! Is anything wrong?"

El Diablo started as if he had been awakened from a deep reverie. He walked to the door and opened it a few inches.

"Everything is all right."

"But, Señor, there was a shot."

"My gun went off by mistake!"

"*Excusa*, Señor, we were worried; but if all is well . . ."

"All is well."

El Diablo shut the door. The only sound was the sobs of the woman who had reached breaking point.

"For God's sake, Skye, don't cry like that!"

She heard his voice far away through the darkness of her misery.

"Skye, can you really care as much as that?" he asked gently.

"Do you . . . imagine . . . that this . . . is a passing . . . fancy?"

"No, I don't believe that," he replied. "But you don't understand what you are asking in wishing to stay here with me."

"With . . . you!" Skye repeated in a whisper. Then she threw back her head and put out her hands beseechingly. "I won't be any trouble . . . only let me stay . . . just for a little while . . ."

"Do you think I would want you for just a little while?" he asked, his voice hoarse with emotion. "If you stay you stay for ever. Do you understand what that means? You, who have wanted so urgently to escape, to be free of me—if you stay now, you will never be free again."

Skye drew a deep breath. It was as if life had suddenly come back into her face.

"I don't want . . . to be . . . free any more."

"Listen," he said. "I married you for the sake of convenience, but I chose you because you were British, fair and lovely and not unlike someone I once loved! I chose you deliberately, meaning to hurt you as I had been hurt. It is not a pretty story, but you had better know the truth.

"Someone once played with me as I meant to play with you. She made me love her, crazily, madly, passionately—but she was not woman enough to give herself to me or to let our love be the beautiful, glorious thing nature had intended it to be. I asked her first to marry me and then, when she was married to someone else, to run away with me, but she preferred to keep me as a plaything.

"Later, when I learnt she was also untruthful and a coward, I saw her for what she was and hated her and everything she stood for in an empty, vicious social life. But because of what she had done to me I vowed revenge on all women and when I saw you, because you were a little like her and because you were English, I wanted to make you suffer!

"I decided to make you fall in love with me so that I could gloat over your misery, laugh at your desires and mock you when you pleaded for my kisses.

"But everything went wrong. You didn't fall in love with me—I fell in love with you."

El Diablo took a step towards Skye as she sat looking up at him, her eyes very wide, both hands laid against her breast, as if to quell the sudden leap of her heart.

"I love you." His voice was deep and compellingly sincere. "I love you as I have never loved a woman before, and as I shall never love a woman again; but because of that love, because I know myself for what I am and you for what you are, I will not keep you here. You must go back to the world you know, to the quietness and security of England, to the easy, undangerous democracy of America."

"Can you really believe I want that sort of existence?" Skye asked breathlessly.

"You think you don't want it now," El Diablo replied; "but you have no idea of what your life here will be when you cannot escape from it. This is my world, this is where I belong, this is where my work lies. I shall never leave Mariposa."

"And this is where I want to stay, too," Skye said.

"With me?" El Diablo asked. "My little sweet, have you forgotten what I am like? I shall not change overnight because I love you. I shall still be cruel and overbearing, autocratic and bad-tempered. You have seen some of the worst of me, do you really believe you could be happy with that, day after day, year after year?"

"I love you," Skye replied softly; "I love you just as you are. I don't want you any different. I wouldn't love you if you were. I only want . . . El Diablo!"

She rose to her feet as she spoke, and with the tears still wet on her cheeks she stood smiling at him the radiant smile of a rainbow across a clouded sky. Still he did not move.

"I dare not touch you," he said hoarsely. "If I do, all my resolutions will go to the wind. Think well before you decide. This is your last chance. If you tempt me now, it will be too late to be sorry afterwards. I want you, Skye; I love you; if you stay with me, I shall never, never let you go."

"I shall never want to go," Skye whispered. "Oh, my darling, won't you understand? I have never been alive until now."

He came towards her then. She felt herself tremble as he took her chin between his fingers and turned up her face to his.

"Say that again," he commanded her; "say those two words that you have never said to me before."

The look in his eyes seemed to squeeze the very breath from her body, yet she managed to obey him.

"My . . . darling."

"My little love, my heart, my own!"

She hardly heard the words for the glory and the wonder of a world that was too dazzling and glorious to be borne.

Then suddenly his lips were on hers and she felt his arms go round her. A flame rose within her to answer the flame within him. She felt his mouth drawing her very soul from her body and making it his.

She felt herself quiver and tremble with passion and happiness. Her whole body ached for him.

She wanted him as he wanted her and her mouth was very soft and yielding beneath the fierceness of his.

He held her closer and closer, kissing her eyes, her cheeks, her neck and again her mouth until it seemed to Skye they were one, their hearts throbbing in unison, their breath a part of one another.

Then he picked her up in his arms.

She put up her hands to check him.

"Your shoulder!" she cried. "Be careful of your shoulder."

But he did not hear her; his eyes were aflame with passion, and there was a wild triumphant look on his face, the expression of a conqueror, of a man who attains that which he most desires.

"You are mine, my love, my wife—my own," he said, as with his lips on hers he carried her away.

ON SALE WHEREVER PAPERBACKS ARE SOLD
—or use this coupon to order directly from the publisher.

BARBARA CARTLAND